SPECIALS

SCOTT WESTERFELD

SIMON AND SCHUSTER

SIMON AND SCHUSTER
First published in Great Britain in 2006 by Simon & Schuster UK Ltd,
1st Floor, 222 Gray's Inn Road, London WC1X 8HB

This edition published in 2014

Originally published in the USA in 2006 by Simon Pulse,
an imprint of Simon & Schuster Children's Division, New York.

A CIP catalogue record for this book is available from the British Library

ISBN: 978-1-47112-396-2

10 9 8 7 6 5 4 3

Printed and bound by CPI Group (UK) Ltd, Croydon, CR0 4YY

www.simonandschuster.co.uk

www.scottwesterfeld.com

To all the fans who've written me about this series.
Thanks for telling me what was right, what was wrong,
and which bits made you throw the book across the room.
(You know who you are.)

Part I

BEING SPECIAL

By plucking her petals you do
not gather the beauty of the flower.
—Rabindranath Tagore, "Stray Birds"

CRASHING A BASH

The six hoverboards slipped among the trees with the lightning grace of playing cards thrown flat and spinning. The riders ducked and weaved among ice-heavy branches, laughing, knees bent and arms outstretched. In their wake glowed a crystal rain, tiny icicles shaken from the pine needles to fall behind, aflame with moonlight.

Tally felt everything with an icy clarity: the brittle, freezing wind across her bare hands, the shifting gravities that pressed her feet against the hoverboard. She breathed in the forest, tendrils of pine coating her throat and tongue, thick as syrup.

The cold air seemed to make sounds crisper: The loose tail of her dorm jacket cracked like a wind-whipped flag, her grippy shoes squeaked against the hoverboard surface with every turn. Fausto was pumping dance music straight through her skintenna, but that was silent to the world outside. Over its frantic beat Tally heard every twitch of her new monofilament-sheathed muscles.

She squinted against the cold, eyes watering, but the tears made her vision even sharper. Icicles whipped past in glittering streaks, and moonlight silvered the world, like an old, colorless movie come flickering to life.

That was the thing about being a Cutter: *Everything* was icy now, as if the world were opening her skin.

Shay swooped in beside Tally, their fingers brushing for a moment, and flashed a smile. Tally tried to return it, but something shifted in her stomach as she looked at Shay's face. The five Cutters were undercover tonight, black irises hidden under dull-eyed contacts, cruel-pretty jaws softened by smart-plastic masks. They had turned themselves into uglies because they were crashing a bash in Cleopatra Park.

For Tally's brain, it was way too soon to be playing dress-up. She'd only been special a couple of months, but when she looked at Shay she expected to see her best friend's new and marvelous cruel beauty, not tonight's ugly disguise.

Tally angled her board sideways to avoid an ice-laden branch, breaking contact. She concentrated on the glittering world, on twisting her body to slip the board among the trees. The rush of cold air helped her refocus on her surroundings rather than the missing feeling inside herself—the one that came from the fact that Zane wasn't here with the rest of them.

"One party-load of uglies up ahead." Shay's words cut through the music, caught by a chip in her jaw and carried through the skintenna network, whisper-close. "You sure you're ready for this, Tally-wa?"

Tally took a deep breath, drinking in the brain-clearing cold. Her nerves still tingled, but it would be totally random to back out now. "Don't worry, Boss. This is going to be icy."

"Should be. It *is* a party, after all," Shay said. "Let's be happy little uglies."

A few of the Cutters chuckled, glancing at each other's fake faces. Tally became aware again of her own millimeters-thick mask: plastic bumps and lumps that made her face zitted and flawed, covering the gorgeously spinning web of flash tattoos. Uneven dental caps blunted her razor-sharp teeth, and even her tattooed hands were sprayed with fake skin.

A glance in the mirror had shown Tally how she looked: just like an ugly. Ungainly, crook-nosed, with baby-fat cheeks, and an impatient expression—impatient for her next birthday, the bubblehead operation, and a trip across the river. Another random fifteen-year-old, in other words.

This was Tally's first trick since turning special. She'd expected to be ready for anything now—all those operations had filled her with icy new muscles and reflexes tweaked to snakelike speed. And then she'd spent two months training in the Cutters' camp, living in the wild with little sleep and no provisions.

But one look in the mirror had shaken her confidence.

It didn't help that they'd come into town through the Crumblyville burbs, flying over endless rows of darkened houses, all the same. The random tedium of the place she'd grown up in gave her a sticky feeling along the inside of her arms, which wasn't helped by the feel of the recyclable dorm uniform against her sensitive new skin. The manicured trees of the greenbelt seemed to press in around Tally, as if the city were trying to grind her down to averageness again. She liked being special, being outside and icy and *better*, and couldn't wait to get back to the wild and strip this ugly mask from her face.

Tally clenched her fists and listened to the skintenna network. Fausto's music and the noises of the others washed over her—the soft sounds of breathing, the wind against their faces. She imagined their heartbeats at the very edge of hearing, as if the Cutters' growing excitement were echoing in her bones.

"Split up," Shay said as the lights of the bash grew close. "Don't want to look too cliquey."

The Cutters' formation drifted apart. Tally stayed with Fausto and Shay, while Tachs and Ho broke off toward the top of Cleopatra Park. Fausto adjusted his soundbox and the music faded, leaving only rushing wind and the distant rumble of the bash.

Tally took another nervous breath, and the crowd's scent flashed through her—ugly sweat and spilled alcohol. The party's dance system didn't use skintennas; it blasted music crudely through the air, scattering sound waves into a thousand reflections among the trees. Uglies were always noisy.

From her training, Tally knew that she could close her eyes and use the merest echoes to navigate the forest blind, like a bat following its own chirps. But she needed her special vision tonight. Shay had spies in Uglyville, and they'd heard that outsiders were crashing the party—New Smokies giving out nanos and stirring up trouble.

That's why the Cutters were here: This was a Special Circumstance.

The three landed just outside the strobing lights of the hoverglobes, jumping off onto the forest's floor of pine needles, which crackled with frost. Shay sent their boards up into the treetops to wait, then fixed Tally with an amused stare. "You smell nervous."

Tally shrugged, uncomfortable in her ugly-dorm uniform. Shay could always smell what you were feeling. "Maybe so, Boss."

Here at the party's edge, a sticky bit of memory

reminded her how she always felt arriving at a bash. Even as a beautiful bubblehead, Tally had hated the trickle of nerves that visited whenever crowds pressed in around her, the heat of so many bodies, the weight of their eyes upon her. Now her mask felt clingy and strange, a barrier separating her from the world. Very unspecial. Her cheeks flashed hot for a second beneath plastic, like a rush of shame.

Shay reached out to squeeze her hand. "Don't worry, Tally-wa."

"They're only uglies," Fausto's whisper sliced through the air. "And we're right here with you." His hand rested on Tally's shoulder, gently pushing her forward.

Tally nodded, hearing the others' slow, calm breaths through the skintenna link. It was just like Shay had promised: The Cutters were connected, an unbreakable clique. She would never be alone again, even when it felt like something was missing inside her. Even when she felt the lack of Zane like head-spinning panic.

She plunged through the branches, following Shay into the flashing lights.

Tally's memories were perfect now, not like when she'd been a bubblehead, confused and muddled all the time. She remembered what a big deal Spring Bash was for uglies. The approach of spring meant longer days for tricks and hoverboarding, and lots more outdoor parties to come.

But as she and Fausto followed Shay through the crowd, Tally felt none of the energy she remembered from last year. The bash seemed so tame, so listless and random. The uglies just stood around, so shy and self-conscious that anyone actually dancing looked like they were trying too hard. They all seemed flat and artificial, like party extras on a video wall, waiting for the real people to arrive.

Still, it was true what Shay liked to say: Uglies weren't as clueless as bubbleheads. The crowd parted easily, everyone sliding out of her way. However zitty and uneven their faces, the uglies' eyes were sharp, full of nervous stabs of awareness. They were smart enough to sense that the three Cutters were different. No one stared for too long at Tally or realized what she was behind her smart-plastic mask, but bodies moved aside at her lightest touch, shivers playing across their shoulders as she passed, as if the uglies sensed something dangerous in the air.

It was easy seeing the thoughts ripple across their faces. Tally could watch the jealousies and hatreds, rivalry and attraction, all of it written on their expressions and in the way they moved. Now that she was special, everything was laid out clearly, like looking down on a forest path from above.

She found herself smiling, finally relaxing and ready for the hunt. Spotting party-crashers was going to be simple.

Tally scanned the crowd, searching for anyone who seemed out of place: a little too confident, overmuscled, and suntanned from living in the wild. She knew what Smokies looked like.

Last fall, back in ugly days, Shay had run away into the wild to escape the bubblehead operation. Tally had followed to bring her back, and they'd both wound up living in the Old Smoke for a few long weeks. Scrabbling like an animal had been pure torture, but her memories came in handy now. Smokies had an arrogance about them; they thought they were better than people in the city.

It took Tally just seconds to spot Ho and Tachs across

the crowded field. They stood out like a pair of cats gliding through a waddling flock of ducks.

"You think we're too obvious, Boss?" she whispered, letting the network carry her words.

"Obvious how?"

"They all look so clueless. We look . . . special."

"We *are* special." Shay looked back at Tally over her shoulder, a grin playing on her face.

"But I thought we were supposed to be in disguise."

"Doesn't mean we can't have *fun*!" Shay suddenly darted away through the crowd.

Fausto reached out and touched Tally's shoulder. "Watch and learn."

He'd been special longer than she had. The Cutters were a brand-new part of Special Circumstances, but Tally's operation had taken the longest. She'd done a lot of very average things in her past, and it had taken a while for the doctors to strip away all the built-up guilt and shame. Random leftover emotions could leave your brain muddled, which wasn't very special. Power came from icy clarity, from knowing exactly what you were, from cutting.

So Tally hung back with Fausto, watching and learning.

Shay grabbed a boy at random, yanking him away from the girl he was talking to. His drink sloshed onto the ground as he started to pull away in protest, but then he caught Shay's gaze.

Shay wasn't as ugly as the rest of them, Tally noticed, the violet highlights in her eyes still visible even through her ugly disguise. They glittered like a predator's in the strobe lights as she pulled the boy closer, brushing against him, a flex of muscles gliding down her body like a flick through a rope.

After that, he didn't look away again, even as he handed off his beer to the random girl, who looked on open-mouthed. The ugly boy placed his hands on Shay's shoulders, his body starting to follow her movements.

People were watching them now.

"I don't remember this part of the plan," Tally said softly.

Fausto laughed. "Specials don't need plans. Not sticky ones, anyway." He stood close behind Tally, his arms around her waist. She felt his breath on the back of her neck, and a tingle started moving through her body.

Tally pulled away. Cutters touched one another all the time, but she wasn't used to that part of being a Special. It made her feel even stranger that Zane hadn't joined them yet.

Through the skintenna network, Tally could hear Shay whispering to the boy. Her breathing deepened, though Shay could run a klick in two minutes without breaking a sweat. A sharp, unshaven sound sliced through the network when she brushed her cheek against the boy's, and Fausto chuckled when Tally flinched.

"Relax, Tally-wa," he said, rubbing her shoulders. "She knows what she's doing."

That much was obvious: Shay's dance was spreading, sucking in the people around her. Until now, the party had been a nervous bubble hovering in the air, and she'd popped its surface tension, releasing something icy inside. The crowd started to pair off, arms wrapping around each other, moving faster. Whoever was crewing the music must have noticed—the volume went higher, the bass deeper, the hoverglobes overhead pulsing from blackness to blinding radiance. The crowd had started jumping up and down with the beat.

Tally felt her heart accelerate, amazed at how effortlessly Shay had brought them all along. The bash was changing, flipping inside out, and all because of Shay. This wasn't like their stupid tricks in ugly days—sneaking across the river or stealing bungee jackets—this was *magic*.

Special magic.

So what if she was wearing an ugly face? Like Shay always said in training, the bubbleheads had it all wrong: It didn't matter what you looked like. It was how you carried yourself, how you *saw* yourself. Strength and reflexes were only part of it—Shay simply *knew* that she was special, and so she was. Everyone else was just wallpaper, a blurred background of listless chatter, until Shay lit them up with her own private spotlight.

"Come on," Fausto whispered, pulling Tally away from the thickening crowd. They retreated toward the party's edge, sliding unseen past the eyes locked on Shay and her random boy. "You go that way. Stay sharp."

Tally nodded, hearing the other Cutters whisper as they spread out across the party. Suddenly, this all made sense. . . .

The bash had been too dead, too flat to cover the Specials or their prey. But now the crowd's arms were up, waving back and forth with the beat. Plastic cups flew through the air, everything a storm of movement. If the Smokies were planning to crash the party, this moment was what they'd been waiting for.

Moving was tricky now. Tally made her way through a swarm of young girls—practically littlies—all dancing together with eyes closed. The glitter sprayed across their uneven skin flashed in the hoverglobes' pulsing light, and they didn't shiver as Tally pushed through them; her special aura had been drowned out by the party's new energy, by Shay's dance-magic.

The ugly little bodies bouncing against hers reminded

Tally how much she had changed inside. Her new bones were made from aircraft ceramics, light as bamboo and hard as diamonds. Her muscles were sheathed whips of self-repairing monofilament. The uglies felt soft and unsubstantial against her, like stuffed toys come to life, boisterous but unthreatening.

A ping sounded inside her head as Fausto boosted the skintenna network's range, and snatches of noise drifted through her ears: screams from a girl dancing next to Tachs, a rumbling beat from where Ho stood close to the speakers, and under it all the distracting things Shay was whispering in her random boy's ear. It was like being five people at once, as if Tally's consciousness were smeared across the party, sucking in its energy in a blend of noise and light.

She took a deep breath and headed toward the edge of the clearing, seeking the darkness outside the hoverglobes' light. She could watch better from out there, keep better hold of her clarity.

As she moved, Tally found it was easier to dance, going with the crowd's motion rather than forcing a path through it. She allowed herself to be pushed randomly through the throng, like when she let high wind currents guide her hoverboard, imagining herself a bird of prey.

Closing her eyes, Tally drank the bash in through her other senses. Maybe this was what being special was *really* all about: dancing along with the rest of them, while feeling like the only real person in the crowd. . . .

Suddenly, hairs stiffened on the back of Tally's neck, her nostrils flaring. A scent, distinct from the human sweat and spilled beer, sent her mind reeling back to ugly days, to running away, to the first time she'd been alone out in the wild.

She smelled *smoke*—the clinging reek of a campfire.

Her eyes opened. City uglies didn't burn trees, or even torches; they weren't allowed to. The party's only light came from the strobing hoverglobes and the half-risen moon.

The scent must have come from somewhere Outside.

Tally moved in widening circles, casting her eyes over the crowd, trying to find the source of the smell.

No one stood out. Just a bunch of clueless uglies dancing their heads off, arms flailing, beer flying. No one graceful or confident or strong . . .

Then Tally saw the girl.

She was slow-dancing with some boy, whispering in his ear intently. His fingers twitched nervously across her back, their movements unconnected to the music's beat—the two looked like littlies on an awkward playdate. The girl's jacket was tied around her waist, as if she didn't mind the cold. And along the inside of her arm lay a pattern of pale squares where sunblock patches had been stuck.

This girl spent a lot of time outside.

As Tally moved closer, she caught the scent of wood smoke again. Her new and perfect eyes saw the coarseness of the girl's shirt, woven from natural fibers, lined with stitched seams and giving off another strange smell . . . detergent. This garment wasn't designed to be worn and then tossed into a recycler; it had to be *washed*, lathered up with soap, and pounded against stones in a cold stream. Tally saw the imperfect shape of the girl's hair—cut by hand with metal scissors.

"Boss," she whispered.

Shay's voice came back sleepily. "So soon, Tally-wa? I'm having *fun*."

"I think I got a Smokey."

"You sure?"

"Positive. She smells like laundry."

"I see her now," Fausto's voice cut through the music. "Brown shirt? Dancing with that guy?"

"Yeah. And she's *tanned*."

There was an annoyed, distracted sigh, a few mumbled apologies as Shay disentangled herself from her ugly boy. "Any more?"

Tally scanned the crowd again, making her way around the girl in a wide circle, trying to catch another whiff of smoke. "Not as far as I can tell."

"Nobody else looks funny to me." Fausto's head bobbed nearby, winding his own path toward the girl. From the other side of the bash, Tachs and Ho were closing in.

"What's she doing?" Shay asked.

"Dancing, and . . ." Tally paused, her eyes catching the girl's hand slipping into the boy's pocket. "She just gave him something."

Shay's breath cut off with a little hiss. Until a few weeks ago, Smokies had brought only propaganda into Uglyville, but now they were smuggling something far more deadly: pills loaded with nanos.

The nanos ate the lesions that kept pretties bubbleheaded, ramping up their violent emotions and raw appetites. And unlike some drug that would eventually wear off, the change was permanent. The nanos were hungry, microscopic machines that grew and reproduced, more of them every day. If you were unlucky, they could wind up eating the rest of your brain. One pill was all it took to lose your mind.

Tally had seen it happen.

"Take her," Shay said.

Adrenaline flooded Tally's bloodstream, clarity blanking out the music and the motion of the crowd. She'd spotted the girl first, so it was her job, her *privilege* to make the grab.

She twisted the ring on her middle finger, felt its little stinger flicking out. One prick and the Smokey girl would be stumbling, passing out like she'd had too much to drink. She'd wake up in Special Circumstances headquarters, ready to go under the knife.

That thought made Tally's skin crawl—that the girl would soon be a bubblehead: pretty, beautiful, and happy. And monumentally clueless.

But at least she'd be better off than poor Zane.

Tally cupped her fingers around the needle, careful not to stab some random ugly in the crowd. A few steps closer, and she reached out with her other hand, pulling the boy away. "Can I cut in?" she asked.

His eyes widened, a grin breaking out on his face. "What? You two want to dance?"

"It's okay," the Smokey girl said. "Maybe she wants some too." She untied the jacket from around her waist, pulling it up over her shoulders. Her hands went through its sleeves and into the pockets, and Tally heard the rustle of a plastic bag.

"Knock yourself out," the boy said, and took a step back, leering at them. The expression brought another flash of heat into Tally's cheeks. The boy was *smirking* at her, amused, like Tally was average and anyone's to think about—like she wasn't special. The uglifying smart plastic on her face began to burn.

This stupid boy thought Tally was here for his entertainment. He needed to find out otherwise.

Tally decided on a new plan.

She stabbed a button on her crash bracelet. Its signal

spread through the smart plastic on her face and hands at the speed of sound, the clever molecules unhooking from each other, her ugly mask exploding in a puff of dust to reveal the cruel beauty underneath. She blinked her eyes hard, popping out the contacts and exposing her wolfen, coal black irises to the winter cold. She felt her tooth-caps loosen, and spat them at the boy's feet, returning his smile with unveiled fangs.

The whole transformation had taken less than a second, barely time for his expression to crumble.

She smiled. "Buzz off, ugly. And you"—she turned to the Smokey—"take your hands out of your pockets."

The girl swallowed, spreading her arms out to either side.

Tally felt the sudden rush of eyes drawn to her cruel features, sensed the crowd's dazzlement at the pulsing tattoos that webbed her flesh in scintillating black lace. She finished the arrest script: "I don't want to hurt you, but I will if I have to."

"You won't have to," the girl said calmly, then she did something with her hands, both thumbs turning upward.

"Don't even think . . . ," Tally started, then she saw too late the bulges sewn into the girl's clothes—straps like a bungee jacket's, now moving of their own accord, cinching themselves around her shoulders and thighs.

"The Smoke lives," the girl hissed.

Tally reached out . . .

. . . just as the girl shot into the air like a stretched-taut rubber band let go from the bottom. Tally's hand passed through empty space. She stared upward, open-mouthed. The girl was still climbing. Somehow, the bungee jacket's battery had been rigged to throw her into the air from a standstill.

But wouldn't she just fall straight back down?

Tally spotted movement in the dark sky. From the edge of the forest, two hoverboards zoomed over the bash, one ridden by a Smokey dressed in crude skins, the other empty. At the top of the girl's arc, he reached out, hardly slowing as he pulled her from midair onto the riderless board.

A shudder went through Tally as she recognized the Smokey boy's jacket, leather and handmade. In a searing flash from a hoverglobe, her special vision caught the line of a scar running through one of his eyebrows.

David, she thought.

"Tally! Heads up!"

Shay's command pulled Tally from her daze, drew her eyes to more hoverboards shooting over the crowd at just above head level. She felt her crash bracelet register a tug from her own board, and bent her knees, timing the jump for its arrival.

The crowd was pulling away from her, shocked by her cruel-pretty face and the girl's sudden ascent—but the boy who'd been dancing with the Smokey grabbed for her. "She's a Special! Help them get away!"

His try for her arm was slow and clumsy, and Tally flicked out her unspent stinger to stab his palm. The boy pulled his hand back, stared at it with a stupid expression for a moment, then crumpled.

By the time he hit the ground, Tally was in the air. With two hands on the grippy edge of her hoverboard, she kicked her feet up onto its riding surface, her weight shifting to bring it around.

Shay was already on board. "Take him, Ho!" she ordered, pointing down at the unconscious ugly boy, her own mask disappearing in a puff of dust. "The rest of you, with me!"

Tally was already zooming ahead, the chill wind sharp against her bare face, an icy battle cry building in her throat, hundreds of faces looking up at her from the beer-soaked ground, astonished.

David was one of the Smokies' leaders—the best prize the Cutters could have hoped for on this cold night. Tally could hardly believe he had dared come into the city, but she was going to make sure he would never leave again.

She weaved among the flashing hoverglobes, soaring out over the forest. Her eyes adjusted swiftly to the darkness, and she spotted the two Smokies no more than a hundred meters ahead. They were riding low, tipped forward like surfers on a steep wave.

They had a head start, but Tally's hoverboard was special too—the best the city could manufacture. She coaxed it onward, brushing the tips of the wind-tossed trees with its leading edge, smashing them into sudden plumes of ice.

Tally hadn't forgotten that it was David's mother who had invented the nanos, the machines that had left Zane's brain the way it was. Or that it was David who'd lured Shay into the wild all those months ago, had seduced first her and then Tally, doing everything he could to destroy their friendship.

Specials didn't forget their enemies. Not ever.

"I've got you now," she said.

HUNTERS AND PREY

"Spread out," Shay said. "Don't let them cut back toward the river."

Tally squinted into the onrushing wind, running her tongue across the uncovered points of her teeth. Her Cutter board had lifting fans front and back, spinning blades that would keep it flying past the edge of the city. But the Smokies' old-fashioned hoverboards would fall like stones once the magnetic grid ran out. That's what they got for living Outside: sunburn, bug bites, and crappy technology. At some point the two Smokies would have to make a dash for the river and its trail of metal deposits.

"Boss? Want me to call back to camp for reinforcements?" Fausto asked.

"Too far away to get here in time."

"What about Dr. Cable?"

"Forget her," Shay said. "This is a Cutter trick. We don't want any regular Specials taking credit."

"Especially this time, Boss," Tally said. "That's David up there."

There was a long pause, and then Shay's razor-bladed laugh came through the network, running an icy finger down Tally's spine. "Your old boyfriend, huh?"

Tally gritted her teeth against the cold, all the embarrassing dramas of ugly days heavy in her stomach for a moment. Somehow, the old guilt never completely faded. "Yours, too, Boss, I seem to remember."

Shay just laughed again. "Well, I guess both of us have scores to settle. No calls, Fausto, no matter what. This boy is ours."

Tally set a determined expression on her face, but the knot in her stomach remained. Back in the Smoke, Shay and David had been together. But then Tally had arrived and David had decided he liked her better, and the jealousy and neediness that went with being an ugly made a mess of things as usual. Even after the Smoke had been destroyed—even when Shay and Tally were clueless bubbleheads—Shay's anger at that betrayal had never completely disappeared.

Now that they were Specials, ancient dramas weren't supposed to matter anymore. But seeing David had somehow disturbed Tally's iciness, making her suspect that Shay's anger might still be buried deep inside too.

Maybe capturing him would end the trouble between them, once and for all. Tally took a deep breath and leaned forward, urging her hoverboard faster.

The edge of the city was growing closer. Below, the greenbelt changed abruptly into suburbia, the rows of boring houses where middle pretties raised their littlies. The two Smokies dropped to street level, zipping around sharp corners, knees bent and arms out wide.

Tally angled into the first hard turn of the chase, a smile growing on her face as her body flexed and twisted. This was how the Smokies usually got away. Regular Specials in their lame hovercars could only move fast in a straight line. But Cutters were *special* Specials: every bit as mobile as the Smokies, and every bit as crazy.

"Stick with them, Tally-wa," Shay said. The others were still long seconds behind.

"No problem, Boss." Tally skimmed the narrow streets, only a meter from the concrete. It was lucky that middle pretties were never out this late—if anyone stumbled into the chase, one glancing blow from a hoverboard would turn them into paste.

The tight spaces didn't slow Tally's quarry. She remembered from her own Smokey days how good David was at this, as if he'd been born on a hoverboard. And the girl probably had plenty of practice in the alleys of the Rusty Ruins, the ancient ghost city from which the Smokies launched their incursions into the city.

But Tally was special now. David's reflexes were nothing compared with hers, and all his practice couldn't make up for the fact that he was random: a creature put together by nature. But Tally had been *made* for this—or *re*made, anyway—built for tracking down the city's enemies and bringing them to justice. For saving the wild from destruction.

She accelerated into a hard bank, clipping the corner of a darkened house, smashing its rain gutter flat. David was so close that she heard the squeak of his grippy shoes shifting on his board.

In another few seconds, she could jump off and grab him, tumbling until her crash bracelets halted them with a shoulder-wrenching spin. Of course, at this speed, even her special body would feel some hurt, and a normal human might break in a hundred random ways. . . .

Tally clenched her fists, but let her board fade back a bit. She'd have to make her move in an open space. She didn't want to kill David, after all. Just see him tamed, turned into a bubblehead, pretty and clueless and out of her life once and for all.

At the next sharp turn, he dared a quick glance over his shoulder, and Tally caught a glimpse of recognition on his face. Her new cruel-pretty features must be quite the icy shock.

"Yeah, it's me, boyfriend," she whispered.

"Ease off, Tally-wa," Shay said. "Wait for the edge of the city. Just stay close."

"Okay, Boss." Tally let herself drop back a bit more, pleased that David knew who was coming for him now.

At top speed, the chase soon reached the factory belt. They all climbed to avoid the automated delivery trucks rumbling through the darkness, orange underlights reading the road markings to find their destinations. The other three Cutters spread out behind her, cutting off any chance of the Smokies doubling back.

With a glance upward at the stars and a lightning calculation, Tally saw that the two were still headed away from the river, zooming toward certain capture at the city's edge.

"This is kind of weird, Boss," she said. "Why isn't he heading for the river?"

"Maybe he got lost. He's just a random, Tally-wa. Not the brave boy you remember."

Tally heard soft laughter over the network, and her cheeks burned. Why did they keep acting like David still meant something to her? He was just some ugly random. And, anyway, it did show *some* bravery, sneaking into the city like this . . . even if it was pretty stupid.

"Maybe they're heading for the Trails," Fausto said.

The Trails were a big preserve on the other side of Crumblyville, the sort of place middle pretties went hiking to pretend they were out in nature. It looked wild, but you could still get picked up by a hovercar when you got tired.

Maybe they thought they could disappear on foot. Didn't David realize that Cutters could fly past the edge of the city? That they could see in the dark?

"Should I move in?" Tally asked. Here in the factory belt,

she could yank David off his board without killing him.

"Relax, Tally," Shay said flatly. "That's an order. The grid ends, no matter which way they go from here."

Tally clenched her fists, but didn't argue.

Shay had been special longer than any of them. Her mind was so icy that she'd practically made herself into a Special—brain-wise, anyway—breaking out of bubble-headness with nothing but a sharp knife against her own skin. And Shay was the one who'd made the deal with Dr. Cable, the arrangement that allowed the Cutters to destroy the New Smoke any way they wanted.

So Shay was the Boss, and obeying wasn't really that bad. It was icier than thinking, which could get you all tangled up.

The neat estates of Crumblyville appeared below. Bare gardens flashed past, waiting for late pretties to plant spring flowers. David and his accomplice dropped to just above ground level, staying low to give their lifters every bit of purchase on the grid.

Tally saw their fingers brush as they hopped a low fence, and wondered if the two of them were together. Probably David had found some new Smokey girl's life to wreck.

That was his thing: going around recruiting uglies to run away, seducing the best and the smartest city kids with the promise of rebellion. And he always had his favorites. First Shay, then Tally . . .

Tally shook her head to clear it, reminding herself that the social life of Smokies was of no interest to a Special.

Leaning forward, she coaxed her board faster. The black expanse of the Trails was just ahead. This chase was almost over.

The two plunged into the darkness, disappearing into dense trees. Tally climbed to skim the forest canopy, watching for signs of their passage in the sharp light of the moon. In the distance beyond the Trails, the true wilds lay, the utter blackness of Outside.

A shiver played across the treetops, the Smokies' two hoverboards streaking like a gust of wind through the forest. . . .

"They're still headed straight out," she said.

"We're right behind you, Tally-wa," Shay answered. "Care to join us down here?"

"Sure, Boss." Tally covered her face with both hands as she dropped, a spray of needles traveling from foot to head, the caress of pine branches shooting along her body. Then she was among the tree trunks, zipping through the forest, knees bent, eyes wide open.

The other three Cutters had caught up with her, arrayed a hundred meters apart, cruel-pretty faces fiendish in the flickering moonlight.

Ahead, at the border between the Trails and the true wilderness, the two Smokies were already descending, their boards' magnetic lifters running out of metal. Their skidding descent echoed through the brush, followed by the sounds of running feet.

"Game over," Shay said.

The lifting fans of Tally's hoverboard kicked in beneath her, a low thrum drifting through the trees like the growl of some hibernating beast. The Cutters slowed, dropping to a few meters' altitude, scanning the dark horizon for movement.

A shiver of pleasure ran down Tally's spine. The chase had become a game of hide-and-seek.

But not exactly a *fair* game. She made a finger gesture, and the chips in her hands and brain responded, laying an infrared channel over Tally's vision. The world was transformed—the snow-patched ground turning a cold blue, the trees emitting soft green halos—every object illuminated by its own heat. A few small mammals stood out, red and pulsing, heads twitching, as if they instinctively knew that something dangerous was nearby. Not far away, a hovering Fausto glowed, his feverish Special-body bright yellow, and Tally's own hands seemed to course with orange flames.

But in the now-purple darkness ahead of her, nothing of human size appeared.

Tally frowned, flicking back and forth between infrared and normal vision. "Where'd they go?"

"They must have sneak suits," Fausto whispered. "Otherwise we could see them."

"Or smell them, at least," Shay said. "Maybe your boyfriend's not so random after all, Tally-wa."

"What do we do?" Tachs said.

"We get off and use our ears."

Tally let her hoverboard drop to the ground, the lifting blades splintering twigs and dry leaves as they spun to a halt. She stepped from the riding surface as it stilled, and the late winter cold leeched up through her grippy shoes.

She wriggled her toes and listened to the forest, watching her breath curl out in front of her face, waiting for the whine of the other boards to peter out. As the silence deepened, her ears caught a soft sound pattering all around her—the wind rattling pine needles in their tiny sheaths of ice. A few birds disturbed the air, and hungry squirrels who'd woken up from a long winter's sleep scrabbled for buried nuts. The breathing of the other Cutters came through on the skintennas' ghostly channel, separate from the rest of the world.

But nothing that sounded like a human moved on the forest floor.

Tally smiled. At least David was making this interesting, standing perfectly still like this. But even with sneak suits hiding their body heat, the Smokies couldn't remain motionless forever.

Besides, she could *feel* him out there. He was close.

Tally silenced her skintenna feed, switching off the noise of the other Cutters, leaving herself in a hushed, infrared world. Kneeling, she closed her eyes, placing one bare palm on the hard, frozen ground. Her special hands had chips in them that caught the slightest vibration, and Tally let her whole body listen for stray sounds.

There was something in the air . . . a hum at the edge of hearing, more an itch in her ears than a real noise. It was one of those ghostly presences she could hear now, like the buzz of her own nervous system or the sizzle of fluorescent lights. So many sounds that were inaudible to uglies and bubbleheads reached a Special's ears, as strange and unexpected as the whorls and ridges of human skin under a microscope.

But what exactly *was* it? The sound ebbed and flowed with the breeze, like the notes that sang out from the high tension lines stretching from the city's solar arrays. Maybe it was some kind of trap, a wire strung between two trees. Or was it a razor-sharp knife angled so that it caught the wind?

Tally kept her eyes closed, listening harder, and frowned.

More sounds had joined the first, ringing from all directions now. Three, four, then five high-pitched notes began to ring, their combined volume no louder than a hummingbird at a hundred meters.

She opened her eyes, and as they refocused in the gloom, Tally suddenly saw them: a slight displacement silhouetting five human figures spread through the forest, their sneak suits blending almost perfectly into the background.

Then she saw how they were standing—legs braced apart, one arm pulled back, the other outstretched—and realized what the sounds were. . . .

Bowstrings stretched taut and ready to fire.

"Ambush," Tally said, then realized she'd cut off her skintenna feed.

She rebooted it just as the first arrow flew.

NIGHTFIGHT

Arrows streaked through the air.

Tally rolled to the ground, flattening herself on a bed of icy, fallen needles. Something whistled past, close enough to ruffle her hair.

Twenty meters away, one of the arrows connected, and an electric buzz shot through her hearing like a network overload, choking off a grunt from Tachs. Then an arrow struck Fausto, and Tally heard him gasp before his feed went silent. She scrambled for cover behind the nearest tree, hearing two bodies thudding against the hard ground. "Shay?" she hissed.

"They missed me," came the answer. "Saw it coming."

"Me too. They've definitely got sneak suits." Tally

shoved herself back against the wide trunk, scanning for silhouettes among the trees.

"And infrared, too," Shay said. Her voice was calm.

Tally looked down at her hands, glowing fiercely in infrared, and swallowed. "So they can see us perfectly and we can't see *them*?"

"Guess I didn't give your boyfriend enough credit, Tally-wa."

"Maybe if you bothered to remember that he was *your* boyfriend too, you'd . . ." Something shifted in the trees ahead, and as her words faded, Tally heard the *snap* of a bowstring. She threw herself to one side as the arrow struck the tree, letting out a buzz like a shock-stick and covering the trunk in a web of flickering light.

She scrambled away, rolling to a spot where two trees' branches wound around each other. Squeezing into a narrow crook between them, she said, "What's the plan now, Boss?"

"The plan is we kick their asses, Tally-wa," Shay chided softly. "We're *special*. They got in the first whack, but they're still just random." Another bowstring snapped and Shay let out a grunt, which was followed by the sound of footsteps sprinting through the brush.

The sound of more bowstrings sent Tally to the ground, but the arrows whipped off into the distance where Shay had retreated. Jittering shadows flickered through the forest, followed by the sounds of electrical discharge.

"Missed again," Shay chuckled to herself.

Tally swallowed, trying to listen through the frantic pounding of her heart, cursing the fact that the Cutters hadn't bothered to bring sneak suits, or throwing weapons, or hardly *anything* Tally could use right now. All she had was her cutting knife, fingernails, special reflexes, and muscles.

The embarrassing thing was, she'd gotten turned around somehow. Was she really hidden *behind* these trees? Or was an attacker looking straight at her, calmly notching another arrow to take her down?

Tally glanced up to try to read the stars, but branches broke the sky into unreadable patterns. She waited, trying to take slow, steadying breaths. If they hadn't fired at her again, she must be out of sight.

But should she run? Or sit tight?

Pressed between the trees, Tally felt naked. The Smokies had never fought this way before; they always ran away and hid when Specials showed up. Her Cutter training was all about tracking and capturing; no one had ever mentioned invisible attackers.

She glimpsed Shay's hot-yellow form slipping deeper into the Trails, moving farther away, leaving her alone.

"Boss?" she whispered. "Maybe we should call in some regular Specials."

"Forget it, Tally. Don't you dare embarrass me in front of Dr. Cable. Just stay where you are, and I'll swing around from the side. Maybe we can pull off a little ambush of our own."

"Okay. But how's that going to work? I mean, they're invisible and were not even—"

"Patience, Tally-wa. And a little quiet, please."

Tally sighed and forced her eyes closed, willing her heart to beat softer. She listened for the hum of drawn bowstrings.

A wavering pitch sounded not far behind her, a bow pulled taut, its arrow notched and ready to fly. Then another pitch joined in, and a third . . . but were they aimed at *her*? She counted a slow ten, waiting for the snap of a loosed arrow.

But no sound came.

She must be hidden here. But she'd counted five Smokies in all. If three had their bows drawn, where were the other two?

Then, even softer than Shay's calm and steady breathing, her ears caught the sound of footsteps moving through the pine needles. But they were too careful, too quiet for a city-born random. Only someone who'd grown up in the wild could move that softly.

David.

Tally stood slowly, sliding her back up the tree trunk, eyes opening.

The footsteps grew closer, coming up on her right. She eased herself sideways, keeping the trees' bulk between herself and the sound.

Daring a quick glance upward, Tally wondered if the branches were thick enough to shield her body heat from infrared optics. But there was no way she could climb without David hearing.

He was close. . . . Maybe if she darted out and stung him before the other Smokies loosed their arrows. After all, they were just uglies, cocky randoms who no longer had the advantage of surprise.

Tally gave her stinger ring a twist, flipping out a freshly charged needle. "Shay, where is he?" she whispered.

"Twelve meters from you." The words were carried on the slightest breath. "Kneeling, looking at the ground."

Even from a standstill, Tally could run twelve meters in a few seconds. . . . Would she be too fast a target for the other Smokies to hit?

"Bad news," Shay breathed. "He's found Tachs's board."

Tally's teeth closed on her lower lip, realizing what the

ambush was all about: The Smokies wanted to get hold of a Special Circumstances hoverboard.

"Get ready," Shay said. "I'm headed back toward you." In the distance her glowing form flickered between two trees, brilliantly obvious but too fast and far away to be caught by anything as slow as an arrow.

Tally forced her eyes closed again, listening hard. She heard more footsteps, louder and clumsier than David's—the fifth Smokey searching for another of the Cutters' boards.

It was time to make her move. She opened her eyes. . . .

A sickening sound rumbled through the forest: the lifting fans of a hoverboard starting up, spitting out chopped-up twigs and pine needles.

"Stop him!" Shay hissed.

Tally was already in motion, streaking toward the noise, realizing with a sick feeling that the lifting fans were loud enough to drown out the snap of bowstrings. The board rose before her, a hot-yellow figure on it sagging in the arms of a black silhouette.

"He's taking Tachs!" she shouted. Two more steps and she could jump. . . .

"Tally, duck!"

She dived for the ground, an arrow's feathers skimming past one shoulder as she twisted through the air, the sizzle of its electric charge raising the hairs on her scalp. Another shot past as Tally rolled to her feet, blindly hoping that more weren't on the way.

The board was three meters up and climbing slowly, wavering under its double load. She jumped straight up, the furious wind of the fans blowing straight down on her. At the last moment Tally imagined her fingers thrusting into the lifting fans—chopped into a spray of blood and gristle—and her nerve faltered. Her fingertips caught the riding surface's edge, barely clinging, and her added weight began to pull the board slowly earthward.

In her peripheral vision, Tally saw an arrow flying toward her, and twisted wildly in midair to dodge it. It shot past, but her fingers had lost their grip. One hand slipped, then the other. . . .

As Tally fell, the growl of a second hoverboard ripped the air. They were stealing another one.

Shay's cry shot through the noise: "Give me a boost!"

Tally landed in a crouch inside the whirlwind of pine needles and saw Shay's yellow-glowing form running full tilt right at her. Tally laced her fingers together and cupped her hands waist-high, ready to throw Shay up at the board, which was straining to climb again.

Another missile streaked toward Tally from the darkness. But if she ducked, Shay would take the arrow in midleap. Her teeth clenched, waiting for the agony of a shock-stick slamming into her spine.

But the board's rotor-wash eased the arrow downward like an invisible hand. It struck between Tally's feet, exploding into a brilliant spiderweb on the icy ground. She tasted electricity in the damp air, and tiny and invisible fingers played across her skin, but her feet were insulated by the soles of her grippy shoes.

Then Shay's weight landed in her cupped hands, and Tally grunted, flinging upward with all her strength.

Shay screamed as she soared into the air.

Tally threw herself to one side, imagining more arrows in flight, her feet skipping across the still-buzzing shock-stick. She spun around and fell backward to the ground.

Another arrow shot past her in a blur, missing her face by centimeters. . . .

She glanced up: Shay had landed on the hoverboard, setting it teeter-tottering wildly. The lifting fans shrieked at its triple load. Shay raised a stinger hand, but David's dark silhouette shoved Tachs toward her, forcing her to catch his limp form. She danced at the board's edge, trying to keep them both from tumbling off.

Then David lashed out, catching Shay in the shoulder with a handheld shock-stick. Another web of sparks lit the night sky.

Tally rose to her feet, running back toward the struggle. The Smokies were *not* fighting fair!

Above her, a bright yellow form was tumbling from the board, headfirst. . . . Tally leaped forward, stretching out her hands. The dead weight thudded into her arms—the special bones as hard as a sack of baseball bats—and sent her sprawling to the ground. "Shay?" she whispered, but it was Tachs.

Tally glanced up. The hoverboard was ten meters up now, hopelessly out of reach, Shay's limp form wrapped around David's sneak-suited darkness in an awkward embrace.

"Shay!" Tally screamed as the hoverboard rose still higher. Then her ears caught the snap of a bowstring, and she threw herself to the ground again.

The arrow missed wildly—whoever had fired it was running. Sneak-suited forms were everywhere, and more boards were buzzing to life all around her, the Smokies lifting into the air.

She twisted her crash bracelet, but there was no responding tug. They had taken all four of the Specials' boards—Tally was stranded on the ground, like some random hiker lost in the forest.

She shook her head in disbelief. Where had the Smokies gotten sneak suits? Since when did they shoot people? How had this easy trick gone so wrong?

She connected her skintenna to the city network, about to call Dr. Cable. Then she hesitated a moment, remembering Shay's orders. No calls, no matter what—she couldn't disobey.

All four hoverboards were in the air now, their lifting fans giving off orange glimmers of heat. She could see Shay unconscious in David's arms, and the glowing form of another Special being carried off on a different board.

Tally cursed. Tachs still lay on the ground, so they'd gotten Fausto, too. She *had* to call for reinforcements, but that would be breaking orders. . . .

A ping came through the network.

"Tally?" the distant voice asked. "What's going on out there?"

"Ho! Where are you?"

"Following your locators. A couple of minutes away." He laughed. "You're not going to believe what that boy at the bash told me. The one your Smokey was dancing with?"

"Never mind! Just get here fast!" Tally scanned the air, watching in frustration as the Cutters' boards lifted higher into the dark sky. In a minute, the Smokies would be gone for good.

It was too late for regular Specials to get here, too late for anything. . . .

Rage and frustration surged through Tally, almost overwhelming her. David was *not* going to beat her, not this time! She couldn't afford to lose her head.

She knew what to do.

Making a claw with her right hand, Tally dug her

fingernails into the flesh of her left arm. The delicate nerves woven into her skin screamed, a torrent of pain piling through her, overloading her brain.

But then the special moment struck, icy clarity replacing panic and confusion. She drew in the cold air in gasps. . . .

Of course. David and the girl had ditched their own hoverboards. They had to have left them close by.

She turned and ran back toward the city, hunting in the darkness for the half-remembered smell of David.

"What happened?" Ho said. "How come you're the only one online?"

"We got jumped. Be *quiet*."

Long seconds later, Tally's nose caught something: David's scent lingering where his hands had polished and tuned, where his sweat had fallen in the chase. The Smokies hadn't bothered to recover their old-fashioned boards. She wasn't completely helpless.

At the snap of her fingers, David's board rose from its hasty covering of pine needles and into the air. She jumped on and it wobbled unsteadily, like the end of a diving board, without the sense of power that the lifting fans gave. But Tally had ridden one just like it all those months ago, and it was enough for now.

"Ho, I'm coming to meet you!" The board shot along the city's edge, speeding up as its lifters grabbed hold of the magnetic grid.

She climbed up through the trees, scanning the horizon. The Smokies flickered in the distance, the bodies of their two captives glowing like embers in a fire.

Glancing up at the stars, she calculated angles and directions. . . .

The Smokies were headed out toward the river, where

they could use magnetics. Carrying two passengers per board, they needed all the lift they could get. "Ho, head for the western edge of the Trails. *Fast!*"

"Why?"

"To save time!" She had to keep her quarry in sight. The Smokies might be invisible, but the two captive Specials shone like infrared beacons.

"Okay, I'm coming," Ho answered. "But what's going on again?"

Tally didn't respond, whipping through the treetops like a slalom rider. Ho wasn't going to like what Tally had to do, but there was no other choice. That was *Shay* out there, being dragged away by David. This was Tally's chance to pay her back for all those old mistakes.

To prove that she was really special.

Ho was there, waiting where the dark trees of the Trails began to thin.

"Hey, Tally," he said as she zoomed toward him. "Why are you riding that piece of junk?"

"Long story." She twisted to a halt beside him.

"Yeah, well, could you *please* tell me what's—" He let out a startled cry as Tally pushed him off his board, sending him tumbling into the darkness below.

"Sorry, Ho-la," she said, stepping from the Smokey board onto his and angling it toward the river. Its lifting fans spun to life as she crossed the city's border. "Need to borrow your ride. Don't have time to explain."

Another grunt reached her ears as Ho's bracelets brought his fall to a halt. "Tally! What the—"

"They've got Shay. Fausto, too. Tachs is back in the Trails, unconscious. Go make sure he's okay."

"*What?*" Ho's voice was fading as Tally shot out into the wild, leaving the city's network repeaters behind. She scanned the horizon and caught distant flickers of infrared, like two glowing eyes ahead—Fausto and Shay.

The hunt was still on.

"We got jumped. Aren't you *listening*?" She bared her teeth. "And Shay said no calls to Dr. Cable. We don't want any help with this." Tally was certain Shay would hate for Special Circumstances to find out that the Cutters—Dr. Cable's very *special* Specials—had been made fools of.

For that matter, a squadron of screaming hovercars would only let the Smokies know that they were being followed. All alone, Tally might be able to sneak up on them.

She leaned forward, coaxing every bit of speed from her borrowed board, Ho's protests fading behind her.

She was going to catch them. There were five Smokies and two captives on four boards; no way could they make top speed. Tally just had to remember that they were random, and she was special.

She still had a chance to rescue Shay, capture David, and make this all okay.

RESCUE

Tally flew low and fast, barely skimming the surface of the river, staring into the dark trees on either side.

Where *were* they?

The Smokies couldn't be that far in front—not with only a couple of minutes' head start. But like her, they were flying low, using the mineral deposits in the winding riverbed for extra push, keeping under cover of the trees. Even the special-hot infrared glow of Shay's and Fausto's bodies couldn't penetrate the dark cloak of the forest. And that was a problem.

What if they'd already pulled off the river, sneaking into the trees to watch her fly past? On their stolen boards, the Smokies could head off in any direction they wanted.

Tally needed a few seconds up in the sky, looking down. But the Smokies also had infrared. To take a peek without giving herself away, she would have to cool her body temperature way down.

She looked into the dark water rushing past her feet and shivered.

This was not going to be fun.

Tally spun to a stop, freezing spray spitting up from the tail of her board, tickling her arms and face, sending another shiver through her bones. The river was running fast, filled to the brim with melted snow rolling down from the mountains, as chill as a champagne bucket back in bubblehead days.

"Wonderful," Tally said with a scowl, then stepped from the board.

With toes pointed, she barely made a splash, but the freezing water set her heart pounding madly. In seconds her teeth began to chatter, her muscles clenching, threatening to snap her bones. She pulled Ho's board down into the water beside her, and the lifting fans spat out tendrils of steam as they cooled.

Tally began an endless, torturous count of ten, wishing bad luck and destruction down on David, the Smokies, and whoever it was who'd first invented freezing water. The cold seeped into her body, making her nerves scream and leeching deep into her bones.

But then it hit her, the special moment. It was like when she cut herself, the pain building until she could hardly stand it anymore . . . then suddenly flipping inside out. And hidden within the agony the strange clarity came again, as if the world had ordered itself into something that made perfect sense.

Just as Dr. Cable had promised so long ago, this was better than bubbly. All of Tally's senses were on fire, but her mind seemed to stand apart from them, observing their sensations without being overwhelmed.

She was non-random, above average . . . almost beyond human. And she had been made to save the world.

Tally stopped counting and let out a slow, calm breath, and bit by bit, her shivering faded away. The icy water had lost its power.

She pulled herself back onto Ho's board, grasping its edges with bone-pale knuckles. It took three tries to snap her numbed fingers loud enough, but finally the hoverboard began to rise into the dark sky, climbing as high as the cool and silent magnetic lifters would take it. As she cleared the trees, the wind hit like an avalanche of cold, but Tally ignored it, her eyes sweeping across the marvelously clear world below.

There they were—only a kilometer or so ahead—a flicker of boards against the black water, a glimpse of a glowing human in infrared. The Smokies seemed to be going slowly, hardly moving at all. Maybe they were resting, unaware that they were being followed. But to Tally, it was as if her moment of icy focus had stopped them in their tracks.

She let the board drop, falling out of sight before her body heat could cut through the chill of soaked clothes. The costume dorm uniform clung to her like a wet woolen blanket. Pulling off the jacket, Tally let it fall into the river.

Her board roared back to life, skimming forward with fans fully engaged, leaving a meter-high wake.

Tally might be soaking and frozen to the bone, and only one against five, but the dunking had cleared her head. She felt her special senses dissecting the forest around her, her instincts spinning, her mind calculating from the stars overhead exactly how long it would take to catch up.

Her hands flexed numbly, but Tally knew that they were the only weapons she needed, no matter what other little tricks the Smokies had brought along.

She was ready for this fight.

Sixty seconds later, she saw it: a lone hoverboard waiting for her, just past a bend in the river. Its rider stood calmly, black silhouette holding the glowing form of a Special.

Tally swirled to a halt, whipping in a tight circle to scan the trees. The forest's deep purple background was filled with half-glimpsed shapes whipped into motion by the wind, but no human forms.

She looked at the dark figure blocking the river before her. The sneak suit hid his face, but Tally remembered the way David stood on a hoverboard: his back foot pointed forty-five degrees out, like a dancer waiting for the music to start. And she could *feel* that it was him.

The glowing-hot form sagging in his arms had to be Shay, still unconscious.

"You saw me following you?" she asked.

He shook his head. "No, but I knew you would."

"What is this? Another ambush?"

"We need to talk."

"While your friends get farther away?" Tally's hands flexed, but she didn't shoot forward and attack. It was strange to hear David's voice again. It traveled clearly over the rushing water, carrying a hint of nerves.

She realized that he was scared of her.

Of *course* he was, but it still felt strange. . . .

"Can you remember me?" he asked.

"What do you think, David?" Tally scowled. "I remembered you even when I was a bubblehead. You always made a big impression."

"Good," he said, like she'd meant that as a compliment. "Then you remember the last time you saw me. You'd figured out how the city had messed up your head. You forced yourself to think clearly again, not like a pretty. And you escaped. Remember?"

"I remember my boyfriend lying on a pile of blankets, half-brain-dead," she said. "Thanks to those pills your mother cooked up."

At the mention of Zane, a tremor went through David's dark form. "That was a mistake."

"A *mistake*? You mean, you sent those pills to me *accidentally*?"

He shifted on the board. "No. But we warned you about the risks. Don't you remember?"

"I remember everything now, David! I can finally *see*." Her mind was clear, Special-clear, untangled from wild, ugly emotions and bubbleheadedness, fully realizing the truth of what the Smokies were. They weren't revolutionaries; they were nothing but egomaniacs, playing with lives, leaving broken people in their wake.

"Tally," he pleaded softly, but she just laughed. Tally's flash tattoos were spinning wildly, pushed into furious motion by the freezing water and her anger. Her mind focused to a razor point, and saw his outline clearer with every beat of her pounding heart.

"You steal *children*, David, city kids who don't know how dangerous it is out in the wild. And you play games with them."

He shook his head. "I never . . . I never meant to play games with you, Tally. I'm sorry."

She started to answer, but saw David's signal just in time. It was nothing but a flicker of one finger, but her mind was so sharp that the tiny movement bloomed like fireworks against the dark.

Tally's awareness shot out in all directions, searching the blackness around her. The Smokies had chosen a spot where half-submerged rocks added to the water's roar, covering any subtle sounds, but somehow Tally *felt* the moment of attack.

An instant later, her peripheral vision caught the arrows on their way: one from each side, like two fingers crushing a bug. Her mind slowed time to a half-dead crawl. Less than a second from hitting, the missiles were too close for gravity to pull her down, no matter how fast she bent her knees. But Tally didn't need gravity. . . .

Her hands shot up from her sides, elbows bending, fingers curling into fists around the arrow shafts. They slid a few centimeters through her palms, the friction burning like snuffing a candle, but their momentum choked in her grip.

The electric buzz in their tips sputtered for an angry moment, close enough that Tally felt the heat on both cheeks, and then the arrows fizzled in frustration.

Her eyes were still locked on David, and even through the sneak suit she saw his jaw drop open, a small, amazed sound carrying across the water.

She let out a sharp laugh.

His voice was shaking. "What have they done to you now, Tally?"

"They made me see," she said

He shook his head sadly, then pushed Shay into the river.

She fell forward limply, smacking the water face-first and hard. David whirled around on his board, kicking up a spray as he bolted away. The two archers zoomed out from the trees and followed, boards roaring to life.

"Shay!" Tally cried, but the unmoving body was already slipping under, dragged down by the weight of crash bracelets and soaked clothing. Shay's infrared colors began to change in the cold water, hands fading from bright yellow to orange. The fast current carried her under Tally, who threw the spent arrows aside, spun on one heel, and dove into the freezing river.

A few panicked strokes brought her up beside the dimly glowing form, and she reached out to grab Shay's hair, yanking her head out of the water. Flash tattoos hardly moved on the pale face, but then Shay shuddered and emptied her lungs with a sudden cough.

"Shay-la!" Tally twisted in the water, getting a better grip.

Shay waved her arms weakly, then coughed up more water. But her flash tattoos were gradually coming back to life, spinning faster as her heartbeat strengthened. Her face glowed brighter in infrared as flowing blood began to warm it back up.

Tally shifted her grip, struggling to keep both their heads above water, signaling with her crash bracelet. Her borrowed board responded with a magnetic tug, on its way.

Shay's eyes opened, blinking a few times. "That you, Tally-wa?"

"Yes, it's me."

"Quit pulling my hair." Shay coughed again.

"Oh, sorry." Tally untangled her fingers from the wet strands. When the hoverboard nudged her from behind, she slung an arm over it, wrapping the other around Shay. A long shiver traveled through them both.

"Water's cold . . . ," Shay said. Her lips were almost blue in Tally's infrared.

"No kidding. But it woke you up, at least." She managed to lift Shay onto the board, getting her upright. She sat there, huddled miserably against the breeze while Tally stayed in the river, staring up into her glassy eyes. "Shay-la? Do you know where you are?"

"You woke me up, so I was . . . asleep?" Shay shook her head, closing her eyes in concentration. "Crap. That means they got me with one of those stupid arrows."

"Not an arrow; David had a shock-stick in his hand."

Shay spat into the river. "He cheated. Throwing Tachs at me." She frowned, opening her eyes again. "Is Tachs okay?"

"Yeah. I caught him before he hit the ground. Then David tried to take you away. But I got you back."

Shay managed a thin smile. "Good job, Tally-wa."

Tally felt a thin, shivery grin on her face.

"What about Fausto?"

Tally sighed again as she pulled herself up onto the board, its fans spinning into motion under her weight.

"They took him, too." She glanced up the river, seeing nothing but darkness. "And they're long gone by now, I guess."

Shay wrapped a shivering, wet arm around Tally. "Don't worry. We'll get him back." She glanced down, confused. "So how did I get in the river?"

"They flew you out here, used you as bait. They wanted to capture me, too. But I was too fast for them, so David pushed you in to distract me, I suppose. Or maybe he was trying to give the other Smokies time to get away, the ones with Fausto."

"Hmm. That's a little insulting," Shay said.

"What is?"

"They used *me* as a decoy instead of Fausto?"

Tally grinned and squeezed Shay harder. "Maybe they were more sure I'd stop for you."

Shay coughed into a fist. "Well, when I catch them, they're going to wish they'd dumped me off a cliff instead." She took a deep breath, her lungs finally drawing clear. "Funny though. It's not like the Smokies, throwing someone into freezing water while they're unconscious. Know what I mean?"

Tally nodded. "Maybe they're getting desperate."

"Maybe." Shay shivered again. "It's like living out in nature is turning them into Rusties. You can *kill* people with bows and arrows, after all. I kind of liked them better the old way."

"Me too," Tally sighed. The razor-sharpness of her anger was fading, leaving her spirit as soggy as her clothing. No matter how hard she'd tried to fix everything, Fausto was still gone, and David too.

"Anyway, thanks for the rescue, Tally-wa."

"That's okay, Boss." Tally took her friend's hand. "So . . . are we even now?"

Shay laughed, wrapping her arm around Tally, her grin widening to reveal every one of her pointed teeth. "You and I don't have to worry about being even, Tally-wa."

Tally felt a burst of warmth, like she always did when Shay smiled. "Really?"

Shay nodded. "We're too busy being special."

They met Ho back at the ambush site. He'd managed to get Tachs awake, and had put in a call to the rest of the Cutters. They were twenty minutes away, bringing extra boards and screaming for revenge.

"Don't worry about getting even, we'll be visiting the Smokies soon enough," Shay said, without bothering to mention the problem with that plan: No one knew where the New Smoke was. In fact, no one was sure if it was anywhere at all. Since the original Smoke had been destroyed, the Smokies kept moving from one spot to another. And now that they had four brand-new Special Circumstances hoverboards, they'd be even harder to pin down.

While Shay and Tally wrung out their wet clothes, Ho and Tachs wandered around the darkness of the Trails, looking for clues. Soon they found the hoverboard that the Smokey girl had abandoned.

"Check the charge on that thing," Shay ordered Tachs. "At least we can figure out how far they had to fly to get here."

"Good idea, Boss," Tally said. "No solar recharging at night, after all."

"Yeah, I'm feeling really brilliant," Shay said. "But a distance doesn't tell us much. We need more."

"We've *got* more, Boss," Ho said. "Like I was trying to tell Tally right before she shoved me off my board, I had a conversation with that ugly kid at the bash. The one the Smokey girl was giving nanos? Before I handed him over to the wardens, I managed to scare him a little."

Tally didn't doubt that. Ho's flash tattoos included a demon's face drawn over his own features, its bloodred lines shifting through a sequence of wild expressions in time with his pulse.

Shay snorted. "*That* little punk knew where the New Smoke was?"

"Not a chance. But he knew where he was supposed to take the nanos."

"Let me guess, Ho-la," Shay said. "New Pretty Town?"

"Yeah, of course." He held up the plastic bag. "But these weren't just for anyone, Boss. He was supposed to take them to the *Crims*."

Tally and Shay looked at each other. All but a few of the Cutters had been Crims back in their pretty days. The clique was all about making trouble: acting like an ugly, beating the lesions, keeping the shallowness of New Pretty Town from erasing your brain.

Shay shrugged. "The Crims are huge these days. There are hundreds of them." She smiled. "Ever since me and Tally made them famous."

Ho nodded. "Hey, I was one too, remember? But that ugly kid mentioned a name, someone he was supposed to give them to specially."

"Anyone we know?" Tally said.

"Yeah . . . Zane. He said the nanos were for Zane."

THE PROMISE

"Why didn't you *tell* me Zane was back?"

"Because I didn't know. It's only been two weeks."

Tally expelled a long sigh through her teeth.

"What's the matter?" Shay said. "Don't believe me?"

Tally turned away to stare into the fire, unsure how to answer. Not trusting other Cutters wasn't very icy—it led to doubts and muddled thoughts. But for the first time since becoming a Special, she felt out of place, uncomfortable in her own skin. Her fingers moved restlessly up and down the cutting scars along her arms, and sounds from the forest around them were making her jumpy.

Zane was back from the hospital, but he wasn't here with her at the Cutters' camp, out in the wild where he should be. And that felt *wrong*. . . .

All around them, the other Cutters were keeping themselves icy. They'd made a bonfire of fallen trees tonight, Shay's way of building morale after last night's ambush. All sixteen of them—minus Fausto—were gathered around, daring one another to dash through the flames barefoot, boasting about what they were going to do to the Smokies when they finally caught them.

And yet Tally felt outside it all, somehow.

Usually, she loved bonfires, the way they made the shadows jump like living things, the real wickedness of burning trees. That was the whole point of being special: You existed to make sure everyone else behaved, but that didn't mean *you* had to.

But tonight the bonfire smell kept triggering memories of her Smokey days. A few of the Cutters had recently switched from cutting to branding, marking their arms with the red-hot ends of firebrands. Like cutting, it kept your mind icy. But for Tally, the smell was too much like when they'd cooked dead animals back in the Smoke. So she stuck to knives.

She kicked a stick into the flames. "Of course I trust you, Shay. But for the last two months I figured that Zane would join Special Circumstances the moment he got better. The thought of him in New Pretty Town, wearing some cookie-cutter face . . ." She shook her head.

"If I could get him here, Tally-wa, I would."

"So you'll talk to Dr. Cable about it?"

Shay spread her hands. "Tally, you know the rules: To join Special Circumstances, you have to *prove* you're special. You have to think your way out of being a bubblehead."

"But Zane was practically special back when he led the Crims. Doesn't Cable understand that?"

"But he didn't really change until after he took Maddy's pill." Shay scooted closer and put her arm around Tally's shoulder, her eyes flickering red in the firelight. "You and I *thought* our way out, without any help."

"Zane and I started changing from the first time we kissed," Tally said, pulling away. "If he hadn't gotten his brain toasted, he'd be one of us by now."

"So what are you worried about?" Shay shrugged. "He did it once, he can do it again."

Tally turned to glare at Shay, unable to say what they were both wondering. Was Zane still the bubbly guy who'd started the Crims? Or had his brain damage changed all that, dooming him to stay a bubblehead for the rest of his life?

The whole thing was totally unfair. Completely random.

*

When the Smokies had brought the first nanos into New Pretty Town, they'd left two pills for Tally to find, along with a letter from herself warning about the dangers, but saying she'd given 'informed consent.' She'd been too scared at first, but Zane was always bubbly, always trying to escape from being pretty-minded. He'd offered to take the untried pills.

The nanos were supposed to free the pretties, turning them from bubbleheads into . . . well, no one had ever bothered to figure out *what* exactly. What would you do with a bunch of spoiled, superbeautiful people with no limits on their appetites? Let them loose on the fragile world, to destroy it the way the Rusties almost had three centuries before?

In any case, the cure hadn't really worked like it was supposed to. Tally and Zane had split the pills, and Zane had gotten the unlucky one. The nanos in it had eaten the lesions that made him a bubblehead, but then they'd kept right on going, eating away more and more of his mind. . . .

Tally shuddered at the thought of how lucky she'd been. The only purpose of her pill had been to switch off the nanos in the other one. Alone, it hadn't done anything—she'd only *thought* she'd taken the cure. And yet she'd managed to stop being a bubblehead all on her own—no nanos, no operation, not even cutting herself like Shay's crew had.

That was why she was in Special Circumstances.

"But either one of us could have taken that pill," Tally said softly. "It's not fair."

"Sure, it's not fair. But that doesn't make it your *fault*, Tally." A laughing, barefoot Cutter ran through the coals before them, scattering sparks. "You were the lucky one.

That's what happens when you're special. Why feel guilty?"

"I never said I felt guilty." Tally snapped a stick in two. "I just want to do something about it. So I'm coming with you tonight, okay?"

"I'm not sure you're up to it, Tally-wa."

"I'm fine. As long as I don't have to stick any plastic on my face."

Shay laughed, reaching out to trace the sweeping lines of Tally's flash tattoos with her pinkie-nail. "I'm not worried about your face—just your brain. Two ex-boyfriends in a row could mess with it."

Tally turned away. "Zane's not an *ex*-boyfriend. He might be a bubblehead right now, but he'll think his way out."

"Look at you," Shay said. "You're shaking. That's not very icy."

Tally looked down at her hands. Made fists to control them.

She kicked a hefty log onto the fire, scattering sparks. Watching as the flames wrapped around it, she opened her hands to the heat. Somehow, the freezing river had given her a chill that wouldn't leave, no matter how close she sat to the blaze.

She just needed to see Zane again, and this weird feeling in her bones would go away.

"Are you shivering because you saw David?"

"David?" Tally snorted. "What gave you that idea?"

"Don't be embarrassed, Tally-wa. No one can be icy all the time. Maybe you just need a cut." Shay drew her knife.

Tally wanted to, but she snorted and spat into the fire. Shay wasn't going to make her feel weak this way. "I handled David just fine . . . better than you did, I seem to remember."

Shay laughed and punched Tally on the shoulder playfully, except it actually *hurt*.

"*Ouch*, Boss," Tally said. Apparently, Shay was still unhappy about being beaten in hand-to-hand combat by a random the night before.

Shay looked down at her fist. "Sorry. Didn't mean that, really."

"Whatever. So are we even now? Can I go see Zane with you?"

Shay groaned. "Not while he's still a bubblehead, Tally-wa. It'll only freak you out. Why don't you go help look for Fausto instead?"

"You don't really think they'll find anything, do you?"

Shay shrugged, then flicked off her skintenna connection to the other Cutters. "Have to give them something to do," she said softly.

Later, the others were going to head out on their hoverboards and scan the wild. The Smokies couldn't remove Fausto's skintenna without killing him, so his signal would read from a kilometer or so away. But mere kilometers meant nothing in the wild, Tally knew. On her way to the Smoke, she'd traveled at hoverboard speeds for days without encountering any sign of humanity, had seen whole cities submerged in desert sands and jungle. If the Smokies wanted to disappear, the natural world was more than big enough.

Tally snorted. "Doesn't mean you have to waste my time too."

"How many times do I have to explain this, Tally-wa? You're *special* now. You shouldn't be mooning over some bubblehead. You're a Cutter, Zane's not—it's as simple as that."

"If it's so simple, then why do I feel this way?"

Shay let out a groan. "Because, Tally, you're up to your usual trick: making things *complicated*."

Tally sighed and kicked at the fire, sending a stream of sparks into the air. She remembered a lot of times when she'd been contented—as a bubblehead, even as a Smokey. But somehow her satisfaction never lasted very long. She always found herself changing, pushing against the limits, and ruining things for everyone around her.

"It's not always my fault," she said softly. "Things just *get* complicated, sometimes."

"Well, trust me on this one, Tally. Seeing Zane is going to make things *really* complicated. Just give him time to find his own way here. Aren't you happy with us?"

Tally nodded slowly—she *was* happy. Her special senses made the whole world icy, and every moment spent in this new body was better than a year of being pretty. But now that she knew Zane was healthy, his absence muddled everything. Suddenly, she felt unfinished and unreal.

"I'm happy, Shay-la. But remember when Zane and I escaped the city last time? And we left you behind? Well, I can't do that again."

Shay shook her head. "Sometimes you have to let people go, Tally-wa."

"So I should have let *you* go last night, Shay? Just let you drown?"

Shay groaned. "Great example, Tally. Look, this is for your own good. Believe me, you don't want this complication."

"Then let's make it simple, Shay-la." Tally put the tip of her thumb between her razor teeth and bit down. With a prick of pain, the iron taste of blood spread across her tongue, and her mind cleared a little.

"Once Zane is special, I'll stop. I'll never make things complicated again." She held out her hand. "I promise, blood for blood."

Shay stared at the little drop of blood. "You swear to that?"

"Yes. I'll be a good little Cutter and do whatever you and Dr. Cable tell me. Just give me Zane."

Shay paused for a moment, then flicked her own thumb across her knife, watching thoughtfully as the blood welled up. "All I ever wanted was for us to be on the same side, Tally."

"Me too. I just want Zane here with us."

"Anything to make you happy." Shay smiled and took Tally's hand, squeezing their thumbs together . . . hard. "Blood for blood."

As the pain pushed through her, Tally felt her mind grow icy for the first time all day. She could see her future now, a clear path with no more reversals or confusions. She'd fought being ugly and she'd fought being pretty, but that was all over—she just wanted to be special from now on.

"Thank you, Shay-la," Tally said softly. "I'll keep this promise."

Shay released her, cleaning the knife with a few quick swipes across her thigh. "I'll make sure that you do."

Tally swallowed, then licked her still-throbbing thumb. "So can I come with you tonight, Boss? Please?"

"I suppose you have to now," Shay said, smiling sadly. "But you might not like what you see."

NEW PRETTY TOWN

After the others headed into the wild, Shay and Tally banked the bonfire, jumped on their boards, and flew toward the city.

New Pretty Town was lit with colorful explosions in the sky, just like every other night. Tethered hot-air balloons floated above the party spires, and gas torches lit the pleasure gardens, like bright snakes ascending the island's sloping sides. The tallest buildings cast jittering shadows in the fireworks' momentary light, reshaping the city's silhouette with every burst.

As they approached New Pretty Town, the ragged cheers of drunken bubbleheads scattered down to meet them. For a moment, the joyous sound made Tally feel like an envious ugly watching from across the river, waiting to turn sixteen. This was her first trip back to New Pretty Town since becoming a Special.

"Do you ever miss pretty days, Shay-la?" she said. They'd only spent a couple of months together in bubblehead paradise before everything had gotten complicated. "It *was* kind of fun."

"It was bogus," Shay said. "I'd rather have a brain."

Tally sighed. She couldn't disagree—but having a brain *hurt* so much sometimes. She licked her thumb, where a red spot still marked her promise.

Climbing the island's slope through a pleasure garden, the two of them kept to the shadows, heading for the center of town. They glided right above a few entangled couples, but no one spotted them overhead.

"Told you we didn't need to switch on our sneak suits, Tally-wa." Shay chuckled softly, letting the skintenna network carry her words. "When it comes to bubbleheads, we're already invisible."

Tally didn't answer, just looked down at the new pretties passing below. They looked so clueless, so completely unaware of all the dangers they had to be protected from. Their lives might be full of pleasure, but they seemed so meaningless to her now. She couldn't let Zane live like this.

Suddenly, laughter and screams came through the trees, approaching fast . . . at hoverboard speed. Flicking her sneak suit on, Tally angled into the thick pine needles of the nearest treetops. A line of boarders came slaloming through the garden, laughing like hysterical demons. She crouched lower, feeling her suit sprout dappled camouflage and wondering how so many uglies had snuck over to New Pretty Town all at once. Not a bad trick . . .

Maybe this bunch would be worth following.

But then she saw their faces: beautiful and huge-eyed, perfect in symmetry, absolutely clear of blemishes. They were *pretties*.

They shot past unaware, shrieking at the top of their lungs, zooming toward the river. Their screams faded, leaving only the smell of perfume and champagne.

"Boss, did you see—"

"Yeah, Tally-wa, I did." Shay was silent for a moment.

Tally swallowed. Bubbleheads didn't hoverboard. You needed all your reflexes to stay on; you couldn't be all fuzzy-brained and easily distracted. When new pretties wanted thrills, they jumped off buildings wearing bungee jackets or rode in hot-air balloons, things that didn't require any skill.

But these pretties hadn't simply been boarding; they'd

been doing it *well*. Things had changed in New Pretty Town since the last time Tally had been here.

She remembered Special Circumstance's latest report, that there were more runaways leaving the city every week, an epidemic of uglies disappearing into the wild. But what would happen if *pretties* got it into their heads to run away?

Shay emerged from her hiding place, her suit shifting from dappled green to matte black. "Maybe the Smokies have been passing out more pills than we thought," she said. "They could be doing it right here in New Pretty Town. After all, if they've got sneak suits, they can go anywhere."

Tally's eyes scanned the trees around them. In a well-tuned suit, as David's ambush had proven, you could hide even from a Special's senses. "That reminds me, Boss. Where did the Smokies get hold of those suits? They couldn't *make* them, could they?"

"No way. And they didn't steal them either. Dr. Cable said that all the cities keep track of their military equipment. But nobody's reporting anything missing, not anywhere on the continent."

"You told her about last night?"

"About the sneak suits, yes. But not about losing Fausto or our boards."

Tally pondered this, floating in a lazy arc above a flickering torch. "So . . . you think the Smokies found some old Rusty technology?"

"Sneak suits are too clever for the Rusties. They were only good at killing." Shay's voice faded, and she stayed silent for a moment as a group of Bashers walked through the trees below, drumming loudly as they headed to some party by the river. Tally peered down, wondering if they looked more lively than normal Bashers. Was *everyone* in town getting more bubbly? Maybe the nanos' effects would rub off even on pretties who hadn't taken a pill—just as being around Zane had always made her bubblier.

After the group had passed, Shay said, "Dr. C thinks the Smokies have some new friends. City friends."

"But only Special Circumstances has sneak suits. Why would one of us—?"

"I didn't say *this* city, Tally-wa."

"Oh," Tally murmured. Cities didn't usually mess with one another's business—that sort of conflict was too dangerous. It could wind up like the wars the Rusties used to have, with whole continents vying for control, trying to kill one another. Just the thought of fighting with another city's Special Circumstances sent a nervous trickle down her spine. . . .

They landed on top of Pulcher Mansion, coming down among solar cells and air extractors. A few bubbleheads stood on the roof, but they were transfixed by the dance of hot-air balloons and fireworks overhead and didn't see a thing.

It felt strange being on the roof of Pulcher again. Tally had practically lived here with Zane last winter, but she saw everything differently now. Smelled it differently too—scents of human habitation came from the spinning air extractors that dotted the roof. Totally unlike the fresh air of the wild, it made her feel anxious and crowded.

"Check this out, Tally-wa," Shay said, sending a vision overlay through her skintenna. Tally opened it, and the building underfoot faded to transparency, revealing a grid of blue lines marked with glowing blobs.

She blinked a few times, trying to make sense of the overlay. "Is this some kind of infrared?"

Shay laughed. "No, Tally-wa. It's a feed from the city interface." She pointed to a cluster of blobs two floors below. "That's Zane-la and some friends. He's still in his old room, see?"

As Tally focused on each blob in turn, a name popped up beside it. She remembered the interface rings that bubbleheads and uglies wore, and how the city used them to keep track of people. Like all troublemaking pretties, though, Zane had probably been fitted with a bracelet, which was basically an interface ring that you couldn't take off.

The other blobs in Zane's room were labeled with names, most of which she didn't recognize. All her old Crim friends had been part of last winter's big escape into the wild. Like Tally, they'd thought their way out of being bubbleheads, so they were Specials now—except for those who were still out in the wild, still Smokies.

Peris's name hovered right next to Zane's. Peris had been Tally's best friend since they were littlies, but during the escape he'd backed out at the last minute, deciding to stay a bubblehead. He was one pretty who would never be special, that much Tally knew.

But at least Zane had a familiar face around.

She frowned. "It must be weird for Zane. Everyone can recognize him from all the tricks we pulled, but he might not even remember any of it. . . ." She let her whisper fade, pushing the awful thoughts away.

"At least he's got some standards," Shay said. "There's about a dozen bashes happening in New Pretty Town tonight, but apparently none of them are bubbly enough for Zane and his crew."

"But they're just sitting around in his room." None of the blobs looked to be moving much. Whatever they were up to, it didn't look very bubbly.

"Yeah. Talking in private is going to be tricky." Shay had planned to trail Zane for a while, then pull him aside in some dark spot between parties.

"Why are they all doing *nothing*?"

Shay touched Tally's shoulder. "Relax, Tally-wa. If they let him come back to New Pretty Town, Zane's fit to party. What would be the point otherwise? Maybe it's too early, and going out would be bogus."

"I hope so."

Shay made a gesture, and the vision overlay faded a little, the real world around them coming back into focus. She pulled on her climbing gloves. "Come on, Tally-wa. Let's go find out for ourselves."

"Can't we hear them through the city interface?"

"Not unless we want Dr. Cable listening in. I'd rather keep this between us Cutters."

Tally smiled. "Okay, Shay-la. So, between us Cutters, what exactly is the plan tonight?"

"I thought you wanted to see Zane," Shay said, then shrugged. "Anyway, Specials don't need plans."

Climbing was easy these days.

Tally didn't fear heights anymore—they didn't even make her icy. There was only the slightest sensation of warning as she looked over the edge of the roof. Nothing panicky or nervous-making—more like a little reminder from her brain to be careful.

She swung both legs over and lowered herself, letting her feet slide down Pulcher Mansion's smooth wall. One grippy-shoed toe wedged into a seam between two sections of ceramic, and she paused, letting the sneak suit turn itself the color of the mansion. She felt its scales shifting to match the building's texture.

When the suit finished its adjustments, Tally released her hold on the roof-ledge. She half-fell and half-slid, hands and feet scraping down the ceramic, darting out madly to catch more seams, the edges of window frames, half-repaired cracks in the wall. None of the imperfections was sturdy enough to hold her weight, but each momentary hand- or foothold slowed her just a little, the descent always under control. It was thrillingly tenuous, as if Tally were a bug running across water too quickly to sink.

By the time she reached Zane's window, Tally was falling fast, but her fingers shot out and caught the ledge easily. She swung in a wide arc, grippy gloves sticking to the ledge as if glued there, her momentum slowly expending itself as she pendulummed back and forth.

When she looked up, Tally saw Shay perched a meter above, balanced on a tiny ridge of window frame that stuck out no more than a centimeter from the wall. Her gloved hands were splayed behind her like five-legged spiders, but Tally couldn't see how there was enough total friction to hold her weight. "How are you *doing* that?" she whispered.

Shay giggled. "Can't tell you all my secrets, Tally-wa. But it's a bit slippy up here. Quick, take a listen."

Hanging from one hand, Tally clamped her other glove's fingertips between her teeth. She pulled it off and stretched out a finger to touch the corner of the window. The chips in her hand registered the vibrations there, turning the expanse of glass into one big microphone. She closed her eyes, hearing the noises inside the room with a sudden intimacy, like pressing one ear to a drinking glass against a thin wall. She heard a ping as Shay listened in through her skintenna.

Zane was talking, and the sound sent a little tremor through Tally. It was so familiar—yet distorted, either by her eavesdropping hardware or the months they'd been apart. She could make out the words, but not what they meant.

"All fixed, fast-frozen relations, with their train of ancient and venerable prejudices and opinions, are swept away," he was saying. "All new-formed ones become antiquated before they can ossify. . . ."

"What's he babbling about?" Shay hissed, adjusting her grip.

"I don't know. Sounds like Rusty-talk. Like some old book."

"Don't tell me Zane's . . . *reading* to the Crims?"

Tally looked up at Shay in puzzlement. A dramatic reading didn't sound very Crim, actually. Or very *anything* but random. And yet Zane's voice kept going, droning on about something melting.

"Take a peek, Tally-wa."

Tally nodded, pulling herself up until her eyes cleared the window ledge.

Zane sat in a big, soft-cushioned chair, holding a tattered old paper book in one hand and waving the other around like an orchestra conductor as he declaimed. But where the city interface had placed the other Crims, there was only empty space.

"Oh, Shay," she whispered. "You're going to love this."

"What I'm going to do is fall on your head, Tally-wa, in about ten seconds. What's going on?"

"He's all alone. Those other Crims are just . . ." She squinted into the gloom outside Zane's reading light. There they were, spread around the room like an attentive audience. "Rings. They're all just interface rings, except for Zane."

Despite Shay's wobbly grip on her perch, she let out a long snicker. "Maybe he's bubblier than we thought."

Tally nodded, grinning to herself. "Should I knock?"

"Please."

"Might startle him."

"Startled is good, Tally-wa. We want him bubbly. Now hurry *up*, I'm starting to slip."

Tally pulled herself higher, getting one knee onto the narrow ledge outside the window. She took a deep breath, then rapped twice, trying to smile without showing the razor sharpness of her teeth.

Zane looked up at the sound, startled for a moment, then his eyes widened. He made a gesture, and the window slid open.

A grin spread across his face.

"Tally-wa," he said. "You've changed."

ZANE-LA

Zane was still beautiful.

His cheekbones were sharp, his stare hungry and intense, like he was still using calorie purgers to keep himself alert. His lips were as full as any bubblehead's, and as Zane stared at Tally, he pursed them in childlike concentration. His hair hadn't changed at all; she remembered how he'd dyed it with calligraphy ink, turning it a bluish black that was way beyond the Pretty Committee's standards of good taste.

But there was something different about his face. Tally's mind spun, trying to figure out what it was.

"You brought Shay-la with you?" he said as the squeak of grippy shoes came from the window behind Tally. "How happy-making."

Tally nodded slowly, hearing in his voice that he wished she'd come alone. Of course. They had so much to talk about, hardly any of which she wanted to say in front of Shay.

It suddenly seemed like years since she'd seen Zane. Tally felt all the differences in her body—the ultralight bones and flash tattoos, the cutting scars along her arms—as reminders of how she'd changed in the time they'd been apart. Of how different they were now.

Shay grinned at the interface rings. "Aren't your friends finding that musty old book a little boring?"

"I've got more friends than you think, Shay-la." His eyes swept across the four walls of the room.

Shay shook her head, pulling a small black device from her belt. Tally's sharp ears caught its barely audible hum, a sizzling like wet leaves thrown onto a fire. "Relax, Zane-la. The city can't hear us."

His eyes widened. "You're allowed to do that?"

"Haven't you heard?" Shay smiled. "We're special."

"Oh. Well, as long as it's just us three . . ." He dropped the book onto the empty chair beside him, where it set Peris's ring jiggling. "The others are off on a little trick tonight. I'm covering, in case the wardens are monitoring us."

Shay laughed. "So the wardens are supposed to believe the Crims have a *reading group*?"

He shrugged. "It's not real wardens, as far as we can tell, only software. As long as someone's talking, it stays happy."

Tally sat down on Zane's unmade bed slowly, a shiver moving through her. Zane wasn't talking like some clueless pretty at all. And if he was covering for his friends while they did something criminal, then he was still bubbly, still the sort of tricky pretty who could one day become a Special. . . .

She breathed in the familiar scent of him from the bedclothes, wondering what her tattoos were doing—probably spinning halfway off her face

But Zane wasn't wearing an interface ring himself, or a bracelet. How were the wardens tracking him?

"Your new face is about a mega-Helen, Tally-wa," Zane said, his gaze traveling the web of flash tattoos on her face and arms. "It could launch a billion ships. But pirate ships, probably."

She smiled at the lame joke, trying to think of something to say. She'd been waiting for this moment for two months, and suddenly all she could do was sit here like an idiot.

But it wasn't just her nerves that were making her word-missing. The more she looked at him, the more Zane looked wrong, somehow, and his voice sounded like it was coming from another room.

"I was hoping you'd come," he added softly.

"She insisted," Shay said, her words whisper-close.

Tally realized why Zane sounded so distant. With no skintenna in his flesh, his words didn't come through like the other Cutters'. He wasn't part of her clique anymore. He wasn't special.

Shay sat down next to Tally on the bed. "But if you don't mind, you two can be all bubbleheaded some other time." She pulled out the small plastic bag of nano pills that Ho had taken from the ugly boy the night before. "We came about these."

Zane half-rose from the chair and held out his hand for them, but Shay just laughed. "Not so fast, Zane-la. You have a bad habit of taking the wrong pills."

"Don't remind me," he said wearily.

Another shudder went through Tally. As he eased himself back into the chair, Zane moved slowly, deliberately, almost like a crumbly.

Tally remembered how Maddy's nanos had damaged his motor control, disrupting the part of his brain in charge of reflexes and motion. Maybe that's all it was, minor tremors left by the tiny machines. Nothing to freak out about.

But again, when she looked into his face, something was missing there, too. It had no gorgeous web of flash tattoos, and gave her none of the thrill she felt when she looked into another Cutter's coal black eyes. He looked sleepy in a way that Specials never did, as if he were wallpaper, just another pretty.

But this was *Zane*, not some random bubblehead. . . .

Tally dropped her eyes to the floor, wishing she could turn off the perfect clarity of her vision. She didn't want to see all these unsettling details.

"Where did those pills come from?" he said. His voice still sounded so far away.

"From a Smokey girl," Shay answered.

He glanced at Tally. "Anyone we know?"

She shook her head, not looking up from the floor. The

girl hadn't been a former Crim or anyone from the Old Smoke. Tally had a flash of wondering if she'd come from another city. Maybe she was one of the Smokies' mysterious new allies. . . .

"But she knew your name, Zane-la," Shay said. "Said these were for you specifically. Expecting a delivery?"

He took a slow breath. "Maybe you should ask her."

"She got away," Tally said, and heard Shay let out a tiny hiss.

Zane laughed. "So Special Circumstances needs my help?"

"We're not the same as . . . ," Tally started, but her voice faded. She *was* in Special Circumstances, Zane could see that for himself. But suddenly she wished she could explain how the Cutters were different, not like the regular Specials who'd pushed him around when he was an ugly. The Cutters played by their own rules. They'd found everything that Zane had always wanted—living in the wild outside the city's dictates, their minds icy, free from the imperfections of ugliness. . . .

Free of the averageness that seemed to be leaking out of Zane.

Her mouth closed, and Shay rested a hand on her shoulder.

Tally could feel her heart beating faster.

"Sure, we need your help," Shay said. "We need to stop these"—she held up the bag of pills—"from making more pretties like *you*." At the last word, she threw it toward him.

Tally saw every centimeter of the bag's flight, watching as it shot past him—his hands coming up a full second too late to catch it. The pills skidded along the wall, dropping into the corner.

Zane let his empty hands fall back into his lap, where they lay curled like dead slugs.

"Nice catch," Shay said.

Tally swallowed. Zane was crippled.

He shrugged. "I don't need pills, anyway, Shay-la. I'm permanently bubbly." He gestured at his forehead. "The nanos damaged me right here, where the lesions are supposed to go. I think the doctors put more in, but as far as I can tell, they don't have much to grab on to. That part of my brain is all new and changing."

"But what about your . . ." Tally's throat closed up around the question.

"My memories? My thoughts?" He shrugged again. "Brains are good at rewiring themselves. The way yours did, Tally, when you thought your way out of being pretty. And yours, Shay-la, when you cut yourself." One hand lifted from his lap, soaring like a trembling bird. "Controlling someone by changing their brain is like trying to stop a hovercar by digging a ditch. If they think hard enough, they can fly right over."

"But Zane . . . ," Tally said. Her eyes felt hot. "You're shaking."

And it wasn't just the infirmity of his movements—it was his face, his eyes, his voice . . . Zane wasn't special.

His gaze fixed on her. "You can do it again, Tally."

"Do what?" she said.

"Undo what they did to you. That's what my Crims are doing—rewiring themselves."

"I don't *have* any lesions."

"Are you sure?"

"Save it for your lame new Crim pals, Zane-la," Shay said. "We're not here to talk about your brain damage. Where did those pills come from?"

"You want to know about the pills?" He smiled. "Why not? You can't stop us. They come from the New Smoke."

"Thanks, genius," Shay said. "But where *is* it?"

He looked down at his quivering hand. "I wish I knew. Could use their help right now."

Shay nodded. "Is that why you're helping them? Hoping they'll fix you?"

He shook his head. "It's a lot more important than me, Shay-la. But, yeah, we Crims are passing out the cure. That's what these five are doing right now while they're supposedly sitting here." He gestured at the interface rings. "But it's bigger than us—half the cliques in town are helping. We've given out thousands so far."

"*Thousands?*" Shay said. "That's impossible, Zane! How're the Smokies making that many? Last I saw, they didn't have flush toilets, much less factories."

He shrugged. "Search me. But it's much too late to stop us. The new pills work too fast. There are already too many pretties who can think."

Tally glanced at Shay. This really was bigger than Zane. If what he was saying was true, no wonder the whole city seemed to be changing.

Zane held out his quivering hands in front of him, the wrists close together. "Want to arrest me now?"

Shay paused for a moment, her flash tattoos pulsing on her face and arms. Finally, she shrugged. "I'd never arrest you, Zane-la. Tally wouldn't let me. And besides, at the moment I don't really care about your little pills."

He raised an eyebrow. "So what *do* you Cutters care about, Shay-la?"

"Other Cutters," Shay said flatly. "Your Smokey pals kidnapped Fausto last night, and we're not happy about it."

Zane's eyebrows rose, and he flashed Tally a look. "That's . . . interesting. What do you think they're going to do with him?"

"Experiment. Make him all shaky like you, probably," Shay said. "Unless we find him in time."

Zane shook his head. "They don't experiment without consent."

"Consent? What part of 'kidnapped' did you not catch, Zane-la?" Shay said. "These aren't the old wimpy Smokies anymore. They've got military gear and an icy new attitude. They ambushed us with shock-sticks."

"They almost drowned Shay," Tally said. "Pushed her into the river unconscious."

"Unconscious?" The smile on Zane's face grew. "Sleeping on the job, Shay-la."

Shay's muscles tensed, and for a moment Tally thought she was going to spring up from the bed and strike—her diamond-hard fingernails and teeth against Zane's defenseless flesh.

But she only laughed, hands uncurling from fighting position to stroke Tally's hair. "Something like that. But I'm very awake now."

Zane shrugged, as if he hadn't noticed how close she'd come to ripping his throat out. "Well, I don't know where the New Smoke is. I can't help you."

"Yes, you can," Shay said.

"How?"

"You can escape."

"Escape?" Zane's fingers went to his throat. Around his neck was a metal chain, its links a dull silver. "That would be tricky, I'm afraid."

Tally closed her eyes for a moment. So that was how they

were tracking him. Zane was not only infirm and unspecial, he was collared like a dog. It was all she could do to keep herself from jumping up and diving out the window. The smell of the room—recycled clothing, the musty book, the sticky sweetness of champagne—all of it was making her sick.

"We can get you something to cut that off," Shay said.

Zane shook his head. "I doubt it. I've tested this in the shop shed; it's the same alloy they use on orbital craft."

"Trust me," Shay said. "Tally and I can do whatever we want."

Tally glanced at Shay. Cut orbital alloy? For technology that serious, they'd have to ask Dr. Cable for help.

Zane fondled the chain. "And for this little favor, you want me to betray the Smoke?"

"You wouldn't do that for your own freedom, Zane," Shay said, and put her hands on Tally's shoulders. "But you'd do it for *her*."

Tally felt the two sets of eyes on her—Shay's black and deep and special, Zane's watery and average.

"What do you mean?" he said slowly.

Shay just stood there silent, but through the skintenna, Tally heard her lips mouth a few words, carried on a breath of air.

"They'll make him special. . . ."

Tally nodded, searching for the words. He'd never listen to anyone else.

She cleared her throat. "Zane, if you escape, it'll prove to them that you're still bubbly. And when they capture you, they'll make you like us. You wouldn't believe how good it feels, how icy. And we can be together."

"Why can't we be together now?" he asked softly.

Tally tried to imagine kissing his childlike lips, stroking

his shaking hands, and the thought disgusted her.

She shook her head. "I'm sorry . . . but not the way you are."

He spoke softly, as if to a child. "You can change yourself, Tally—"

"And *you* can escape, Zane," Shay interrupted. "Get out into the wild and let the Smokies find you." She pointed into the corner. "You can even keep that bag of pills, bubbly up some of your Crim friends if you want."

His eyes didn't leave Tally. "And then betray them?"

"You don't have to do anything, Zane. Along with the cutting tool, I'll give you a tracker," Shay said. "Once you reach the New Smoke, we'll come get you, and the city will make you strong and fast and perfect. Bubbly forever."

"I'm already bubbly," he said coldly.

"Yeah, but you're not strong, or fast, or perfect, Zane-la," Shay said. "You're not even *average*."

"Do you really think I'll betray the Smoke?" he said.

Shay squeezed Tally's shoulders. "For her, you will."

He looked at Tally, a lost expression on his face for a moment, like he really was unsure. Then he stared down at his hands and sighed, nodding slowly.

But Tally saw them clear as day, the thoughts passing across Zane's face: He would accept the offer, then try to trick them once he had escaped. He really believed that he could fool them both, then somehow rescue Tally and bring her back to averageness.

It was so simple seeing into his mind, as easy to read as the uglies' pathetic rivalries back at the Spring Bash. His infirm body let his thoughts leak out, like a random sweating on a hot day.

Tally looked away.

"Okay," he said. "For you, Tally."

"Meet us at midnight tomorrow, where the river splits," Shay said. "The Smokies are going to be suspicious of runaways, so bring enough supplies for a long wait. But they'll eventually come for *you*, Zane."

He nodded. "I know what to do."

"And bring as many friends as you want, the more the better. You might need some help out there."

He didn't argue with the insult, just nodded, trying to catch Tally's eyes. She looked away, but forced a weak smile onto her face. "You'll be happier when you're special, Zane-la. You don't understand how good it is." She flexed her hands, watching the tattoos spin. "Every second is so icy, so beautiful."

Shay stood, pulling Tally to her feet and striding to the window. She paused, one foot on the sill.

Zane just looked at Tally. "We'll be together soon."

All Tally could do was nod.

THE CUT

"You were right. That was horrible."

"Poor Tally-wa . . ." Shay swept her hoverboard closer. In the water below, the moon's reflection kept pace with them, warping madly with the ripples of the current. "I'm really sorry."

"Why does he look so different? It's like he's not the same person."

"*You're* not the same person, Tally. You're special now, and he's just average."

Tally shook her head, trying to remember Zane back in their pretty days. How bubbly he was, how his face glowed with excitement as he talked, and how that thrilled her, made her want to touch him. . . . Even when he was being annoying, there'd never been anything *average* about Zane. But tonight he'd seemed emptied of something essential, like champagne with all the bubbles gone flat.

There was a split screen in her brain: the way she remembered Zane and the way she saw him now, two pictures crashing against each other. The endless minutes with him had left her feeling as if her head were about to break in half.

"I don't want this," she said softly. Her stomach was uneasy and the moonlight on the water was too bright, its lines too sharp in her perfect vision. "I don't want to be this way."

Shay angled her board sideways, sweeping directly into Tally's path and spinning to a sudden, dangerous stop. Tally leaned back, and both hoverboards shrieked like buzz saws as they halted, coming to rest only centimeters apart.

"What way? Annoying? *Pathetic?*" Shay shouted, her voice all razors and ground glass. "I tried to tell you not to come!"

Tally's heart was pounding from the near collision, and anger rushed through her in a torrent. "You *knew* that seeing him would do this to me!"

"You think I know everything?" Shay said coldly. "*I'm* not the one in love. Haven't been since you stole David from me. But maybe I thought love might make a difference. Well, Tally-wa, did it make Zane *special* for you?"

Tally flinched, something inside her flipping over. She looked down at the black water, feeling like she was going to throw up. She tried to stay icy, to remember how Zane had made her feel back in pretty days. "What did Dr. Cable do to us, Shay? Do we have some kind of special lesions in our brains? Something that makes everyone else look pathetic? Like we're better than them?"

"We *are* better than them, Tally-wa!" Shay's eyes shone like coins, reflecting the lights of New Pretty Town. "The operation gives us the clarity to see that. That's why everyone else looks confused and pitiful, because that's how most people *are*."

"Not Zane," Tally said. "He was never pitiful."

"He's changed too, Tally-wa."

"But it's not his fault. . . ." Tally turned away. "I don't want to *see* this way! I don't want to be disgusted by everyone who's not part of our clique, Shay!"

Shay smiled. "You'd rather be all happy and loving, like a clueless bubblehead? Or live like a Smokey, crapping in holes and eating dead rabbits and feeling all virtuous about it? What part of being special don't you like?"

Tally's fingers curled into fighting position. "I don't like the part where Zane looks *wrong* to me."

"Do you think he looks right to *anyone*, Tally? His brain's a mess!"

Tally felt tears burning inside, but the heat didn't spill into her eyes. She'd never seen a Special cry, and didn't even know if she could. "Just answer me: Is there something in my head that makes him look wrong? What did Cable do to us?"

Shay let out a frustrated sigh. "Tally, in every conflict both sides do things to people's heads. But at least our side gets it right. The city makes bubbleheads the way they are to keep them happy and the planet safe. They make us Specials see the world so clearly that its beauty almost *hurts*, so we won't let humanity try to destroy it again." Shay edged her board closer, reaching out to take Tally's shoulders. "But the Smokies are amateurs. They experiment on people, turn them into freaks like Zane."

"He's not a . . . ," Tally began, but couldn't finish. The part of her that despised his weakness was too strong—she couldn't deny the way Zane sickened her, like something that shouldn't be allowed to live.

But it wasn't his fault. It was Dr. Cable's, for not making him special. For following her stupid rules.

"Stay icy," Shay said softly.

Tally took a deep breath, trying to get her anger and frustration under control. She let her senses expand, until she could hear the wind playing in the pine needles. Scents rose up from the water—the algae on its surface, the ancient minerals down below. Her heartbeat slowed a little.

"Tell me, Tally: Are you certain you really love Zane, and not just some leftover memory of him?"

Tally winced, closing her eyes. Inside her, the images of Zane still warred with each other. She was trapped between them, and clarity wouldn't come.

"It makes me sick to look at him," she whispered. "But I know that's not right. I want to go back . . . to how I felt before."

Shay's voice lowered. "Then listen, Tally. I have a plan—a way to get that necklace off."

Tally opened her eyes again, gritting her teeth at the thought of the collar around his throat. "I'll do anything, Shay."

"But it has to look like Zane escaped on his own—otherwise Cable won't want him. Which means tricking Special Circumstances."

Tally swallowed. "And we can really do that?"

"You mean will our brains let us?" Shay snorted. "Of course. We're not bubbleheads. But we're risking everything we have. Understand?"

"And you'd do that for Zane?"

"For you, Tally-wa." Shay grinned, her eyes flashing. "And for the fun of it. But I need you absolutely icy."

Shay drew her knife.

Tally closed her eyes again, nodding. She wanted clarity so *badly*. She reached out to grasp Shay's knife by the blade.

"Hang on, not your hand . . ."

But Tally squeezed down hard, driving the razor edge into her flesh. The delicate and fine-tuned nerves woven into her palm, a hundred times more sensitive than any random's, split apart, screaming. She heard herself cry out.

The special moment came with its wild clarity, and Tally could finally see through her own tangled thoughts: Deep inside herself were threads of permanence, the things that had remained unchanged whether she was ugly or pretty or special—and love was one of them. She longed to be with Zane again, feeling everything she'd felt with him before, but amplified a thousandfold by her new senses. She wanted Zane to know what it was like to be a Special, to see the world in all its icy clarity.

"Okay." Her breath was ragged. She opened her eyes. "I'm with you."

Shay's face was radiant. "Good girl. But it's traditional to use the arms."

Tally opened her hand, the skin of her palm tugging free from the knife, setting off a fresh wave of pain. She sucked in breath.

"I know it hurts, Tally-wa." Shay was whispering now, staring in fascination at the blood-slicked blade. "It made me sick too, seeing Zane like that. I didn't know he'd be so messed up, *honest*." Her board slid a little closer, and she placed her hand softly over Tally's wounded palm. "But I'm not going to let this break you, Tally-wa. I don't want you turning all mushy and average. We'll make him one of us and save the city too; we'll fix everything." She pulled her medical kit from a sneak-suit pouch. "Just like I'm going to fix you now."

"But he won't give the Smokies up."

"He doesn't have to." Shay sprayed the wound, and the pain quickly faded to a faraway tingling. "He only has to prove he's bubbly, and we'll do the rest—get him and Fausto back, then capture David and the rest of them. It's the only way to stop what's happening. Like Zane said, arresting a bunch of pretties won't help. We have to cut this off at the source: We have to find the New Smoke."

"I know." Tally nodded, her mind still icy. "But Zane's so crippled, the Smokies will know that we *let* him escape. They'll pull apart everything he's carrying, scan every bone in his body."

Shay smiled. "Of course they will. But he'll be clean."

"Then how will we track him?" Tally asked.

"The old-fashioned way." Shay turned her board around, reaching out to take Tally by her unbloodied hand. They climbed, lifting fans thrumming to life underfoot as Shay pulled her higher and higher, until the city was spread out around them, a great bowl of light surrounded by darkness.

Tally glanced down at her hand. The pain had faded to a dull pounding that throbbed in time with her heartbeat, and the medspray was congealing her spilled blood, turning it to a dust that blew away as they rose. The wound had already sealed, leaving nothing but a ridge of raised skin. The scar cut straight across her flash tattoos, breaking the dermal circuitry that made them dance. Her palm was a jittering mess of lines, like a computer screen after a hard crash.

But Tally's thoughts were still clear. She flexed her fingers, sending little pings of pain up her arm.

"See that blackness out there, Tally-wa?" Shay pointed toward the city's nearest edge. "That's *our* space, not the randoms'. We were designed for the wild, and we're going to be tracking Zane-la and his pals every step of the way."

"But I thought you said—"

"Not with *electronics*, Tally-wa. We'll use sight and smell, and all the other old ways of the forest." Her eyes flashed. "Like the pre-Rusties used to do."

Tally looked across the orange glow of factories, out to where darkness marked the Outside. "Pre-Rusties? You mean, look for *bent branches* or something? People on hoverboards don't leave a lot of footprints behind, Shay-la."

"True. Which is why they'll never suspect someone's following them, because no one's done that kind of tracking for at least three hundred years." Shay's eyes flashed. "But you and I can smell an unwashed human from a kilometer away, a burnt-out campfire from ten. We can see in the dark and hear better than bats." Her sneak suit flickered to night black. "We can make ourselves invisible and move without a sound. Think about it, Tally-wa."

Tally nodded slowly. The Smokies would never imagine anyone watching from the darkness, listening for every step, sniffing out every campfire and chemically cooked meal.

"And with us along," Tally said, "Zane will be okay even if he gets lost or hurt."

"Exactly. And after we find the New Smoke, you two can be together."

"Are you sure Dr. Cable will make him special?"

Shay pushed off from Tally, laughing as her board dropped. "After what I've got planned, she'll probably give him *my* job."

Tally looked down at her still-tingling hand. Then she reached out with it and touched Shay's cheek. "Thank you."

Shay shook her head. "No thanks necessary, Tally-wa. Not after the way you looked back in Zane's room. I hate seeing you all miserable like that. It's just not special."

"Sorry, Boss."

Shay laughed and tugged her into motion again, off the river and toward the factory belt, descending to normal flying height. "Like you said, you didn't leave me behind last night, Tally-wa. So we're not leaving Zane behind either."

"And we'll get Fausto back, too."

Shay turned back toward her and half-grinned. "Oh right, let's not forget about poor Fausto. And that other little bonus . . . what was that again?"

Tally took a deep breath. "The end of the New Smoke."

"Good girl. Any more questions?"

"Yeah, one: Where are we going to find something that can cut orbital alloy?"

Shay spun in one complete circle on her board, holding a finger in front of her lips.

"Somewhere *very* special, Tally-wa," she whispered. "Follow me, and all will be revealed."

THE ARMORY

"You weren't kidding about dangerous, were you, Boss?"

Shay chuckled. "Backing out already, Tally-wa?"

"Not a chance," Tally whispered. The cutting had left her restless, full of energy demanding to be expended.

"Good girl." Shay grinned at her through the tall grass. Their skintennas were shut down so that the city records wouldn't reveal they'd been here tonight, and Shay's voice sounded tinny and far away. "Zane will get *mega*-bubbly points if they think he organized a trick like this."

"That's for sure," Tally whispered, staring up at the formidable building before them.

Back when she was little, older uglies had sometimes joked about sneaking into the Armory. But no one had ever been stupid enough to actually try.

She remembered all the rumors. The Armory held every registered piece of hardware the city possessed: handguns and armored vehicles, spy-tech, ancient tools and technologies, even strategic, city-killing weapons. Only a select few people had ever been allowed inside; the defenses were mostly automatic.

The dark, windowless building was surrounded by a wide-open field marked with the flashing red lights of a no-fly zone. The grounds were ringed with sensors, and four auto-cannon guarded the Armory's corners, serious defenses in case some unthinkable war ever broke out between the cities.

This place wasn't designed to warn trespassers off. It was designed to kill them.

"Ready for some fun, Tally-wa? "

Tally looked at Shay's intense expression, and felt her own heart beating faster. She flexed her wounded hand. "Always, Boss."

They crept back through the grass to their hoverboards, which waited behind a giant, automated factory. As they ascended toward its roof, Tally zipped up the front of her sneak suit and felt its scales do a little boot-up dance. Her arms turned black and blurry-looking, the scales angling themselves to deflect radar waves.

She frowned. "They'll know that whoever did this had sneak suits, won't they?"

"I already told Dr. Cable about the Smokies going invisible on us. So maybe they loaned the Crims some toys." Shay flashed a razor smile, then pulled her hood over her head, turning herself into a faceless silhouette. Tally did the same.

"Ready to go ballistic?" Shay asked, pulling on gloves. Her voice was altered by the mask, and she looked like a person-shaped smudge against the horizon, her outline blurred by the random angles of the scales.

Tally swallowed. The hood over her mouth made her breath hot against her face, like she was suffocating. "Ready when you are, Boss."

Shay snapped her fingers, and Tally crouched, counting off ten long seconds in her head. The boards began to buzz as they slowly built magnetic charge, the fan blades spinning up to just below take-off speed. . . .

On *ten*, Tally's board leaped into the air, pushing her down into a squat. The fans screamed all the way up to maximum, angling her toward the Armory like an arcing firework. A few seconds later, they shut down, and Tally found herself soaring through the dark sky in silence, excitement rushing through her once again.

She knew this plan was crazy, but the danger filled her mind with iciness. And soon Zane would be able to feel this way too. . . .

Halfway across, Tally grabbed the board and pulled it to her body, hiding its surface behind her radar-deflecting suit. Tally glanced over her shoulder—she and Shay were soaring over the no-fly barrier, high enough to escape the motion sensors on the ground. No alarms sounded as they passed the perimeter, falling silently toward the Armory's roof.

Maybe this was going to be easy. It had been two centuries since there had been any serious conflict among the cities—no one really believed that humanity would ever go to war again. Besides, the Armory's automatic defenses were designed to repel a major attack, not a couple of burglars looking to borrow a handheld tool.

She felt another smile grow on her face. This was the first time the Cutters had dared to trick the city itself. It was almost like ugly days again.

The roof rushed toward her, and Tally held her board over her head, hanging from it like a parachute. A few seconds before she hit, the lifting fans burst to life, bringing her to a sudden halt. Tally landed softly, as easy as stepping from a slidewalk.

The board cut off and settled into her hands. She lowered it gently to the roof. They could make no sound from now on, communicating only with sign language and through their suits' contacts.

A few meters away, Shay held both thumbs up.

With soft, careful steps, the two made their way to the

doors in the center of the roof, where hovercars entered and exited. Tally saw a seam down the middle where they would open up.

She touched her fingertips to Shay's, letting the suits carry her whisper. "Can we cut through this?"

Shay shook her head. "This whole building's made of orbital alloy, Tally. If we could cut through it, we could free Zane ourselves."

Tally scanned the roof, seeing no signs of access doors. "I guess we go with your plan then."

Shay drew her knife. "Get down."

Tally flattened herself against the roof, feeling her suit's scales shift to match its texture.

Shay threw the knife hard, then hit the ground herself. It arced beyond the building's edge, spinning out into the darkness and toward the sensor-strewn grass.

Seconds later, earsplitting alarms shrieked from all directions. The metal surface beneath them jolted, the doors parting with a rusty groan. A tornado of dust and dirt leaped from the gap, a monstrous machine rising in its midst.

It was barely bigger than a pair of hoverboards lashed together, but it looked heavy—four lifting fans screamed with the effort of hauling it through the air. As it emerged, the machine seemed to grow, unfolding wings and claws with shuddering alien movements, like a giant metal insect being born. Its bulbous body bristled with weaponry and sensors.

Tally was used to robots; cleaning and gardening drones were everywhere in New Pretty Town. But those looked like amiable toys. Everything about the mechanism above her—its jerky movements, its black armor, the shrieking blades of its fans—seemed inhuman and dangerous and cruel.

It hovered for a nervous-making moment, and Tally thought it had spotted them, but then the fans twisted at a sharp angle, and the thing shot off in the direction that Shay had thrown her knife.

Tally turned just in time to see Shay rolling through the still-open hovercar doors. She followed, slipping into darkness just as they began to lurch closed. . . .

And found herself falling, tumbling down a lightless shaft. Her infrared only transformed the blackness into an incomprehensible riot of shapes and colors flying past.

She dragged her feet and hands against the smooth metal wall, trying to slow herself, but skidded downward until one grippy toe jammed into a fissure. She came to a momentary halt.

Scrambling for a handhold, Tally found nothing but slick metal. She was tipping over backward, her toe losing its grip. . . .

But the shaft wasn't much wider than she was tall—Tally thrust out her arms overhead, spreading her fingers as both hands struck the opposite wall. The traction of the climbing gloves brought her to a halt, facing upward, muscles straining.

Her back was arched, her body wedged across the width of the shaft like a playing card bent between two fingers. Dull pain throbbed in her wounded hand from the impact.

She twisted her head around, trying to see where Shay had fallen.

There was nothing but darkness below. The shaft smelled of stale air and corrosion.

Tally struggled to get a better look. Shay had to be

close—the shaft couldn't go down *forever*, after all, and Tally hadn't heard anything hit the bottom. But it was impossible to judge perspective; all around her was a mass of meaningless infrared shapes.

Her spine felt like a chicken bone about to snap. . . .

Suddenly, fingertips touched her back.

"Take it easy," Shay's whisper came through the suits' contacts. "You're making *noise*."

Tally sighed. Shay was just below her in the darkness, invisible in her sneak suit. "Sorry," she whispered.

The hand pulled away for a second, then the touch returned. "Okay. I'm steady. Let yourself drop."

She hesitated.

"Come *on*, scaredy-cat. I'll catch you."

Tally took a breath, squeezed her eyes shut, then let go. An instant of free fall later, she found herself cradled in Shay's arms.

Shay chuckled. "You are one *heavy* baby, Tally-wa."

"What are you standing on, anyway? I can't see anything down here."

"Try this." Shay sent an overlay through the suit contacts, and everything shifted around Tally, infrared frequencies rebalancing before her eyes. Slowly the glowing silhouettes around her began to make sense.

The shaft was lined with hovercraft crouched in holding bays, their outlines bristling like the one they'd seen above. There were dozens in all shapes and sizes, a swarm of deadly machines. Tally imagined them all springing to life at once and chopping her to pieces.

She placed a tentative foot on one of the machines, then slipped out of Shay's arms, hands clinging to the barrel of the craft's auto-cannon.

Shay reached out and touched her shoulder, whispering, "How about all this firepower? Icy, huh?"

"Yeah, great. I just hope we don't wake them up."

"Well, our infrared's all the way up, and it's still hard to see, so everything must be pretty cold. There's actually *rust* on some of them." Against the jumbled background, Tally saw Shay's head turn upward. "But that one outside is plenty awake. We should get moving before it comes back."

"Okay, Boss. Which way?"

"Not down. We need to stay close to our hoverboards." Shay pulled herself upward, grasping weaponry, landing legs, and airfoils like handholds in a climbing gym.

Up was fine with Tally, and now that she could see, the spiny shapes of the sleeping hovercraft made for easy climbing. Clinging to gun barrels was a little nervous-making, though, like entering some sleeping predator's body through its own razor-toothed mouth. She avoided the grasping claws and fan blades, and anything else that looked sharp. The slightest tear in her suit would leave behind dead skin cells, revealing Tally's identity like a fresh thumbprint.

About halfway up, Shay reached down to touch her shoulder. "Access hatch."

Tally heard a metal *cha-chunk*, and blinding light filled the shaft, falling across two hovercraft. In the light they seemed less threatening—dusty and ill-kept, like stuffed predators in some old nature museum.

Shay slipped through the hatch, and Tally scrambled after her, dropping into a narrow hallway. Her vision adjusted to the orange work lights overhead, her suit shifting to match the pale color of the walls.

The hallway was too narrow for people—hardly wider

than Tally's shoulders—and the floor was covered with bar codes, navigation markers for machines. She wondered what nasty contraptions were roaming these halls, searching for intruders.

Shay started up the hallway, waving a finger for Tally to follow.

The hallway soon opened onto a room that was *huge*—bigger than a soccer field. It was full of motionless vehicles that towered around them like frozen dinosaurs. Their wheels were as tall as Tally, and their bowed cranes brushed the high ceiling. Lifting claws and giant blades shone dully in the orange work lights.

She wondered why the city would keep a bunch of Rusty construction equipment around. These old machines would only be useful for building beyond the city's magnetic grid, where hoverstruts and lifters wouldn't work. The claws and earthmoving scoops around her were tools for attacking nature, not maintaining the city.

There were no doors, but Shay gestured to a column of metal rungs set into the wall—a ladder leading up and down.

One floor up, they found themselves in a small, crowded room. Floor-to-ceiling shelves were stuffed with a wild assortment of equipment: scuba breathers and night-vision goggles, firefighting canisters and body armor . . . along with a whole slew of things that Tally didn't recognize.

Shay was already scrabbling through the gear, slipping objects into her sneak suit's pouches. She turned around and tossed something to Tally. It looked like a Halloween mask, with huge googly eyes and a nose like an elephant's trunk. Tally squinted to read the tiny label tied to it:

CIRC. 21 CENT.

She puzzled over the words for a moment, then remembered the old-style dating system. This mask was from the Rusties' twenty-first century, a little over three hundred years ago.

This part of the Armory wasn't a storehouse. It was a museum.

But what *was* this thing? She turned the label over:

BIOWARFARE FILTER MASK, USED

Biowarfare? *Used?* Tally quickly dropped the mask on the shelf beside her. She saw Shay watching, the shoulders of her suit moving.

Very funny, Shay-la, she thought.

Biological warfare had been one of the Rusties' more brilliant ideas: engineering bacteria and viruses to kill each other. It was about the stupidest kind of weapon you could make, because once the bugs were finished with your enemies, they usually came for you. In fact, the whole Rusty culture had been undone by one artificial oil-eating bacterium.

Tally hoped that whoever ran this museum hadn't left any civilization-ending bugs around.

She crossed the floor, took Shay's shoulder, and hissed, "Cute."

"Yeah, you should have seen your face. Actually, *I* should have seen your face. Stupid sneak suits."

"Find anything?"

Shay held up a shiny tubelike object. "This should do the job. The label says it works." She slipped it into one of her sneak-suit pouches.

"So what's all that other stuff for?"

"To throw them off the scent. If we only steal one thing, they might figure out what we want it for."

"Oh," Tally whispered. Shay might be making stupid jokes, but her mind was still icy.

"Take these." Shay shoved an armful of objects at her and went back to puzzling over the shelves.

Tally looked down at the jumble of equipment, wondering if any of it was infected with Tally-eating bacteria. She slipped a few pieces that would fit into the sneak suit's carrying pouches.

The largest object looked like some kind of rifle, with a thick barrel and long-range optics. Tally peered down its sight and saw Shay's silhouette in miniature, crosshairs marking where the bullets would hit if she squeezed the trigger. She felt a moment of disgust. The weapon was designed to make any average person into a killing machine, and life and death seemed like a lot to risk on a slip of some random's finger.

Her nerves were jumping. Shay had already found what they needed. It was time to get out of here.

Then Tally realized what was making her nervous. She smelled something through the sneak suit's filter, something human. She took a step toward Shay. . . .

The lights overhead began to flicker, bright white chasing away the room's orange glow, and footsteps clanged from the ladder rungs. Someone was climbing toward the museum.

Shay crouched, rolling onto the lowest shelf beside her, stretching across the jumble of tools. Tally looked around frantically for a place to hide, then wedged herself into a corner where two shelves didn't quite meet, the rifle hidden behind her. Her sneak suit's scales writhed, trying to fade into the shadows.

Across the room, Shay's suit was sprouting jagged lines

to break up her outline. By the time the light steadied overhead, she was almost invisible.

But Tally was not. She looked down at herself. Sneak suits were designed for hiding in complex environments—jungles and forests and battle-wrecked cities, not in the corners of brightly lit rooms.

But it was too late to find another spot.

A man was stepping off the ladder.

BREAK OUT

He wasn't very scary.

He seemed to be an average late pretty, with the same gray hair and wrinkled hands as Tally's great-grandfathers. His face showed the usual signs of life-extension treatments: crinkly skin around the eyes, and veiny hands.

But he didn't seem calm or wise to Tally, the way crumblies had before she'd become a Special—just old. She realized that she could knock him cold without regret if she had to.

More nervous-making than the crumbly were the three little hovercams that floated above his head. They shadowed him as he strode unseeing past Tally toward one of the shelves. He reached to take something down, and the cameras shifted in the air, zipping in closer, like a rapt audience watching a magician's every movement, always staying focused on his hands. He ignored the cameras, as if he was used to their attentions.

Of course, Tally thought. The hovercams were part of the building's security system, but they weren't looking for intruders. They were designed to watch the staff, making sure nobody snuck off with any of the horrible old weapons stored here. They glided smoothly over his head, watching everything this historian—or museum curator, or whatever he was—did here in the Armory.

Tally relaxed a little. Some crumbly boffin who himself was under guard was a lot less threatening than the squad of Specials she'd been expecting.

He handled the objects delicately, and the care he took with them made her vaguely nauseous, as if he saw them as valuable works of art instead of killing machines.

Then suddenly the crumbly froze, a frown on his face. He checked a glowing palmbook in his hand, then started sifting through the objects one by one. . . .

He'd noticed something missing.

Tally wondered if it was the rifle poking into her back. But it couldn't be: Shay had taken the weapon from the other side of the museum.

But then he picked up the biowarfare filter mask. Tally swallowed—she'd put it back in the wrong place.

His eyes slowly swept the room.

Somehow, he didn't see Tally wedged into her corner. The sneak suit must have melded her outline into the shadows on the wall, like an insect against a tree limb.

He carried the mask over to where Shay was hidden, his knees centimeters from her face. Tally was certain he'd notice all the objects she'd borrowed, but once the crumbly had put the mask back in its proper place, he nodded and turned around, a satisfied expression on his face.

Tally breathed a slow sigh of relief.

Then she saw the hovercam staring down at her.

It still floated just above the crumbly's head, but its

little lens was no longer watching him. Either Tally's imagination was running wild, or it was pointed straight at her, slowly focusing and refocusing.

The crumbly walked back to where he'd started, but the camera stayed where it was, no longer interested in him. It drifted closer to Tally, flitting back and forth, like some hummingbird unsure about a flower. The old man didn't notice its nervous little dance, but Tally's heart was pounding, her vision blurring as she struggled not to breathe.

The camera flew still closer, and past its flitting eye Tally saw Shay's form shifting. She'd also seen the little hovercam—things were about to get very tricky.

The camera stared at Tally, still unsure. Was it smart enough to know about sneak suits? Would it just chalk her up to a smudge on its lens?

Apparently, Shay wasn't waiting to find out. Her suit's camouflage had changed into the sleek black of armor. She pulled herself silently out into the open, pointed at the camera, and drew her finger across her throat.

Tally knew what she had to do.

In a single motion, she whipped the rifle from behind her back. It struck the hovercam with a *crack*, sending it flying across the museum, past the astonished crumbly's head, and careening into a wall. It dropped to the floor, stone-cold dead.

Instantly, a screaming alarm filled the room.

Shay burst into motion, running toward the ladder. Tally squeezed out of her corner and followed, ignoring the astonished crumbly's cries. But as Shay jumped for the ladder, a metal sheath snapped shut around it. She bounced back with a hollow *clang*, her suit cycling through a sequence of random colors from the impact.

Tally swept her eyes around the museum—there was no other way out.

One of the two remaining hovercams buzzed straight up to her face, and she smashed it with another blow from the rifle butt. She swung at the other one, but it shot away into a corner of the ceiling, like a nervous housefly trying not to get swatted.

"What are you *doing* here?" the crumbly shouted.

Shay ignored him, gesturing at the remaining hovercam. "Kill that!" she ordered, her voice distorted by the sneak suit's mask, then spun back toward the shelves, rifling through them as fast as she could.

Tally grabbed the heaviest-looking object she could find—some sort of power hammer—and took aim. The camera was flitting back and forth in a panic, swinging its lens one way and then the other, trying to keep track of both her and Shay. Tally took a deep breath, watching the pattern of its movements for a moment, her mind racing through calculations. . . .

The next time the hovercam's lens left her for Shay, she threw.

The hammer hit the camera dead center, and it dropped to the floor, sputtering like a dying bird. The crumbly jumped away from it, as if a wounded hovercam were the most dangerous thing in this museum of horrors.

"Be careful!" he shrieked. "Don't you know where you are? This place is *deadly*!"

"No kidding," Tally said, looking down at the rifle. Was it powerful enough to cut through metal? She took aim at the sheath that had covered the ladder, braced herself, and pulled the trigger. . . .

It made a clicking sound.

Bubblehead, thought Tally. No one kept *loaded* guns in a museum. She wondered how long it would be before the ladder would open back up to reveal one of the evil machines from the shaft, fully awake and primed to kill.

Shay knelt in the middle of the museum, a small ceramic bottle clutched in her hands. She placed it on the floor and grabbed the rifle from Tally, lifting it over her head.

"No!" the crumbly cried as the rifle butt swung down, hitting the bottle with a dull thud. Shay raised the weapon for another swing.

"Are you crazy?" the crumbly yelled. "Do you know what that is?"

"Actually, I do," Shay said, and Tally could hear the smirk in her voice. The bottle was making its own beeping noise, the little red warning light on it flashing furiously.

The crumbly turned away and started climbing up the shelves behind him, throwing aside ancient weapons to clear space for his hands.

Tally turned to Shay, remembering not to use her name aloud. "Why is that guy climbing the walls?

Shay didn't respond, but on the next swing of the rifle, Tally got her answer.

The bottle broke open, and a silvery liquid streamed from it, spreading out across the floor. The liquid flowed into many rivulets, stretching out like some hundred-legged spider after a long nap.

Shay hopped away from the spill, and Tally took a few steps back herself, unable to take her eyes from the mesmerizing sight.

The crumbly looked down and let out a horrible howl. "You let it out? Are you *insane*?"

The liquid began to sizzle, and the smell of burning plastic filled the museum.

The alarm changed tone, and in one corner of the room a tiny door popped open, disgorging two little hoverdrones. Shay leaped toward them and whacked one with the rifle butt, sending it into the wall. The second dodged around her and let loose a spray of black foam at the silver liquid.

Shay's next swing choked the spray off. She leaped across the growing silver spider on the floor. "Get ready to jump."

"Jump *where*?"

"Down."

Tally looked at the floor again, and saw that the spilled liquid was *sinking*. The silvery spider was melting its way straight through the ceramic floor.

Even inside the cool of her sneak suit, Tally felt the heat from wild chemical reactions. The smell of burnt plastic and charred ceramic had become choking.

Tally took another step back. "What *is* that stuff?"

"It's hunger, in nano form. It eats pretty much everything, and makes more of itself."

Tally took another step back. "What *stops* it?"

"What am I, a historian?" Shay rubbed her feet in a patch of the black foam. "This stuff should help. Whoever runs this place probably has an emergency plan."

Tally looked up at the crumbly, who had reached the top shelf, his eyes wide with fear. She hoped that climbing the walls and panicking wasn't the *whole* plan.

The floor groaned underneath them, then cracked, and the center of the slivery spider dropped out of sight. Tally gawked for a moment, realizing that the nanos had eaten their way through the floor in less than a minute. Tendrils of silver remained behind, still spreading in all directions, still hungry.

"Down we go," Shay cried. She stepped gingerly to the edge of the hole, peered down, then cannonballed through.

Tally took a step forward.

"Wait!" the crumbly cried. "Don't leave me!"

She looked back—one of the tendrils had reached the shelf he was clinging to, and was swiftly spreading up into the jumble of ancient weapons and equipment.

Tally sighed, leaping up onto the shelf next to him. She whispered in his ear, "I'm saving you. But if you mess with me I'll feed you to that stuff!"

The voice distortion that hid her identity turned the words into a monstrous growl, and the man only whimpered. She prized his fingers from the shelf, balanced his weight across her shoulders, and jumped back down to an untouched part of the museum floor.

Smoke filled the room now, and the crumbly was coughing hard. It was as hot as a sauna, and it was dripping inside Tally's sneak suit, the first time she'd sweated since turning special.

Another section of the museum floor fell through with a crash, leaving a gaping view of the room below. The soccer field full of machines was ribboned with silver tendrils, one of the giant vehicles already half-consumed.

The Armory was fighting back against the hungry nanos in earnest now. Small flying craft filled the air, frantically spraying black foam. Shay hopped from machine to machine, whacking them with the rifle, helping the goo spread.

It was a long drop, but Tally didn't have much choice. The shelves had begun to tilt as the nanos consumed their bases.

She took a deep breath and jumped, the old man on her shoulders screaming the whole way down.

Landing atop one of the machines, she grunted under the crumbly's weight, then dropped to an untouched bit of floor. The hungry silver goo was close, but she managed to dance to a halt, grippy shoes squeaking like panicked mice.

Shay paused in her battle with the sprayer drones for a moment and pointed over Tally's head. "Watch out!"

Before Tally could even look up, she heard the creaking sound of another collapse. She hopped away, avoiding tendrils of silver and blotches of slippery-looking black foam. It was like some littlies' game of hopscotch, but with lethal consequences if she made a mistake.

Reaching the other end of the room, Tally heard more of the ceiling collapse behind her. The contents of the museum's shelves rained down on the construction machines, two of which had been turned into boiling masses of silver. The sprayer drones were trying to cover them with black foam.

Tally dumped the crumbly into a heap on the floor and checked the ceiling directly overhead. They weren't below the museum anymore, but the silver stuff would keep spreading even through the walls. Was it going to eat the whole building?

Maybe that was Shay's plan. The foam seemed to be working, but Shay leaped from safe spot to safe spot laughing, swinging at the sprayer drones, preventing them from getting the outbreak under control.

The alarm changed tone again, shifting to an evacuation warning.

Which seemed like a good idea to Tally.

She turned to the crumbly. "How do we get out of here?"

He coughed into a fist. The smoke was filling even this giant room. "The trains."

"Trains?"

He pointed downward. "Subways. Just below ground level. How did you get in here? Who *are* you, anyway?"

Tally groaned. *Subway trains?* Their boards were on the roof, but the only way up was through the hovercraft bay, full of deadly machines that would be *very* awake by now. . . .

They were trapped.

Suddenly, one of the huge vehicles sprang to life.

It looked like some piece of old farm equipment, the sharp metal threshers across its front slowly beginning to spin. It struggled to turn, working its way out of its cramped parking space.

"Boss!" Tally called. "We need to get out of here!"

Before Shay could answer, the whole building rumbled. One of the construction machines had been turned entirely into silver goo and was starting to sink through the floor.

"Look out below," Tally said softly.

"This way!" Shay cried, her voice barely audible in all the commotion.

Tally turned to pick up the crumbly.

"Don't touch me!" he cried. "They'll save me if you *just get away from me*!"

She paused, then saw that two little sprayer drones were hovering protectively over his head

Tally dashed across the room, hoping the floor wasn't about to collapse. Shay was waiting for her, swinging the rifle to protect a growing web of silver on the wall. "We can get through here. Then past the next wall. We have to reach outside sooner or later, right?"

"Right . . . ," Tally said. "Unless *that* thing crushes us."

The farming machine was still struggling free of its parking space. As they watched, a bulldozer next to it started up, rolling out of its way. The larger machine untangled itself and began to roll toward them.

Shay looked back at the wall. "Almost big enough!"

The hole was widening quickly now, its silver edges glowing with heat. Shay pulled something from one of her sneak suit's pouches and hurled it through.

"Duck!"

"What was that?" Tally shouted, crouching down.

"An old grenade. I just hope it still—"

A flash of light and a deafening roar came through the hole.

" . . . works. Come on!" Shay ran a few steps toward the lumbering farm machine, skidded to a halt, then turned and faced the hole.

"But it's not big enough. . . ."

Shay ignored her, diving through. Tally swallowed. If one drop of the silver stuff had gotten on Shay . . .

And she was supposed to follow?

The rumble of the farm machine reminded her that she didn't have much choice. It had detoured around the sinking, infected vehicles, and was in the clear now, gaining speed every second. One of wheels was ribboned with silver goo, but wouldn't be eaten away until long minutes after it had smashed Tally flat.

She took two steps back, put her palms together like a diver going into water, and threw herself through the hole.

On the other side, Tally rolled to a stop and sprang to her feet. The floor shook as the farming machine hit the wall, and the glowing hole behind her was suddenly much bigger.

Through it, she saw the huge machine backing up for another attack.

"Come on," Shay said. "That thing's going to get in here pretty quick."

"But I . . ." Tally strained to turn and look at her own back, her shoulders, the bottoms of her feet.

"Relax. No silver ickies on you. Me either." Shay stuck the barrel of the rifle into a drop of silver goo, then grabbed Tally and dragged her across the room. The floor was covered with the charred remains of foam sprayers and security drones that had been destroyed by Shay's grenade.

At the opposite wall, Shay said, "The building *can't* be much bigger than this." She pushed the half-consumed rifle against the wall. "Hope not, anyway."

A glob of silver clung, already beginning to grow . . .

The floor shook with a mighty *boom* again, and Tally spun around to see the front end of the threshing machine pulling back from the hole. The gap was much wider now, big enough to walk through. Between the hungry goo and the pummeling, the wall wasn't going to last much longer.

The farming machine was now thoroughly infected. Glowing tendrils traveled across its threshers like spinning lightning. She wondered if it would be consumed before it could pound its way through. But a pair of spraying drones shot into view and began to douse it with black foam.

"This place really wants to kill us, huh?" Tally said.

"That's my guess," Shay said. "Of course, you can try surrendering if you want."

"Hmm." The ground shook, and Tally watched as more of the wall crashed to the floor. The hole was almost big enough for the huge machine to roll through. "Got any more grenades?"

"Yeah, but I'm saving them."

"What the hell *for*?"

"For *those*."

Tally turned back toward the spreading silver web. The night sky showed through at its center, and Tally saw the running lights of hovercraft outside.

"We're dead," she said softly.

"Not yet." Shay pressed a grenade against the sliver nanos, watched them spread for a moment, then tossed it underarm through the gap, pulling Tally down.

The *boom* of an explosion battered their ears.

Across the room, the thresher struck for the last time, the entire wall collapsing into glowing silver rubble. The machine rolled forward slowly now, struggling along on half-eaten wheels covered with black foam and shimmering sliver.

Through the hole behind her, Tally saw the shapes of more hovercraft than she could count.

"They'll kill us if we go out there!" Tally said.

"Get *down*!" Shay barked. "That goo could hit a lifting fan any second."

"Hit a what?"

At that moment, a horrible sound came from outside, like gears grinding wrong on a bicycle. Shay pulled Tally down again as another explosion rang out. A spray of silver droplets came through the hole.

"Oh," Tally said softly. The nanos on Shay's grenade had been blown onto some unlucky hovercraft's lifting fans, which had let loose a deadly shower as they'd been consumed. By now, every machine waiting for them outside must have been infected.

"Call your hoverboard!"

Tally flicked her crash bracelet. Shay was readying to

jump, hopping between the spreading droplets of silver that covered the room. She took three careful steps, then threw herself into the gap.

Tally took one step back from the hole—all she had room for. The lumbering threshing machine was so close that she could feel the heat of its disintegration.

She took a breath and dived into the breach. . . .

FLIGHT

Tally tumbled into darkness.

The night silence enveloped her, and for a moment she simply let herself fall. Maybe she'd brushed against the deadly silver goo on her way through the hole, or was about to be blown from the sky, or was falling to her death, but at least it was cool and *quiet* out here.

Then a tug came on her wrist, and the familiar shape of her hoverboard hurtled out of the darkness. Tally spun herself in midair, landing in a perfect riding stance.

Shay was already speeding toward the closest edge of the city. Angling her board to follow, Tally engaged its lifting fans, the thrum beneath her feet building swiftly to a howl.

The sky around them was filled with glowing shapes, all headed away from Tally. Every single hovercraft was trying to put distance between itself and its fellow machines; none of them knew which had been spattered with the silver goo and which were clean. The most obviously contaminated were grounding themselves in the no-fly area, stilling their spinning fans before they infected the rest.

She and Shay would have a few minutes' head start while the armada got itself organized.

Imagining pinpricks of heat on her arms and hands, Tally glanced down to check herself for growing silver dots. She wondered if the sprayers inside were getting the hungry nanos under control, or whether the whole building was going to sink into the earth.

If the silver goo was the sort of stuff the Armory kept in its museum, what were the "serious" weapons stored deep underground like? Of course, destroying one building wasn't much by Rusty standards. They'd killed whole cities with a single bomb, sickened generations with radioactivity and poisons. Next to that, the silver stuff really was a museum piece.

Behind her, firefighting hovercars from the city were arriving, spraying out vast clouds of the black foam across the whole Armory.

Tally turned away from the chaos and shot after Shay in the dark sky, relieved to see that no glowing droplets clung to her night black sneak suit. "You're clean," she called out.

Shay took a quick spin around Tally. "You too. Told you that Specials are born lucky!"

Tally swallowed, glancing over her shoulder. A few surviving hovercraft were zooming out from the pandemonium of the Armory grounds, chasing them. She and Shay might be invisible in their suits, but their hoverboards would still show up as bright slivers of heat. "I wouldn't call this good luck yet," she yelled across the void.

"Don't worry, Tally-wa. If they want to play, I've got more grenades." As the two of them hit the edge of Crumblyville, Shay dropped to roof level to take better advantage of the grid.

Tally followed her down, taking a slow breath. That Shay in possession of hand grenades was a *comforting* thought showed what kind of a night this had turned into.

She could hear the roar of hovercraft building now. Apparently, the goo hadn't gotten them all. "They're getting closer."

"They're faster than we are, but they won't mess with us over the city. They don't want to kill any innocent bystanders."

Which doesn't include us, Tally thought. "So how do we get away?"

"If we can find a river outside of town, we can jump."

"*Jump?*"

"They can't see *us*, Tally—just our boards. Falling through the air in sneak suits, we'll be completely invisible." She was fiddling with one of the grenades. "Just find me a river."

Tally flipped a map overlay across her vision.

"All that firepower will chop our boards to pieces," Shay said. "They won't have enough left to . . ." Shay's voice faded. All at once, the hovercraft had winked out of existence, leaving the night sky empty.

Tally flipped through various infrared overlays, but could see nothing. "Shay?"

"They must have turned their lifting fans off. They're running on magnetics, totally stealthy."

"But why? We *know* that they're following us."

"Maybe they don't want to freak out the crumblies," Shay said. "They're pacing us, surrounding us, waiting for us to leave the city. Then they'll start shooting."

Tally swallowed. In the momentary silence, her adrenaline was fading, and the magnitude of what they'd done finally struck home. Because of them, the military was in an uproar, probably thinking the city was under attack. For a moment, the icy glamour of being special slipped away. "Shay, if this goes wrong, thanks for trying to help Zane."

"Hush, Tally-wa." Shay hissed. "Just find me that river."

Tally counted down the seconds. The city limit was less than a minute away.

She remembered the other night, the thrill of chasing the Smokies to the edge of the wild. But now she was the one being hunted, outnumbered, and outgunned. . . .

"Here we go," Shay warned.

As they shot out over the dark edge of the city, glowing forms winked into existence all around them. First Tally heard the roar of lifting fans spinning to life, and then bright lances of heat began to streak across the sky.

"Don't make it easy for them!" Shay cried.

Tally began to weave, slipping around the arcs of blazing projectiles that filled the air. A stream of cannon fire shot past her, hot as a desert wind on her cheek, splintering the trees below like matchsticks. She veered and climbed, barely avoiding another barrage from the opposite direction.

Shay threw a grenade straight up into the air. A few seconds later, it burst behind them, and a concussion wave hit Tally like a fist, setting her board wobbling. She heard the plaintive shrieking of lifting fans knocked awry—Shay had hit one of the hovercraft without even aiming!

Which only proved, of course, how many of them there were. . . .

Two arcing trails of cannon fire streaked across Tally's path, searing the air, and she twisted hard to avoid them, barely staying on her board.

In the distance ahead, a band of reflected moonlight glimmered.

"The river!"

"I see it," Shay called. "Set your board to fly straight and level once you jump."

Tally banked again, another spray of projectiles narrowly missing her. She stabbed at her crash bracelets' controls, setting the board to fly ahead without her.

"Try not to make a splash!" Shay cried. "Three . . . two . . ."

Tally jumped.

The dark river shone below her as she fell, a winding black mirror reflecting the chaos in the sky. She sucked in deep breaths, storing up oxygen, pressing her hands together to split the water cleanly.

The river's surface slapped her hard, then its watery roar erased the screams of gunfire and lifting fans. Tally plunged deep into the darkness, its cold and silence enveloping her.

She waved her arms in circles to keep herself from floating too quickly to the top, staying down as long as her lungs could stand it. When she finally surfaced, her eyes scanned the sky, but found only flickers on the dark horizon, kilometers away. The river's current was brisk and smooth.

They had escaped.

"Tally?" a shout bounced across the water.

"Over here," she answered softly, paddling to face the sound.

Shay reached her with a few powerful strokes. "You okay, Tally-wa?

"Yeah." Tally did a quick internal diagnostic on her bones and muscles. "Nothing broken."

"Me neither." Shay was smiling tiredly. "Let's head for shore. We've got a long walk ahead of us."

As they swam slowly shoreward, Tally watched the sky anxiously—she'd had enough of fighting off the city's armed forces for one night.

"That was truly icy, Tally-wa," Shay said as they dragged themselves onto the muddy riverbank. She pulled out the tool she'd found in the museum. "By this time tomorrow night, Zane will be on his way into the wild. And we'll be right behind him."

Tally looked at the alloy-cutter, hardly believing they'd almost gotten killed for something smaller than a finger. "But after everything we did back there, will anyone really believe it was a bunch of Crims?"

"Maybe not." Shay shrugged, then giggled. "But by the time they get around to stopping that silver goo, they won't have much evidence left. And whether they think it was Crims or Smokies or a bunch of commando Specials from another city, they'll know Zane-la has some bad-ass friends."

Tally frowned. They'd only meant to make Zane seem bubbly, not involve him in a major attack.

Of course, with the city threatened this way, Dr. Cable would probably be thinking about recruiting a few more Specials as soon as possible. And Zane would make a logical candidate.

Tally smiled. "He does have some bad-ass friends, Shay-la. He has you and me."

Shay laughed as they started into the woods, sneak suits shifting to match the dappled shafts of moonlight. "Tell me about it, Tally-wa. That boy doesn't know how lucky he is."

Part II

TRACKING ZANE

When the people of the world all know beauty as beauty,
There arises the recognition of ugliness.
When they all know the good as good,
There arises the recognition of evil.
—Lao Tzu, *The Tao Te Ching*

CUT FREE

The next night, they found Zane and a small group of Crims waiting for them, clustered in the shadow of the dam that calmed the river before it encircled New Pretty Town. The sound of falling water and the nervous smells of the Crims set Tally's senses abuzz, her flash tattoos spinning like pinwheels on her arms.

After last night's adventures, her old random body would've been dead tired. She and Shay had walked all the way into the city center before calling Tachs to bring new boards, a hike that would have laid up any normal human for days. But a few hours' sleep had mostly restored Tally's body, and their exploits at the Armory now seemed like a practical joke—one that had gotten a little out of hand, maybe. . . .

Her skintenna was crackling with the city's high alert: wardens and regular Specials out in force, the newsfeeds openly wondering if the city was at war. Half of Crumblyville had seen the inferno on the horizon, and the giant pile of black foam where the Amory had once stood was hard to explain away. There were military hovercraft visible over the center of town, stationed to protect the city government from any further attacks. The nightly fireworks displays had been canceled until further notice, leaving the skyline strangely dark.

Even the Cutters had been called in and told to search for any connection between the Smokies and the Armory's destruction, which Tally and Shay thought was pretty funny.

The buzz of the emergency energized Tally; she found the whole thing icy, like back when school was canceled because of a blizzard or a fire. Even with her sore muscles, she felt ready to follow Zane into the wild for weeks or months, whatever it took.

But as her board touched down, Tally made sure not to catch his watery-eyed gaze. She didn't want this icy feeling sucked out of her, randomized by his infirmity. So she turned her eyes to the rest of the Crims.

There were eight in all. Peris was among them, his big eyes widening as he took in Tally's new face. He was holding a cluster of toy balloons, like an entertainer at some littlie's birthday party.

"Don't tell me *you're* going," she snorted.

He returned her gaze without blinking. "I know I wimped out on you, Tally. But I'm bubblier now."

Tally looked at Peris's full lips, the softness of his trying-to-be-defiant expression, and wondered if his new attitude had come from one of Maddy's pills. "So what are those balloons for? In case you fall off your hoverboard?"

"You'll see," he answered, mustering a smile.

"You bubbleheads better be ready for a long trip," Shay said. "The Smokies may wait a while before they pick you up. I hope that's survival gear in those packs and not champagne."

"We're ready," Zane answered. "Water purifiers and sixty days of self-heating meals each. Lots of SpagBol."

Tally winced. Ever since her first trip into the wild, the merest thought of Spagbol made her stomach flip. Luckily, Specials gathered their own food in the wild; their rebuilt stomachs could extract the nutrition out of practically anything that grew. A few Cutters had actually taken up hunting, though Tally stuck to wild plants—she'd eaten her share of dead animals back in Smokey days.

The Crims started hoisting their backpacks, keeping their faces solemn, trying to look serious. She just hoped they didn't chicken out in the middle of the wild and leave Zane alone. He already looked a little shaky, even with his board still on the ground.

A few of the other Crims were staring at her and Shay. They wouldn't have seen a Special before, much less a scarred and wildly tattooed Cutter. But they didn't seem scared—like normal bubbleheads would be—just curious.

Of course, Maddy's nanos had been making the rounds for a while now. And the Crims would be the first to try anything to make themselves bubbly.

How would you run a city where everyone was Crim? Instead of most people going along with the rules, they'd always be stealing and doing tricks. Wouldn't you eventually wind up with *real* crimes—random violence and even murders—like back in Rusty days?

"All right," Shay said. "Get ready to move." She pulled out the alloy-cutter.

The Crims slipped their interface rings from their fingers, and as Peris handed each a balloon, they tied their rings to the dangling strings.

"Clever," Tally said, and Peris beamed a satisfied smile at her. When the balloons were let go with the rings attached, it would look to the city interface as though the

Crims were taking a slow hoverboard trip together, letting the wind push them along in typical bubblehead fashion.

Shay took a step toward Zane, but he held up his hand. "No, I want Tally to set me free."

Shay let out a short, barked laugh and tossed Tally the tool. "Your boy wants you."

Tally took a slow breath as she crossed to where Zane stood, vowing to herself that she wouldn't let him randomize her brain. But when she reached out to grasp the metal chain, her fingers brushed his bare throat, and a shudder passed through her. Her eyes stayed on the necklace, but standing this close, fingertips centimeters from his flesh, brought up old and dizzy-making memories.

But then she saw the trembling in Zane's hands, and the repulsion rose in her once more. The war in her brain wouldn't end until he was a Special—his body as perfect as her own.

"Hold steady," she said. "This is hot."

Tally dimmed her vision as the tool sparked to life, a sputtering blue-and-white rainbow in the darkness. The heat hit her face like opening an oven, and a smell like burnt plastic filled the air.

Her own hands were shaking.

"Don't worry, Tally. I trust you."

She swallowed, still not looking up into his eyes. She didn't want to see their watery color, or Zane's thoughts so obvious on his face. She just wanted him to get moving, out into the wild where he could be found by the Smokies, recaptured, and then finally remade.

As the bright arc touched metal, Tally heard an alert ping go through her. Standard city procedure: The necklace was wired to send a signal if damaged. Any warden in the vicinity would have heard the ping too.

"Better let those balloons go," Shay said. "They'll come looking soon."

The arc sliced through the last few millimeters of the chain, and Tally lifted it from around his neck with both hands, careful to keep the glowing tips from his bare flesh.

Her arms were halfway around him when Zane took her wrists. "Try to change your mind, Tally."

She pulled away, his grip no stronger than the strands of a spider web. "My mind is fine the way it is."

His fingertips slid down her arm, along the ridges of cutting scars. "Then why do you do this?"

She looked at his hands, still afraid to meet his eyes. "It makes us icy. It's like being bubbly, but much better."

"What is it that you're not feeling, that you have to do that?"

She frowned, unable to answer the question. He just didn't understand cutting because he'd never *done* it. On top of which, her skintenna was carrying every word to Shay. . . .

"You can rewire yourself again, Tally," he said. "The fact that they made you into a Special *means* you can change."

She stared at the still-glowing cutting tool, remembering what they'd gone through to get it. "I've already done more than you think."

"Good. Then you can choose what side you're on, Tally."

She looked up into his eyes at last. "This isn't about what side I'm on, Zane. I'm not doing this for anyone but us."

He smiled. "Neither am I. Remember that, Tally."

"What do you . . . ?" Tally dropped her gaze, shaking her head. "You have to get moving, Zane. You won't look very bubbly if the wardens catch you here before you've even taken a step."

"And speaking of being caught," Shay whispered, handing the tracker to Zane. "Give that a twirl when you find the Smoke, and we'll come running. It also works if you throw it into a fire, doesn't it, Tally-wa?"

He looked at the tracker, then slipped it into his pocket. All three of them knew that he wouldn't use it.

Tally dared another glance into Zane's eyes. He might not be special, but his fierce expression didn't look like a bubblehead's either.

"Try to keep changing, Tally," he said softly.

"Just *go*!" She turned and took a few steps away, snatching the last few balloons away from Peris, twisting their strings around the still-glowing necklace. When she let them go, the balloons struggled against the necklace's weight at first, until a gust of wind buoyed their strength.

By the time she looked back at Zane, his board was rising, his arms outstretched unsteadily, like a littlie walking a balance beam. One Crim flew on either side of him, ready to help.

Shay let out a sigh. "This is going to be *way* too easy."

Tally didn't answer, keeping her eyes on Zane until he disappeared into the darkness.

"We better get moving," Shay said. Tally nodded. When the wardens came sniffing, they might think it was somewhat random to find a couple of Specials hanging around Zane's last known location.

The scales of her sneak suit shuddered through their

little boot-up dance, and Tally pulled on her gloves, drawing the hood down over her face.

Within seconds, Tally and Shay were as perfectly black as the midnight sky above.

"Come on, Boss," she said. "Let's go find the Smoke."

OUTSIDE

Zane's escape went much easier than Tally had expected.

The rest of the Crims and their pretty allies must have been in on the trick—hundreds of them released their interface rings on toy balloons at the same time, filling the air with false signals. Another hundred or so uglies did the same. The wardens' channel was full of irritated chatter as they went around collecting rings and putting a halt to dozens of pranks. The authorities weren't in the mood for practical jokes after last night's attack.

Shay and Tally finally switched off the wardens' babble.

"Pretty icy so far," Shay said. "Your boyfriend should make a good Cutter."

Tally smiled, feeling relieved to have Zane's shakiness out of her sight. The excitement of the chase was beginning.

They followed the little group of Crims from a kilometer back, the eight figures so clear in infrared that Tally could tell Zane's glowing silhouette apart from the others'. She noticed that at least one of them always flew close to him, ready to lend a hand.

The runaways didn't speed up the river toward the Rusty Ruins, but made their unhurried way to the southern edge of the city. When they ran out of grid, they descended into the forest and hiked, carrying their hoverboards toward the same river that Tally and Shay had jumped into the night before.

"That's bubbly of them," Shay said. "Not taking the usual way out."

"Must be tough on Zane, though," Tally said. Hoverboards were heavy carrying without a grid beneath them.

"If you're going to worry about him this whole trip, Tally-wa, it's going to be *extremely* boring."

"Sorry, Boss."

"Relax, Tally. We won't let anything happen to your boy." Shay dropped into the pine trees. Tally stayed up high for another moment, watching the little group's slow progress. It would be an hour before they made the river and could use their boards again, but she was reluctant to lose sight of the runaways out here in the wild.

"A little early in the trip to burn your fans out, don't you think?" Shay's voice came from below, intimate in the skintenna network's feed.

Tally sighed softly, then let herself descend.

An hour later, they were sitting on the riverbank waiting for the Crims to catch up.

"Eleven," Shay said, tossing another rock. Spinning wildly, it skipped across the water as she counted aloud, finally sinking after the eleventh bounce.

"Hah! I win again!" Shay announced.

"No one else is playing, Shay-la."

"It's me against nature. Twelve." Shay threw again, the rock bouncing happily out into the middle of the river, dropping to the bottom after exactly twelve skips. "Victory is mine! Come on, you try."

"No thanks, Boss. Shouldn't we check on them again?"

Shay groaned. "They'll be here soon, Tally. They were almost at the river last time you checked, which was about five minutes ago."

"So why aren't they here yet?"

"Because they're *resting*, Tally. They're all tired after lugging their crappy boards through the forest." She smiled. "Or maybe they're cooking up a delicious feast of Spagbol."

Tally grimaced. She wished the two of them hadn't flown ahead. The whole point of this trick was to stay close to the runaways. "What if they went the other way? Rivers go two ways, you know?"

"Don't be so random, Tally-wa. Why would they head *away* from the ocean? Once you get past the mountains, there's nothing but desert for hundreds of kilometers. The Rusties called it Death Valley even before the weeds took over."

"But what if they arranged to meet the Smokies back there? We don't know how much contact the Crims have had with outsiders."

Shay sighed. "Fine. Go and check." She kicked at the dirt between her feet, trying to find another flat rock. "Just don't stay up too long. They might have infrared."

"Thanks, Boss." Tally stood, snapping for her board.

"Thirteen," Shay answered, and threw.

From up high, Tally could make out the runaways. As Shay had suspected, they were on the riverbank, unmoving, probably resting their feet. But as she tried to figure out which was Zane, Tally frowned.

Then she realized what was bothering her: There were *nine* glowing blobs of heat, not eight. Had they built a fire? Was some self-heating meal tricking her infrared?

She adjusted her vision to bring them into focus. The silhouettes sharpened until Tally was certain that all of them were human-size.

"Shay-la," she whispered. "They *did* meet someone."

"Already?" Shay answered from below. "Huh. I didn't think the Smokies would make it *this* easy."

"Unless it's another ambush," Tally said softly.

"Let them try. I'm coming up."

"Hang on, they're moving." The glowing forms were slipping out onto the river, headed toward her and Shay at hoverboard speed. But one remained behind, walking into the cover of the forest. "They're on their way here, Shay. Eight of them, anyway. Somebody's going the other direction."

"Okay, you follow that one. I'll stick with the Crims."

"But—"

"Don't argue with me, Tally. I won't lose your boyfriend. Just get moving, and don't let them see you."

"Okay, Boss." Tally dropped toward the river to let her hoverboard's fans cool. Zooming toward the approaching Crims, she booted her suit, pulling the hood over her face. Tally angled closer to the bank and its cover of overhanging plants, slowing almost to a halt.

Within a minute, the Crims shot past, unaware, and she recognized Zane's unsteady form among the others.

"Got them," Shay said a moment later. Her voice was already fading. "If we go off river, I'll leave a skintenna beacon for you."

"Okay, Boss." Tally leaned forward, heading toward the mysterious ninth figure.

"Be careful, Tally-wa. I don't want to lose two Cutters in the one week."

"No problem there," Tally said. She wanted to get back to following Zane, not get captured herself. "See you soon."

"Miss you already . . . ," Shay said as her signal faded.

Tally's senses scanned the forests on either side of the river. The dark trees crowding the banks were full of infrared phantoms; small animals and nesting birds flashed past as random flickers of heat. But nothing human-size . . .

As Tally neared the spot where the Crims had met their mysterious friend, she slowed, crouching low on her board. She smiled, beginning to feel icy and excited. If this was another ambush, the Smokies were going to discover that they weren't the only ones who could turn invisible.

She glided to a halt on the muddy riverbank, stepping from her board and sending it into the sky to wait for her.

The spot where the Crims had stood was marked by a swarm of footprints. The smell of an unwashed human lingered in the air, someone who had been days or longer without a bath. That couldn't be one of the Crims, who'd smelled like recyclable clothes and nervousness.

Tally moved carefully into the trees, following the trail of scent.

Whoever she was following knew something about woodcraft. No broken branches marked a clumsy passage, and the undergrowth showed no telltale signs of footsteps. But the smell grew stronger as Tally moved ahead, enough to make her nose wrinkle. Running water or not, even Smokies didn't smell *this* bad.

A flicker of infrared glow came through the trees, a human form ahead of her. She paused a moment to listen, but hardly a sound carried through the forest: Whoever it was could move as silently as David.

Tally crept forward slowly, eyes scanning the ground for the subtle markers of a trail. Seconds later she found it—an almost invisible channel through the dense trees, the path that the figure was following.

Shay had warned her to be careful, and whoever this person was—Smokie or not—they wouldn't be easy to sneak up on. But perhaps one ambush deserved another. . . .

Tally veered off the trail, running deeper into the forest. She moved silent and light-footed through the soft undergrowth, sweeping around her quarry in a slow arc until she found the trail again. Then she crept forward, ahead of them now, until she spotted a high tree branch that stretched directly over the path.

The perfect spot.

As she climbed, her suit-scales sprouted the rough texture of bark, its colors shifting into a dappled moonlit pattern. She clung to an overhanging branch, invisible and waiting, her heartbeat quickening.

The glowing figure came through the trees in total silence. There were no synthetic smells among those of unwashed humanity: no sunblock patches, insect repellent, or even a trace of soap or shampoo. As Tally flipped through vision overlays, she detected no signs of electronics or a heated jacket, and her ears didn't catch the slight buzz of night-vision goggles.

Not that equipment would help her quarry. Absolutely motionless in her sneak suit, hardly breathing, Tally was undetectable even to the best technology. . . .

And yet, just as the figure passed below her, it slowed, cocking its head as if listening for something.

Tally held her breath. She *knew* she was invisible, but her heart beat faster, her senses amplifying the sounds of the forest around her. Was there someone else out here? Someone who'd spotted her climbing the tree? Phantoms flickered at the corners of her vision. Her body longed to act, not hide up here among the leaves and branches.

For a long moment, the figure didn't move. Then, very slowly, its head tipped back to gaze upward.

Tally didn't hesitate—she dropped, flattening her scales to night black armored mode, wrapping both arms around the figure, pinning its arms as she dragged it to the ground. This close, the unwashed smell was almost choking.

"I don't want to hurt you," she hissed through the suit's mask. "But I will if I have to."

The young man struggled for a moment, and Tally saw the flash of a metal knife in his hand. She squeezed harder, pushing the breath from his lungs with a cracking of ribs until the knife slipped from his fingers.

"Sayshal," he hissed.

His accent sent a shudder of recognition through Tally. *Sayshal?* She remembered that strange word from somewhere. She flipped off her infrared, pulled him to his feet, and pushed him backward, taking in his face in a stray beam of moonlight.

He was bearded and dirty-faced, his clothing nothing but strips of animal skins sewn crudely together.

"I know you . . . ," she said softly.

When he didn't answer, Tally pulled off her hood, letting him see her face.

"Young Blood," he said, smiling. "You have changed."

BARBARIAN

His name was Andrew Simpson Smith, and Tally had met him before.

When she'd escaped the city back in her pretty days, she'd stumbled across a sort of reservation, an experiment maintained by the city's scientists. The people inside the reservation lived like pre-Rusties, wearing skins and using only Stone Age tools—clubs and sticks and fire. They inhabited small villages that were constantly at war with each other, an endless cycle of revenge killings for the scientists to study, like a purified layer of human violence squeezed between the halves of a petri dish.

The villagers didn't know about the rest of the world, or that every problem they faced—illness and hunger and bloodshed—had been solved by humanity centuries before. That is, they hadn't known until Tally had stumbled into one of their hunting parties, been mistaken for a god, and told a holy man named Andrew Simpson Smith all about it.

"How did you get out?" she asked.

He smiled proudly. "I crossed the edge of the world, Young Blood."

Tally raised an eyebrow. The reservation was bounded by "little men," dolls strung from the trees and armed with neural scramblers that caused terrific pain to anyone who got too close. The villagers were far too dangerous to be let loose into the real wild, so the city had given their world impassable borders.

"How did you manage that?"

Andrew Simpson Smith chuckled as he bent to pick up

his knife, and Tally fought an urge to kick it from his hand. He had called her a *Sayshal*, the villagers' word for hated Specials. Of course, now that he'd seen her face, he remembered Tally as a friend, an ally against the gods of the city. He had no idea what her new lace of flash tattoos meant, no understanding that she had become one of the gods' feared enforcers.

"After you told me how much lay beyond the edge of the world, Young Blood, I began to wonder if the little men were afraid of anything."

"Afraid?"

"Yes. I tried many ways to scare them. Songs, spells. The skulls of bears."

"Um, they're not really men, Andrew. Just machines. They don't exactly get afraid."

His expression grew more serious. "But *fire*, Young Blood. I learned they fear fire."

"Fire?" Tally swallowed. "Um, Andrew, was this a really *big* fire, by any chance?"

His smile returned. "It burned many trees. When it was done, the little men had run away."

She groaned. "I think the little men were *burned* away, Andrew. So you're saying you started a forest fire?"

"Forest fire." He considered this for a moment. "Those are good words for it."

"Actually, Andrew, those are *bad* words. You're just lucky it's not summer, or that fire could've taken out your whole . . . world."

He smiled. "My world is bigger now, Young Blood."

"Yeah, but still . . . that wasn't what I had in mind."

Tally sighed. Her attempt to explain the real world to Andrew had resulted in massive destruction instead of enlightenment, and his fire had probably released several villages full of dangerous barbarians into the wild. There were Smokies and runaways and even campers from the city out here. "How long ago did you do this?"

"Twenty-seven days." He shook his head. "But the little men came back. New ones, who are not afraid of fire. I have been outside my old world ever since."

"But you've made some new friends, haven't you? City friends."

He looked at Tally suspiciously for a moment. He must have realized that if she'd seen him with the Crims, she had been following them. "Young Blood," he said cautiously. "By what fortune do we meet?"

Tally didn't answer right away. The concept of lies had hardly seemed to exist in Andrew's village, at least until Tally had explained the big lie they were all living in. But surely by now he was more wary of city people. She decided to choose her words carefully. "Those gods you just met, some of them are friends of mine."

"They are not gods, Tally. You taught me that."

"Right. Good for you, Andrew." She wondered what else he understood these days. He had grown more comfortable with the city's language, as if he'd been practicing a lot. "But how did you know they were coming? You didn't just run into them accidentally, did you?"

He looked at her warily for a moment, then shook his head. "No. They're running from the Sayshal, and I offered help. They are your friends?"

She chewed her lip. "One of them was . . . I mean, *is* . . . my boyfriend."

Comprehension spread across Andrew's face, and he let out a low chuckle. Reaching out one hand, he patted her shoulder roughly. "I see now. That's why you follow, making yourself as invisible as a Sayshal. A *boy*friend."

Tally tried not to roll her eyes. If Andrew Simpson Smith wanted to think she was a jilted lover tagging along after the runaways, it was certainly simpler than explaining the truth. "So how did you know to meet them here?"

"After I found I could not go home, I set off to look for you, Young Blood."

"Me?" Tally asked.

"You were trying to get to the Rusty Ruins. You told me how far, and in what direction."

"And you made it there?"

Andrew's eyes widened as he nodded, a shiver passing through his frame. "A huge village, full of the dead."

"And met the Smokies there, didn't you?"

"The New Smoke Lives," he said gravely.

"Yeah, it sure does. And now you help runaways for them?"

"Not just me. The Smokies know how to fly above the little men. Others from my village have joined us. One day, we'll all be free."

"Well, that's great news," Tally said. The Smokies had really gone crazy now, letting a bunch of deadly savages out into the wild. Of course, the villagers would make useful allies. They knew woodcraft better than any city kids could ever hope to, probably even better than the oldest Smokies. They knew how to gather food on the trail and make clothes from natural materials, all the skills the cities had lost. And after generations of tribal warfare, they'd be experts in the art of ambush as well.

Andrew Simpson Smith had somehow sensed Tally

overhead, even in her sneak suit. Instincts like that took a lifetime in the wilderness to hone.

"How did you help those runaways just now?"

He smiled proudly. "I gave them the way to the New Smoke."

"Great. Because, you see, I've sort of been out of the loop. And I was kind of hoping you'd help me out with that too."

He nodded. "Of course, Young Blood. Just speak the magic word."

Tally blinked. "A magic word? Andrew, it's *me*. I may not know any magic words, but I've been trying to get to the Smoke since you met me."

"True. But I've made a promise." He shifted uncomfortably from foot to foot. "What happened to you, Young Blood, after you left? When I reached the ruins, I told the Smokies how you had appeared to us. They said the city had taken you away again. Had done things to you." He gestured at her face. "Is that another fashion statement?"

Tally sighed, looking into his eyes. He was just a random, and a particularly *random* random at that, with his uneven teeth and spotty, never-washed skin. But for some reason, she didn't want to lie to Andrew Simpson Smith. For one thing, it seemed way too easy, tricking someone who couldn't even read, who'd spent all but the last few weeks of his life trapped in an experiment.

"Your heart is beating fast, Young Blood."

Tally's hand went to her face, which was no doubt spinning. Andrew hadn't forgotten how flash tattoos revealed excitement and distress. Maybe it was pointless to lie to him. Instincts that could detect someone in a sneak suit were not to be underestimated.

She decided to tell the truth. The part that was important to her, anyway.

"Let me show you something, Andrew," she said, peeling off her right glove. She held out her palm, the short-circuited flash tattoos sputtering in time with her heartbeat in the moonlight. "See those two scars? They're marks of my love . . . for Zane."

He stared at her hand wide-eyed, nodding slowly. "I've never seen scars on your people before. Your skin is always . . . perfect."

"Yeah. We only have scars if we want to, so they always *mean* something. These mean that I love Zane. He's the one who looked unwell, kind of shaky? I need to follow him, to make sure he's okay out here."

Andrew nodded slowly. "And he's too proud to accept the help of a woman?"

Tally shrugged. The villagers were pretty much Stone Age about the whole gender thing, too. "Well, let's just say he doesn't exactly want *my* help right now."

"I was not too proud when you taught me about the world." He smiled. "Maybe I'm smarter than Zane."

"Maybe you are." She made a fist with her bare hand. The ridges of scarring across her palm still felt stiff. "I'm asking you to break your promise, Andrew, and tell me where they're headed. I think I can cure Zane of his shakes. And I'm worried about him being out here with a bunch of city kids. They don't understand the wild like you and I do."

He still stared at her hand, thinking hard. Then his eyes raised to meet hers. "Without you, I'd still be trapped inside a false world. I want to trust you, Young Blood."

Tally forced herself to smile. "So you'll tell me where the New Smoke is?"

"I don't know. It's too big a secret for me. But I can give you a way." He reached into a pouch at his belt and withdrew a handful of tiny chips.

"Position-finders," Tally said softly. "With a route programmed in?"

"Yes. This one brought me here to meet these young runaways. And this one will lead you to the New Smoke. Do you know how it works?" Andrew's calloused, grubby forefinger hovered over the boot button of one of the finders, and there was an eager look on his face.

"Yeah, no problem. I've used them before." Tally smiled back at him, reaching for the device.

He pulled it away. She looked up, hoping she wouldn't have to take it by force.

His fist stayed closed. "Do you still challenge the gods, Young Blood?"

Tally frowned. Andrew knew that she had changed, but how much?

"Answer me," he said, his eyes bright in the moonlight.

She took a moment before answering. Andrew Simpson Smith wasn't like the non-Specials in the city, the blank-eyed mass of uglies and pretties. Living in the wild had made him more like her: a hunter, a warrior, a survivor. With the scars of a dozen fights and accidents, he almost looked like a Cutter.

Somehow, Tally didn't see Andrew as wallpaper. Whether or not she could deceive him, she realized now that she didn't want to.

"Do I still challenge the gods?" Tally thought of what she and Shay had done the night before, breaking into the city's most guarded facility and practically destroying it in the process. They had set off on their own without telling

Dr. Cable their true plans. And this whole journey was, for Tally at least, more about fixing Zane than winning the city's war against the Smoke.

The Cutters might be Specials, but over the last few days Tally Youngblood had reverted to her own nature: thoroughly Crim.

"Yes. I still challenge them," she said softly, realizing that it was true.

"Good." He grinned, relieved, and handed her the position-finder. "Go then, follow your boyfriend. And tell the New Smoke that Andrew Simpson Smith was very helpful."

SPLIT

As Tally made her way back down the river, she held the position-finder tightly in her scarred hand, thinking hard.

Once she told Shay about her encounter with Andrew Simpson Smith, the plan would change. With the finder the two of them could fly ahead of the slow-moving runaways, reaching the New Smoke long before Zane and his crew. By the time the Crims arrived, their destination would be a Special Circumstances encampment, full of imprisoned Smokies and recaptured runaways. Showing up after the rebellion had already been crushed wouldn't make Zane look very bubbly.

Worse, he'd be out here on his own for the rest of the trip, with only his Crim friends to help if something went seriously wrong. One bad fall from his hoverboard and Zane might not survive to see the New Smoke at all.

But how much would Shay care about all that? What she really wanted was to find the New Smoke, save Fausto, and get her revenge on David and the rest of them. Babysitting Zane wasn't her idea of an important mission goal.

Tally slowed to a stop, suddenly wishing she hadn't run into Andrew Simpson Smith at all.

Of course, Shay didn't know about the position-finder yet. Maybe she didn't need to know. If they stuck with the original plan, tracking the Crims the old-fashioned way, Tally could save the finder as a backup in case they lost the trail. . . .

She opened her hand, looking down at the finder and at her scars, wishing for some of the clarity she'd felt the night before. She thought of drawing her knife, but remembered the expression on Zane's face as he stared at her scars.

It wasn't that she *needed* to cut herself, after all.

Tally closed her eyes, willing herself to think clearly.

Back in ugly days, Tally had always wimped out on decisions like this one. She'd always avoided any confrontation. That's how she'd wound up betraying the Old Smoke by accident, too afraid to tell anyone about the tracker she carried. And how she'd lost David, by never telling him she'd been a spy.

Lying to Shay now was what the old Tally would have done.

She took a deep breath. She was special now; she had clarity and strength. This time, she would tell Shay the truth.

Closing her fist, Tally urged her board forward again.

Ten kilometers upriver, her skintenna pinged as it picked up Shay's.

"I was getting worried about you, Tally-wa."

"Sorry, Boss. I ran into an old friend."

"Really? Anyone I know?"

"You never met him. Remember my campfire stories about the Restricted Experimental Area? The Smokies have started freeing the villagers and training them to help with runaways."

"That's crazy!" Shay paused. "But wait a second. You *knew* him? He was from the same village you stumbled into?"

"Yeah, and I'm afraid it's no coincidence, Shay-la. It's the holy man who helped me, remember? I told him where the Rusty Ruins were. He was the first to escape, and he's an honorary Smokey now."

Shay whistled in amazement. "Very random, Tally. So how was he supposed to help the Crims? Teach them to skin rabbits?"

"He's sort of a guide. Runaways give him a code word, and he gives them position-finders that lead you to the Smoke." She took a deep breath. "And for old times' sake, he gave me one too."

By the time Tally caught up with Shay, the Crims had made camp.

Tally watched from the darkness as one by one they made their way to the river's edge, dipping their purifiers into the silty water. She and Shay had hidden themselves downwind, and smells of self-heating food packs drifted from the runaways' camp. Tally vividly remembered all the tastes and textures from her own days in the wild, catching the scents of CurryNoods, PadThai, and the hated SpagBol on the breeze. Her ears picked up snatches of the Crims' still-excited chatter as they prepared to sleep the 'day' away.

"They did a good job on this thing—it won't tell me the

final destination." Shay was playing with the position-finder. "It only gives you one waypoint at a time; it waits till you get there to give you the next one. We'll have to follow the whole path to find out where it ends." She snorted. "It'll probably take us the scenic route."

Tally cleared her throat. "It won't be *us*, Shay-la."

Shay looked up. "What's that, Tally?"

"I'm staying with the Crims. With Zane."

"Tally . . . that's a waste of time. We can travel twice as fast as they can."

"I know." She turned to face Shay. "But I'm not going to leave Zane out here with a bunch of city kids. Not in his condition."

Shay groaned. "Tally-wa, you're *so* pathetic. Don't you have any faith in him? Don't you keep telling me how *special* he is?"

"It's not about being special. This is the wild, Shay-la. Anything can happen: accidents, dangerous animals, his condition getting worse. You go ahead alone. Or call the rest of the Cutters—you won't have to worry about getting spotted, after all. But I'm staying close to Zane."

Shay's eyes narrowed. "Tally . . . this is not your choice. I'm giving you an order."

"After what we did last night?" Tally let out a choked laugh. "It's a little late to lecture me about the chain of command, Shay-la."

"This isn't about the chain of command, Tally!" Shay cried. "This is about the Cutters. About Fausto. You're choosing those bubbleheads over *us*?"

Tally shook her head. "I'm choosing Zane."

"But you *have* to come with me. You promised you'd stop making trouble!"

"Shay, I promised that if they made Zane special, I'd stop trying to change things. And I'll keep that promise, once he's a Cutter. But until then . . ." Tally tried to smile. "What are you going to do? Report me to Dr. Cable?"

Shay let out a long hiss. Her hands were curled into fighting position, her teeth bared to show their points. She jerked her chin at the runaways. "What I'm going to do, Tally-wa, is go over there and tell Zane that he's a joke, a dupe, and that you've been tricking him—*laughing* at him. Let him run home scared while we end the Smoke forever, and see if he ever becomes a Special then!"

Tally clenched her own fists, holding Shay's gaze. Zane had already paid enough for her lack of courage; she had to stand her ground this time. Her mind spun for an answer to Shay's threat.

A moment later she saw it, and shook her head. "You can't do that, Shay-la. You don't know where that finder leads. It could take you to another test of some kind—not some barbarian, but a Smokey who'll know what you are, and who won't give you the next set of directions." Tally gestured at the runaways. "One of us has to stay with them. Just in case."

Shay spat on the ground. "You don't give a damn about Fausto, do you? He's probably being experimented on right now, and you want to waste time tracking these bubbleheads!"

"I know that Fausto needs you, Shay. I'm not asking you to stay with me." She spread her hands. "One of us has to go ahead, and the other stay with the Crims. It's the only way."

Shay made another hissing sound and stalked away to the river's edge. She yanked a flat stone from the mud and hoisted it, ready to throw it out across the water.

"Shay-la, they might see," Tally whispered. Shay paused, her arm still cocked. "Look, I'm sorry about this, but I'm not being totally random, am I?"

Shay's response was to stare at the stone for a moment, then drop it back into the mud and draw her knife. She began to roll up the arm of her sneak suit.

Tally turned away, hoping that once her mind was clear, Shay would understand.

She watched the runaway camp, where everyone was eating carefully, apparently having realized that self-heating meals could burn their tongues. That was the first lesson everyone got out in the wild: Nothing could be trusted, not even your own dinner. It wasn't like the city, where every sharp corner had been rounded off, every balcony equipped with a resistance field in case you fell, and where the food never came boiling hot.

She couldn't leave Zane out here alone, even if staying with him made Shay hate her.

A moment later, Tally heard Shay standing up, and turned to face her. Her arm was bleeding, her flash tattoos in dizzying motion, and as she approached, Tally saw the telltale sharpness of her eyes.

"All right. We split up," she said. Tally tried to smile, but Shay shook her head. "Don't you dare get happy about this, Tally-wa. I thought making you into a Special would change you. I thought if you could see the world clearly, you'd think about *yourself* a little less. It wouldn't just be you and your latest boyfriend; I thought you might let something else matter every once in a while."

"I care about the Cutters, Shay, honest. I care about *you*."

"You did until Zane reappeared. Now, nothing else matters." She shook her head in disgust. "And I've been trying so hard to please you, to make this work for you. But it's pointless."

Tally swallowed. "But we have to split up—it's the only safe way to make sure the finder works."

"I know that, Tally-wa. I can see your *logic*." Shay looked at the runaways, disgust all over her wildly spinning face. "But answer me this: Did you think it all through and *then* realize we should split up? Or had you already decided to stick with Zane, no matter what?"

Tally opened her mouth, then closed it.

"Don't bother lying, Tally-wa. We both know the answer." Shay snorted, turned away, and snapped her fingers for her hoverboard. "I really thought you'd changed. But you're still the same self-centered little ugly you've always been. That's what's *amazing* about you, Tally—even Dr. Cable and her surgeons don't stand a chance against your ego."

Tally felt her hands begin to tremble. She had expected an argument, but not this. "Shay . . ."

"You're even a failure as a Special, always worrying about everything. Why can't you just be *icy*?"

"I always tried to do what you—"

"Well you can stop trying now." Shay reached into the storage compartment of her board and pulled out medspray, giving her bleeding arm a long squirt. Then she pulled out a few more sealed packages, tossing them into the mud at Tally's feet. "Here's a pack of smart plastic, if you have to go undercover. A couple of skintenna beacons and a satellite booster." She let out a bitter laugh, her voice still quivering with contempt. "I'll even give you one of my left-over grenades. Just in case something big gets between you and shaky-boy."

The grenade dropped to the ground with a *thud*, and Tally flinched.

"Shay, why are you—"

"Stop *talking* to me." The order silenced Tally, who could only stare as Shay rolled her sneak suit down her arm and drew its hood over her face, replacing her furious expression with a mask of midnight darkness. Her voice came distorted through the mask. "I'm not waiting around any longer. Fausto's my responsibility, not that pack of bubbleheads."

Tally swallowed. "I hope he's okay."

"I'm sure you do." Shay leaped onto her board. "But I'm all done with caring what you hope or think, Tally-wa. Forever."

Tally tried to speak, but Shay's last word had come out so coldly that she couldn't.

Shay rose into the sky, her silhouette barely visible against the dark trees on the other bank. She slipped out over the river, then shot into the blackness, disappearing instantly, like something winking out of existence.

But Tally could still hear her breathing through the skintenna link. It sounded harsh and angry as it began to fade, as if Shay's teeth were still bared in hatred and disgust. Tally tried to think of one more thing to say, something that would explain why she had to do this. Staying with Zane was more important than being a Cutter, more important than any promise she'd ever made.

This decision was about who Tally Youngblood was inside, whether ugly or pretty or special. . . .

But a moment later Shay was out of range, and Tally still hadn't said a word. She found herself alone and in hiding, waiting for the Crims to fall asleep.

INCOMPETENCE

The Crims tried to build a fire, and failed.

All they managed to do was set a few wet branches smoldering, the angry hiss so loud that Tally could hear it from her hiding place. They never got a real blaze going, and the pile was still sputtering desultorily as dawn began to break. That's when the Crims noticed the dark column of smoke rising into the lightening sky, and tried to put it out. They wound up dumping handfuls of mud on the half-alive fire. By the time they had it under control, their city clothes looked like they'd been sleeping rough for a week.

Tally sighed, imagining Shay's chuckle as they struggled with the simplest things. At least they had realized that it was smarter to sleep during the day and travel at night.

As the runaways wrestled their way into sleeping bags, Tally allowed herself to fall into catnap mode. Specials didn't need much sleep, but she could still feel the Armory break-in and the long hike afterward in her muscles. The Crims would be bone tired after their first night in the wild, so now was probably the best time to catch up on her rest. Without Shay along to trade watches with, Tally might have to stay alert for days at a time.

She sat with her legs crossed, facing the runaway camp and setting her internal software to ping every ten minutes. But sleep didn't come easily. Her eyes burned with unshed tears from the fight with Shay. Accusations still echoed in her mind, making the world fuzzy and distant. She took slow, deep breaths, until finally her eyes fell closed. . . .

Ping. Ten minutes already.

Tally checked the Crims, who hadn't moved, then tried to fall asleep again.

Specials were designed to sleep this way, but being roused every ten minutes still did weird things to time. As if Tally was watching a fast-motion video of the day, the sun seemed to rise quickly into the sky, the shadows shifting around her like living things. The soft sounds of the river blurred into a single droning note, and her mind drifted uneasily between worry for Zane and dejection about the fight. It seemed like no matter what happened, Shay was destined to hate her. Or maybe Shay had been right, and Tally Youngblood had a talent for betraying her friends. . . .

When the sun was almost at its peak, Tally awakened not from the sound of a ping, but from a blinding flash hitting her eyes. She jolted upright, hands curled in fighting position.

The light was coming from the Crims' camp. As she rose, it winked out again.

Tally relaxed. It was only the runaways' solar-powered hoverboards spread out across the riverbank to recharge. As the sun moved across the sky, it had caught the reflective cells at just the right angle to shine in Tally's eyes.

Watching the boards sparkle, Tally felt uneasy. After only a few hours on board, the runaways didn't really need to recharge yet—they should be a lot more worried about staying invisible.

Shielding her eyes, Tally looked up. To any passing hovercar, the unfurled boards would glitter like a distress beacon. Didn't the Crims realize how close to the city they were? Their few hours of boarding had probably seemed like an eternity to them, but they were still practically on the doorstep of civilization.

Tally felt another a wave of shame. She had disobeyed Shay and betrayed Fausto to babysit these *bubbleheads*?

She opened her skintenna to the city's official channels, and instantly picked up chatter coming from a warden's car on a slow, lazy patrol along the river. The city had realized by now that last night's pranks had been diversions for yet another escape. All the obvious routes away from the city—rivers and old rail lines—would be under scrutiny. If the wardens spotted the unfurled hoverboards, Zane's escape would come to an ignominious end, and Tally would have gone against Shay for nothing.

She wondered how to get the Crims' attention without revealing herself. She could throw a few rocks, hoping to wake them up with a convincingly random noise, but they probably didn't have a city-band radio with them. The runaways wouldn't recognize the danger they were in—they'd just go back to sleep.

Tally sighed. She was going to have to fix this herself.

Pulling her hood down, she took a few steps to the riverbank and slipped into the water. The sneak suit's scales began to undulate as she swam, mimicking the ripples around her and turning as reflective as the slow, glassy river.

Closer to the camp, the smell of extinguished fire and discarded food packs met her nostrils. Tally took a deep breath and submerged completely, swimming underwater until she reached the riverbank.

She belly-crawled up from the water, raising her head slowly, letting the suit adjust itself to every change around her. It turned brown and soft, scales burrowing into the mud and pushing her along like a slug.

The Crims were asleep, but buzzing flies and the occasional stir of wind brought soft murmurs from them. New pretties might have lots of practice sleeping until noon, but never on hard ground. The slightest noise could bring them all awake.

Their camo-mottled sleeping bags would be invisible from the air, at least. But the unfurled boards only shone brighter as the sun climbed, eight of them crowding the riverbank. Wind tugged at the corners, which were weighted with stones and clumps of mud, making them flash like glitterbombs.

To recharge a hoverboard, you pulled it apart like a paper doll, exposing the maximum surface area to the sun. Fully unfurled, they were as thin and light as kite plastic, and a gust of wind might carry them into the trees—at least, if the Crims woke up and found their boards moved into the forest, they might *believe* that was what had happened.

Tally crawled to the nearest board and plucked the rocks from its corners. Rising slowly to her feet, she dragged it into the shade. After a few minutes' work, she had it wedged between two trees in a way that she hoped looked random, but was secure enough that the wind wouldn't carry it away for good.

Only seven more to go.

The work was excruciatingly slow. Tally had to consider every step she took among the sleeping bodies, and every accidental sound made her heart flutter. All the while she half-listened to the warden's car approaching on her skintenna feed.

Finally, the last of the eight hoverboards had been carefully dragged into the shade. They were tangled together, like crumpled umbrellas after a windstorm, the bright solar arrays turned facedown in the brush.

Before slipping back into the river, Tally stood for a

moment regarding Zane. Asleep, he looked more like his old self; the random shakes didn't trouble him in unconsciousness. Without his thoughts traveling across his face, he looked smarter, almost special. She imagined his eyes sharpened to cruel-pretty angles, and let her mind trace lacework flash tattoos across his face. Tally smiled and turned, taking a step back toward the river. . . .

Then she heard a sound, and froze.

It was a soft, sudden intake of breath, a noise of surprise. She waited motionless, hoping it had been a nightmare, and that the breathing would settle back into sleep. But her senses told her that someone was awake.

Finally she turned her head with excruciating slowness to look over her shoulder.

It was Zane.

His eyes were open, sleepy and squinting in the sunlight. He stared straight at her, dazed and half-asleep, unsure if she was real.

Tally stood absolutely still, but the sneak suit didn't have much to work with. It might show a blurry version of the water behind Tally, but in broad daylight Zane would still see a transparent humanoid figure, like a statue of solid glass standing half in the river. To make things worse, mud still clung to the suit, clods of brown hovering against the background.

He rubbed his eyes and looked around the empty riverbank, realizing that the hoverboards were missing. Then he looked up at her again, a puzzled expression still on his face.

Tally remained motionless, hoping that Zane would decide this was nothing but a strange dream.

"Hey," he said softly. His voice came out croaking, and he cleared his throat to speak louder.

Tally didn't let him. She took three swift steps through the mud, whisking off one glove, flicking out the stinger from her ring.

As the tiny needle plunged into his throat, Zane managed to let out a soft and startled cry, but then his eyes rolled back up into his head and he sank back to the ground, fast asleep again. He began to snore softly.

"Just a dream," Tally whispered into his ear. Then she lowered herself onto her belly and slithered back into the river.

Half an hour later, the warden's hovercar passed, moving from side to side like a lazy snake. It didn't spot the Crims, never pausing for a moment in the sky.

Tally stayed close to the camp, hidden in a tree about ten meters away from Zane, her sneak suit prickly with the texture of pine needles.

As the afternoon wore on, the Crims started to wake up. No one appeared to worry too much about the windblown hoverboards, just dragged them back out into the sunlight and went on with the process of breaking camp.

As she watched, the runaways wandered off into the woods to pee, cooked themselves meals, or took quick swims in the cold river, trying to clean off the mud and sweat of travel and the general greasiness of sleeping rough.

All except Zane. He stayed unconscious longer than the rest, the knockout drugs slowly working their way through his system. He didn't wake up until the sun was setting, when Peris finally leaned over him to give him a shake.

Zane sat up slowly, holding his head in his hands, the perfect picture of a pretty with a bad hangover. Tally wondered what he remembered. Peris and the others so far believed the wind had moved their hoverboards, but they might change their minds after hearing about Zane's little dream.

Peris and Zane huddled together for a while, and Tally slid slowly around her tree, gaining a vantage where she could almost read their lips. Peris seemed to be asking if Zane was all right. New pretties hardly ever got sick—the operation made them too healthy for trivial infections—but with his condition and all . . .

Zane shook his head and gestured down at the riverbank, where the hoverboards were soaking up the last rays of sun. Peris pointed toward the spot where Tally had arranged them. The two walked over to it, coming alarmingly close to where Tally clung to her tree. The expression on Zane's face looked unconvinced. He knew that at least one part of his dream—the missing boards—had been real.

After a few long, tense minutes, Peris returned to packing up camp. But Zane stayed, sweeping his gaze slowly around the horizon. Even invisible in her suit, Tally flinched as his eyes slid past her hiding place.

He wasn't certain of anything, but Zane suspected what he'd seen had been more than a dream.

Tally would have to be very careful from now on.

INVISIBLE

Over the next few days, Tally's pursuit of the Crims fell into a steady rhythm.

The runaways stayed up later each night, their random

bodies slowly adjusting to traveling in darkness and sleeping during the day. Soon they managed to ride all night, making camp only when the first rays of dawn broke on the horizon.

Andrew's position-finder was leading them south. They followed the river to the ocean, then hopped onto the rusting rails of an old high-speed train line. Someone had made the coastal tracks safe for hoverboarding, Tally noticed, with no dangerous gaps in the magnetic field. Wherever the line was broken, buried metal cables kept the Crims from crashing. They never even had to hike.

She wondered how many other runaways had used this path, and from how many other cities David and his allies were recruiting.

The New Smoke was certainly farther away than she'd expected. David's parents were originally from Tally's city, and he had always hidden within a few days' travel of home. But Andrew's position-finder had led them halfway to the southern continent, the days visibly growing longer and the nights warmer as they headed south.

As the coast began to rise into high cliffs, the waves crashing far below faded to a dull roar, and tall grasses choked the ancient train tracks. In the distance huge fields of the white weed glimmered in the sun. The weed was a form of engineered orchid that some Rusty scientist had let loose upon the world. It grew everywhere, leeching the ground of nutrients and choking whole forests in its path. But something about the ocean, perhaps the salt air, kept it away from the coast.

The Crims seemed to grow used to the routine of travel. Their hoverboarding skills improved, though following them was never a challenge. The steady practice didn't hurt

Zane's coordination, but compared to the others he was still unsteady on his board.

Shay had to be getting farther ahead every hour. Tally wondered if the rest of the Cutters had joined her. Or was she being cautious and traveling alone, waiting until she'd found the New Smoke before calling in reinforcements?

Every day that the Crims didn't reach their goal, it became more likely that Special Circumstances was already there, and that their entire journey was a cruel joke, just like Shay had said.

Traveling alone gave Tally a lot of time to think, and she spent most of it wondering if she really was the self-centered monster Shay had described. It didn't seem fair. When had she even had a *chance* to be selfish? Ever since Dr. Cable had recruited her, other people had made most of Tally's choices for her. Someone was always forcing her to join their side in the conflict between the Smokies and the city. Her only real decisions so far had been staying ugly in the Old Smoke (which hadn't worked out at all), escaping from New Pretty Town with Zane (ditto), and splitting up with Shay to protect Zane (not great so far). Everything else had happened because of threats, accidents, lesions in her brain, and surgery changing her mind for her.

Not exactly her fault.

And yet she and Shay always seemed to wind up on opposite sides. Was that a coincidence? Or was there something about the two of them that always turned them from friends into enemies? Maybe they were like two different species—hawks and rabbits, say—and could never be allies.

So who was the hawk? Tally wondered.

Out here alone, she felt herself changing again.

Somehow the wild made her feel less special. She still saw the world's icy beauty, but something was missing: the sounds of the other Cutters around her, the intimacy of their breathing in the skintenna network. She began to realize that being a Special wasn't just about strength and speed; it was about being part of a group, a clique. Back at camp Tally had felt *connected* to the others—always reminded of the powers and privileges they shared, and of the sights and smells only their superhuman senses could detect.

Among the Cutters, Tally had always felt special. But now that she was alone in the wild, her perfect vision only made her feel minuscule. In all its glorious detail, the natural world seemed big enough to swallow her.

The distant group of runaways weren't impressed or terrorized by her wolflike face and razor fingernails. How could they be when they never even glimpsed her? She was invisible, an outcast fading away.

She was almost relieved when the Crims made their second mistake.

They'd stopped to make camp on one side of a tall rocky outcrop, protected from the wind coming off the ocean. The weeds were close here, glowing softly as the sun rose, turning the inland hills as white as sand dunes.

The Crims unfurled their boards and weighted them down, made a halfway competent fire and ate their meals. Tally watched them drop off to sleep with their usual speed, exhausted from a long day of travel.

This far from the city, she no longer had to worry about the boards being spotted. Her skintenna hadn't picked up traffic from the wardens for days. But as she settled in for a long day of watching, Tally noticed that one of the boards—Zane's—had been left out in the ocean breeze whipping around the outcrop.

The board fluttered, and one of the stones weighting its corners rolled off.

Tally sighed—after a week on the trail, the runaways *still* hadn't learned to do this right—but inside she felt a ping of eagerness. Fixing this would give her *something* to do, at least, and maybe make her feel less insignificant. For those few moments she wouldn't be completely alone. She would hear the breathing of the sleeping Crims and take a closer look at Zane. Seeing him still and asleep, untroubled by his shaking, always reminded Tally of why she had made the choices she had.

She crawled toward the camp, her sneak suit turning the color of the dirt. The sun was rising behind her, but this would be much easier than the riverbank, where all eight boards had gone astray. Zane's hoverboard was still fluttering, another corner having freed itself, but it hadn't leaped into the air just yet. Perhaps its magnetics had found purchase with some underground vein of iron, and were dutifully holding it down.

When Tally reached the board, it was flapping like a wounded bird, the breeze swirling around it smelling of seaweed and salt. Strangely, someone had left an old leather-bound book open next to the hoverboard. Its pages snapped noisily in the wind.

Tally squinted. It looked like the one that Zane had been reading, that first night she'd seen him back from the hospital.

Another corner of the board slipped free, and Tally raised a hand to snatch it before the wind pulled it away.

But the hoverboard didn't budge.

Something was wrong here. . . .

Then Tally saw why it wasn't moving. The fourth corner was tied to a stake, secured against the wind, as if whoever had placed it out here in the breeze had known the stone weights would fail.

Then she heard something over the fluttering pages of the book—the stupid, noisy book that had *obviously* been left here to cover other sounds. One of the Crims was breathing less evenly than the others . . . someone was awake.

She turned and saw Zane watching her.

Tally jumped to her feet, whipping off her glove and flicking out her stinger in one motion. But Zane raised one hand: It held a collection of metal stakes and firestarters. Even if Tally somehow made it those five meters and stung him, all that metal would fall clattering to the ground, waking the rest of them.

But why hadn't he just cried out? She tensed, waiting for him to raise an alarm, but instead he lifted a finger slowly to his lips.

His sly expression said, *I won't tell if you don't.*

Tally swallowed, scanning the other Crims in the darkness. None of them watched through slitted eyes; they were all fast asleep. He wanted to talk to her alone.

She nodded, her heart beating fast.

The two crept out of the camp and around the outcrop, to where the breeze and crash of waves would cloak their words in a steady roar. Now that Zane was moving, his trembling had started again. As he settled himself next to her in the scrubby grass, Tally didn't look at his face. She already felt revulsion threatening to rise up inside her.

"Do the others know about me?" she asked.

"No. I wasn't sure myself. Thought I was imagining things." He touched her shoulder. "I'm glad I wasn't."

"Can't *believe* I fell for that stupid trick."

He chuckled. "Sorry to take advantage of your better nature."

"My *what*?"

In the corner of her eye, Tally saw him smile. "You were protecting us that first day, weren't you? Moving the hover-boards out of sight?"

"Yeah. A warden was about to spot you. Bubbleheads."

"Thought so. That's why I figured you'd help out again. Our own personal protector."

Tally swallowed. "Yeah, great. It's nice to be appreciated."

"So is it just you?"

"Yeah, I'm all alone." It was true now, after all.

"You're not supposed to be out here, are you?"

"You mean am I disobeying orders? Afraid so."

Zane nodded. "I knew you and Shay had some trick up your sleeves, letting me go. I mean, you didn't really expect me to use that tracker." He reached out and took her arm, his fingers pale against the dull gray of the sneak suit. "But how are you following us, Tally? It's not something inside me, is it?"

"No, Zane. You're clean. I'm just staying close, watching you every minute. Eight city kids in the wild aren't very hard to spot, after all." She shrugged, still staring out into the crashing waves. "I can smell you too."

"Oh." He laughed. "Not too bad yet, I hope."

She shook her head. "I've been in the wild before, Zane. I've smelled worse. But why didn't you . . . ?" She turned toward him but lowered her gaze, focusing on the zipper of his jacket. "You set a trap for me, but didn't mention it to the other Crims?"

"I didn't want to panic everybody." Zane shrugged. "If a whole bunch of Specials were following us, there wasn't much they could do about it. And if it was just you, I didn't want the others to know. They wouldn't understand."

"Understand what?" Tally said softly.

"That this whole trip wasn't a trap," he continued. "That it was just you. Protecting us."

She swallowed—of course, it *had* been a trap. But what was it now? Just a joke? A pointless waste of time? Shay, Dr. Cable, and the rest of Special Circumstances were probably already waiting for them at the Smoke.

He squeezed her arm. "It's changing you again, isn't it?"

"What is?"

"The wild. That's what you always said—traveling to the Smoke that first time, it's what made you what you are."

Tally turned away to stare out at the ocean, tasting its salt in her mouth. Zane was right—the wild was changing her again. Every time she crossed the wilderness alone, the beliefs the city had instilled in her were shaken up. But this time around, Tally's realizations weren't making her particularly happy. "I'm not sure *what* I am anymore, Zane. Sometimes I think I'm nothing but what other people have done to me—a big collection of brainwashing, surgeries, and cures." She looked down at her scarred hand, the tattoos flickering brokenly across her palm. "That, and all the mistakes I've made. All the people I've disappointed."

He traced the scar with a quivering fingertip; she closed her hand and looked away. "If that were true, Tally, you wouldn't be out here now. Disobeying orders."

"Yeah, well, I'm pretty good at the disobeying part."

"Look at me, Tally."

"Zane, I'm not sure if that's a good idea." She swallowed. "You see . . ."

"I know. I saw your face that night. I've noticed how you haven't looked at me. It makes perfect sense that Dr. Cable would pull something like that—Specials think everyone else is worthless, right?"

Tally shrugged, not wanting to explain that it was worse with Zane than anyone else. Partly because of the way she'd felt about him before, the contrast between now and then. And partly . . . the other thing.

"Try, Tally," he said.

She turned away, almost wishing for a moment that she wasn't special, that her eyes weren't so perfectly tuned to capture every detail of his infirmity. That her mind hadn't been turned against everything random and average and . . . crippled.

"I can't, Zane."

"Yes you can."

"What? So you're an expert on Specials now?"

"No. But remember David?"

"David?" She glared at the sea. "What about him?"

"Didn't he once tell you that you were beautiful?"

A chill went through her. "Yeah, back in ugly days. But how did you . . . ?" Then Tally remembered their last escape, how Zane had gotten to the Rusty Ruins a week before her. He and David had had plenty of time to get to know each other before she'd finally shown up. "He *told* you about that?"

Zane shrugged. "He'd seen how pretty I was. And I guess he was hoping that you could still see him, the way you had back in the Old Smoke."

Tally shuddered, a rush of old memories sweeping through her: that night two operations ago when David had looked at her ugly face—thin lips and frizzy hair and squashed-down nose—and said that she was beautiful. She'd tried to explain how it couldn't be true, how biology wouldn't *let* it be true. . . .

But still he'd called her beautiful, even when she was ugly.

That was the moment that Tally's whole world had started to unravel. That was the first time she'd switched sides.

She felt an unexpected ping of pity for poor, random-faced David. Raised a Smokey, he'd never had the operation, hadn't even seen any city pretties back then. So of course he might think that ugly Tally Youngblood would be okay to look at.

But after she'd been turned pretty, Tally had given herself up to Dr. Cable just to stay with Zane, and had pushed David away.

"That's not why I chose you, Zane. Not because of your face. It's because of what you and I did together—how we freed ourselves. You know that, right?"

"Of course. So what's wrong with you now?"

"What do you mean?"

"Listen, Tally. When David saw how beautiful you were, he took on five million years of evolution. He saw past your imperfect skin and asymmetry and everything else our genes select against." Zane held out his hand. "And now you can't even look at me just because I'm *shaking a little*?"

She stared at his sickening, quivering fingers. "It's worse than being a bubblehead, Zane. Bubbleheads are just clueless, but Specials are . . . single-minded about some things. But at least I'm trying to fix the situation. Why do you think I'm out here following you?"

"You want to take me back to the city, don't you?"

She groaned. "What's the alternative? Having Maddy try one of her half-baked cures?"

"The alternative is inside you, Tally. This isn't about *my* brain damage; it's about *yours*." He slid closer, and she closed her eyes. "You freed yourself once before. You beat the pretty lesions. In the beginning, all it took was a kiss."

She felt the heat of his body next to her, smelled the campfire smoke on his skin. She turned away, eyes still shut tight. "But it's different being special—it isn't just some little piece of my brain. It's my whole body. It's the way I see the world."

"Right. You're so special no one can touch you."

"Zane . . ."

"You're so special you have to cut yourself just to feel anything."

She shook her head. "I don't do that anymore."

"So you *can* change!"

"But that doesn't mean . . ." She opened her eyes.

Zane's face was centimeters from hers, his gaze intense. And somehow the wild had changed him, too—his eyes no longer looked watery and average to her. His stare was almost icy.

Almost special.

She leaned closer . . . and their lips met, warm in the chill of the outcrop's shadow. The roar of the waves filled her ears, drowning out her nervous heartbeat.

She slid closer, hands pushing inside his clothes. She wanted to be out of the sneak suit, no longer alone, no longer invisible. Arms around him, she squeezed tight, hearing his breath catch as her lethal hands gripped harder. Her senses brought her everything about him: his heart pulsing softly in his throat, the taste of his mouth, the unwashed scent of him cut by the salt spray.

But then his fingers brushed her cheek, and Tally felt their trembling.

No, she said silently.

The tremors were soft, almost nothing, as faint as the echoes of rain falling a kilometer away. But they were everywhere, on the skin of his face, in the muscles of his arms around her, in his lips against hers—his whole body shivering like a littlie's in the cold. And suddenly Tally could *see* inside him: his damaged nervous system, the corrupted connections between body and brain.

She tried to blot the image from her mind, but it only grew clearer. She was designed to spot weaknesses, after all, to take advantage of the frailties and flaws of randoms. Not ignore them.

Tally tried to pull away a little, but Zane's grip on her arm tightened, as if he thought he could *hold* her there. She broke the kiss and opened her eyes, glaring down at the pale fingers grasping her, a sudden, unstoppable flash of anger rising.

"Tally, wait," he said. "We can—"

But he hadn't let go. Rage and disgust filled her, and Tally sent a flutter of razor spines rolling across her sneak suit. Zane cried out and pulled back, his fingers and palms bleeding.

She rolled away, springing to her feet and running. She'd *kissed* him, let herself be touched by him—someone unspecial and barely average. Someone crippled . . .

Bile rose in her throat, as if the memory of kissing him was trying to tear itself free of her body. She stumbled and fell to one knee, her stomach heaving, the world spinning.

"Tally!" He was coming after her.

"Don't!" She raised one hand, not daring to look up at him. Breathing in the cold, pure sea air, the nausea was beginning to pass. But not if he got any closer.

"Are you okay?"

"Does it *look* like I'm okay?" A wave of shame whipped through Tally. What had she done? "I just can't, Zane."

She pulled herself up and ran toward the ocean, away from him. The outcrop ended on a chalky cliff, but Tally didn't slow down. . . .

She jumped, barely clearing the rocks below, hitting the waves with a slap, diving down into the icy embrace of the water. The churning ocean spun her around, almost dumping her back on the jagged shore, but Tally pulled herself deeper with a few powerful strokes, until her hands brushed the dark and sandy bottom. The roiling water began to fall back, shifting into a riptide around her. It pulled Tally outward, rumbling in her ears, erasing her thoughts.

She held her breath, letting the ocean claim her.

A minute later Tally let herself break the surface, gasping for air. She was half a kilometer from where she'd started, well offshore and being carried south by the current.

Zane was at the cliff's edge, scanning the water for her, his bleeding hands wrapped in his jacket. After what she'd done, Tally couldn't face him, didn't even want to be *seen* by him. She wanted to disappear.

She drew down her hood and let the suit take on the rippling silver of the water, let herself be pulled farther away.

Finally, when he'd gone back to camp, Tally swam toward shore.

BONES

After that, the journey seemed to take forever.

Some days, she became convinced the position-finder was nothing but a Smokey trick leading them around the wild forever: crippled Zane struggling to make it through the long nights of travel; psycho Tally alone inside her sneak suit, detached and invisible. Both of them in separate hells.

She wondered how Zane felt about her now. After what had happened, he must have realized how weak she really was: Dr. Cable's feared fighting machine undone by a kiss, sickened by something as simple as a quivering hand.

The memory of it made her want to cut herself, to tear at her own flesh until she had become something different inside. Something less special, more human. But she didn't want to go back to cutting after telling Zane she'd stopped. It would be like breaking a promise to him.

Tally wondered if he'd told the other Crims about her. Were they already planning something—a way to ambush Tally and turn her over to the Smokies? Or would they try to escape, leaving her behind, alone in the wild forever?

She imagined sneaking into camp again while the others were sleeping, and telling Zane how bad she felt. But she couldn't bear to face him. She might have gone too far this time, almost throwing up in his face, not to mention cutting up his hands.

Shay had already given up on her. What if Zane also decided he'd had enough of Tally Youngblood?

Toward the end of two weeks, the Crims came to a halt on a cliff that jutted out high above the sea.

Tally glanced up at the stars. It was well before dawn, and the rail line stretched before them unbroken. But the runaways all jumped from their boards and gathered around Zane, looking down at something in his hand.

The position-finder.

Tally watched and waited, hovering just below the edge of the sea cliff, lifting fans keeping her aloft above the crashing waves. After a few long minutes, she saw campfire smoke; it was clear the Crims weren't going any farther tonight. She drifted closer and pulled herself onto the cliff.

Circling around in the high grass, she made her way closer to the encampment. Flares of infrared erupted as the Crims heated their meals.

Finally, Tally reached a spot where the wind carried sounds and the smell of city food to her.

"What do we do if no one comes?" one of the girls was saying.

Zane's voice answered. "They'll come."

"How long?"

"I don't know. But there's nothing else we can do."

The girl started talking about their water supply, and the fact that they hadn't seen a river for the last two nights.

Tally sank back into the grass, relieved—the position-finder had told them to stop here. This wasn't the New Smoke, obviously, but perhaps this awful journey was coming to an end soon.

She looked around, sniffing the air, wondering what was special about this place. Among the scents of self-heating meals, Tally smelled something that made her skin crawl . . . something rotten.

She crawled toward the scent through the high grass,

eyes sweeping the ground. The stench grew and grew, finally so strong it almost made her gag. A hundred meters from the camp she found the source: a pile of dead fish, heads and tails and picked-clean spines with flies and maggots crawling all over them.

Tally swallowed, telling herself to stay icy as she searched the area around the pile. In a small clearing, she discovered the remains of an old campfire. The charred wood was cold, the ash all blown away, but someone had camped here. Many people, in fact.

The lifeless fire was in a deep pit, banked against the sea breeze, and built to give off heat efficiently. Like all city pretties, the Crims always optimized their fires for light instead of heat, burning through wood carelessly. But this fire had been made by practiced hands.

Tally glimpsed something white among the ashes, and reached in to gently draw it out. . . .

It was a bone, about as long as her hand. She couldn't tell what species it belonged to, but it was marked with small depressions where human teeth had gnawed into the marrow.

Tally couldn't imagine city kids eating meat after only a couple of weeks in the wild. Even the Smokies rarely *hunted* for food—they raised rabbits and chickens, nothing as big as whatever this bone had come from. And the teeth had left uneven marks; whoever they were, they didn't know a lot about dentistry. One of Andrew's people had probably built this fire.

A shiver went through her. The villagers she'd met thought of outsiders as enemies, like animals to be hunted and killed. And pretties weren't "gods" to them anymore. Tally wondered how the villagers felt about discovering that they'd lived inside an experiment all their lives, and that their beautiful gods were nothing but human beings.

She wondered if any of the Smokies' recruits ever thought about getting revenge on the city pretties.

Tally shook her head. The Smokies had trusted Andrew enough to put him in charge of guiding the runaways here. Surely the others they had recruited weren't homicidal maniacs.

But what if other villagers had learned to escape from their "little men"?

As dawn approached, Tally stayed awake, not bothering with her usual catnaps. She watched the sky for signs of hovercars as always, but she also kept an eye on the inland approach to the cliffs, infrared at full power. The unpleasant rumble in her stomach from seeing the pile of rotten fish never completely went away.

They came three hours after sunrise.

NEW ARRIVALS

Fourteen figures showed in infrared, slowly climbing the lazy inland hills, all but hidden by the long grass.

Tally booted her sneak suit, and felt its scales ripple up to mimic the grass, like the hackles of a nervous cat. The only figure she could see clearly was the woman at the front of the group. She was definitely a villager—clad in skins and carrying a spear.

Tally sank lower into the grass, remembering the first time she'd met the villagers—they'd jumped her in the middle of the night, ready to kill for the crime of being an outsider. The Crims would be fast asleep by now.

If there was any violence, it would happen suddenly, leaving little time for Tally to save anyone. Maybe she should wake up Zane now and tell him what was approaching. . . .

But the thought of how he might look at her, her own disgust mirrored in his eyes, sent her head spinning.

Tally took a deep breath, ordering herself to stay icy. The long nights of traveling—invisible and alone, trying to protect someone who probably didn't even want her around—had started to make her paranoid. Without a better look, she couldn't assume that the approaching group posed a threat.

She crawled on hands and knees, moving swiftly in the tall grass, giving the pile of rotten fish a wide berth. A little closer, Tally heard a clear voice ring out across the fields, carrying an unfamiliar tune in the random-sounding syllables of the villagers' language. The song didn't sound particularly warlike—more happy, like something you'd sing when your team was winning a soccer game.

To these people, of course, random violence pretty much *was* a soccer game.

As they grew closer, Tally raised her head. . . .

And breathed a sigh of relief. Only two of the approaching group wore skins. The rest were city pretties—bedraggled and tired-looking, but definitely not savages. The whole group balanced water packs on their shoulders, the bubbleheads hunched under the weight, the villagers carrying it effortlessly. Tally looked into the distance the way they'd come, and saw the glimmer of water from an ocean inlet. They'd only been away on a provisions run.

Remembering how Andrew had detected her, Tally stayed well clear of the group. But she was close enough to make out their clothes. The city pretties' seemed all wrong, totally fashion-missing, or maybe a few years out of style. But these kids hadn't been out here *that* long.

Then Tally heard one boy asking how far it was back to camp, and the strangeness of his accent sent a shiver through her. They were from another city, somewhere far enough away that they talked differently. Of course, she was halfway to the equator. The Smokies had been spreading their little rebellion far and wide.

But what were they doing here? she wondered. Surely this little patch of cliff wasn't the New Smoke. Tally crawled along behind the group, still watching them warily as they approached the sleeping Crims.

Suddenly, she came to a halt, feeling something in her bones—something all around, as if the earth were rumbling under her.

A strange noise came from the distance, low and rhythmic, like huge fingers drumming on a table. It faded in and out for a few moments before steadying.

The others could hear it now. The villager heading up the little party let out a cry, pointing toward the south, and the city pretties all looked up expectantly. Tally could already see it, thundering across the hills toward them, its engines glowing hot in infrared.

She raised herself into a half crouch and started running for her board, the thrumming sound building around her. Tally remembered her first trip into the wild, when she'd gotten a lift to the Smoke in a strange Rusty flying vehicle. The rangers, naturalists from another city, had used old contraptions like this one to fight the white weed.

What were they called again?

It wasn't until she had made it back to her hoverboard that Tally remembered the name.

The "helicopter" landed not far from the cliff's edge.

Twice the size of the one Tally had ridden to the Smoke, it descended with an awesome fury, the whirlwind battering down the grass in a wide circle. The helicopter kept itself aloft with two huge spinning blades that mercilessly beat the air, like huge lifting fans. Even in her hiding place, their sound rattled Tally down to her ceramic bones, her hoverboard bucking beneath her like a nervous horse in the windstorm.

The Crims were awake by now, of course, shaken to consciousness by the thundering beat. Whoever was flying the helicopter had spotted them from up high, and had waited for them to furl their boards before landing. By the time the machine came down, the other group had made its way back to the cliffs. The two sets of runaways were eyeing each other warily as the helicopter's crew jumped out onto the beaten grass.

The rangers, Tally remembered, came from a city with different attitudes from her own, one that didn't particularly care whether the Smoke existed or not. Their main concern was preserving nature from the engineered plagues that the Rusties had left behind, especially the white weed. The rangers had traded favors with the Old Smoke sometimes, giving runaways lifts in their flying machines.

Tally had liked the rangers she'd met. They were pretties but, like firefighters or Specials, they didn't have the bubblehead lesions. Thinking for themselves was a part of their job description, and they possessed the calm competence of the Smokies—without the ugly faces.

The helicopter's blades kept spinning as it sat on the ground, stirring the air beneath her board and making it impossible to hear a thing. But from her vantage hovering just below the edge of the sea cliff, it was obvious that Zane was introducing himself and the other Crims. The rangers didn't seem to care, one listening as the others checked over their ancient, cantankerous machine. The two villagers regarded the newcomers suspiciously, though, until Zane produced the position-finder.

At the sight of it, one of them pulled out a scanning wand and began to wave it around Zane's body. She took special care to check his teeth, Tally noticed. The other villager was busy scanning another Crim, the two of them checking all eight of the new arrivals thoroughly.

Then they began to herd the runaways, all twenty of them, onto the helicopter. The thing was much bigger than a warden's hovercar, but it was so crude and loud and *ancient*-looking . . . Tally wondered how it could carry them all.

The rangers didn't seem worried. They were busy sticking the city kids' hoverboards onto the machine's undercarriage, sandwiching them together magnetically.

As crowded as the runaways would be inside, it had to be a short trip. . . .

The problem was, Tally wasn't sure how she could tag along. The helicopter she'd ridden in was faster and could go much higher than any hoverboard. And if she lost sight of them, there would be no way to follow the Crims the rest of the way to the New Smoke.

Tracking the old-fashioned way had its disadvantages.

She wondered what Shay had done when she'd reached

this point. Tally boosted her skintenna, but found no trace of another Special nearby; no waiting beacons pulsed a message for her.

But Andrew's position-finder must have led Shay here as well. Had she disguised herself as an ugly and tried to fool the villagers? Or had she managed to follow the helicopter somehow?

Tally peered at the undercarriage again. Among the twenty sandwiched hoverboards was just enough space for a human being.

Maybe Shay had snuck a ride. . . .

Tally pulled on her grippy gloves, readying herself. She could wait until the helicopter took off, then pursue it in a short chase across the hills, followed by a quick climb up through the windstorm of its spinning blades.

She felt a smile spreading across her face. After two weeks of skulking after the Crims, it would be a relief to face a real challenge, one that would make her feel like a Special again.

And even better, the New Smoke had to be close. She had almost reached the end of the line.

PURSUIT

Soon the pretties were all loaded into the helicopter, and the two villagers stepped back, waving and smiling.

Tally didn't wait for it to take off. She headed southward down the coast, back in the direction it had come from, staying below the cliffs to keep out of sight. The trick would be waiting until the machine was far enough from the villagers before climbing into the open sky. After weeks of hiding, she didn't want to be spotted this close to her goal.

The helicopter's spinning blades changed pitch, the whine building slowly to a thunderous beating in the air. She resisted the urge to look back, keeping her eyes on the winding and rugged cliff wall. She snaked along it, only an arm's length away, staying low and out of sight.

Tally's ears told her when the helicopter lifted into the air behind her. She urged her hoverboard faster, wondering what the Rusty contraption's top speed was.

Tally had never pushed a Special Circumstances board as fast as it could go. Unlike hoverboards designed for randoms, the Cutters' didn't have safety features to keep you from doing anything stupid. If you let them, the lifting fans would spin until they overheated, or worse. She knew from Cutter training that fans didn't always fail gracefully—you could push them until they tore themselves apart in a shower of white-hot metal. . . .

Tally flicked on her infrared vision and glanced down at the fan in front of her left foot; it already had the red-hot glow of campfire embers.

The helicopter was catching up, its thunder closing in behind and above her, battering the air. She dropped farther below the cliff level, the crashing waves passing beneath her in a wild blur, every outcrop of rocks threatening to take off her head.

By the time the helicopter drew even overhead, it was a hundred meters off the ground and still climbing. She had to make her move now.

Tally angled back and shot up over the cliff's edge, skimming the earth to a spot directly below the helicopter, out of view of its bulbous windows. Behind her the two villagers had shrunk to mere dots. Her sneak suit was tuned sky blue, so even if they were still watching, they would only see the sliver of her hoverboard.

As Tally climbed toward the thundering machine, her board began to shiver, the vortex beneath the helicopter flailing at her with invisible fists. The air pulsed around her, like a sound system with the bass turned way too high.

Suddenly, her board dropped out from under her, and Tally found herself falling for a moment. Then its grippy surface bucked up under her feet again. She glanced down to check if one of her fans had failed, but they were both still spinning. Then the board dropped again, and Tally realized that she was hitting random pockets of low pressure in the maelstrom, the board abruptly finding itself without enough air to push against.

Tally bent her knees and climbed faster, ignoring the white-hot glow of her lifting fans and the buffeting blows of the tempest around her. She didn't have time for caution—the helicopter was still climbing, still gaining speed, and would soon be out of reach.

Suddenly, the wind and noise quieted—she had reached a zone of calm, like the eye of a hurricane. Tally glanced up. She was directly underneath the machine's belly, sheltered from the turbulence created by the spinning blades. This was her chance to climb aboard.

She climbed higher, reaching out with grippy-gloved hands. Her crash bracelets tugged upward, connecting with the metal in the craft. Another meter higher and she would be there. . . .

Out of the blue, the world seemed to tilt around Tally. The helicopter's belly dipped to one side, then pulled away. The machine was banking hard, making a sudden turn inland, stripping her of the protection of its massive body, like coming around a corner into the path of a storm.

The wind hit Tally in a roiling wave, whipping her legs out from under her and sending the hoverboard fluttering away. Her ears popped in the eddies and currents of the helicopter's vortex, and for a terrifying second she saw the giant blades loom close to her in a great blurred wall of force, their ear-shattering beat pounding through her body.

But instead of cutting her to ribbons, the blades' fury flung her away; she spun in midair, the horizon wheeling around her. For a moment, even her special sense of balance failed, as if the world was whirling into chaos.

After a few seconds of freefall, Tally felt a tug on her wrists, and made the gesture to recall her hoverboard. It had leveled itself off and was shooting toward her at top speed, its lifting fans so hot they had turned whiter than the sun.

She made a grab for the board, and the superheated riding surface burned her hands even through gloves, the scent of grippy plastics at their melting point assaulting her nostrils. The heat was so intense that her sneak suit switched itself to armored mode, trying to offer some protection.

Still spinning, Tally hung from the board for a moment, until its winglike shape stabilized her. Then she rolled herself up onto it and rose to a riding stance.

She switched the sneak suit back to sky blue and looked ahead—the helicopter was receding into the distance.

Tally hesitated, realizing that she should give up now, return to the pickup point, and wait for the next group of runaways. Surely helicopters made this trip regularly.

But Zane was in there, and she couldn't abandon him

now. Shay and the rest of Special Circumstances might already be on their way.

Tally urged her overheating board faster. The helicopter had lost altitude and speed during its turn, and soon she was catching up.

The heat of her hoverboard's surface began to burn the soles of her feet, and Tally felt its vibration shifting beneath her. The metal fans were expanding in the white heat, changing the board's sound and feel. She pushed it forward, until the tempest swirling around the helicopter began to batter her again, the air rumbling as she made another approach.

But this time Tally knew what to expect; she had learned the shape of the invisible vortex in her first trip through. Instinct guided her through its whorls and eddies and into the small bubble of protection underneath the machine.

Her hoverboard was whining furiously now, but she urged it upward toward the undercarriage, arms outstretched. . . .

Closer and closer.

Tally felt the moment of breakdown through the soles of her feet, the board's unsteady vibration changing all at once into a wild shudder. A metal scream reached her ears as the lifting fans disintegrated, and she realized it was too late to go any direction but up. She bent her knees and leaped . . .

At the peak of her jump, Tally scrambled for something to grab on to, her fingers brushing against the stored hoverboards. But they were packed into thick sandwiches without any handholds, and the helicopter's landing struts were out of reach on either side.

Tally began to fall. . . .

She stabbed at her crash bracelets' controls, setting them to exhaust their batteries, to pull her toward the tons of metal above as hard as they could. A sudden, crushing force seized her wrists—the combined magnetics of twenty boards booting up and taking hold. The bracelets dragged her upward, pinning Tally against the nearest riding surface, her arms almost ripped from their sockets by the sudden jerk.

Below, the screech of her hoverboard turned into a wracking cough, then it dropped away. Tally's ears caught the metal squeal of the board, tearing itself to pieces as it fell, until the helicopter's portable maelstrom whisked the noise away.

Tally found herself stuck to the underside of the helicopter, its vibration rumbling through her like crashing waves.

For a moment, she wondered if the pilots and passengers had heard her board disintegrate, but then Tally remembered her own helicopter flight the year before. To make themselves heard, she and the rangers had been forced to shout over the roar of the blades.

After a few minutes of hanging from her wrists, Tally turned off the magnetics in one of her bracelets and swung out both feet, wrapping them around a landing strut. She switched off the other, then dangled head-down from the strut for a nervous-making moment in the furious wind before pulling herself up into a small gap between the runaways' boards. From there, she watched as the trip unfolded.

The helicopter proceeded on its inland course, the world growing more lush and forested as the sea slipped away behind. It climbed still higher, moving faster until the trees were nothing but a green blur below. Only a few spots had been touched by the white weed here.

Keeping a careful grip, Tally pulled off her gloves and checked her hands. The palms were burned, with a few pieces of melted plastic stuck to them, but the flash tattoos still pulsed, even those already broken by her cutting scar. Her medspray had gone down with the hoverboard, along with everything else. Only her crash bracelets, ceremonial knife, and sneak suit had survived.

But she'd made it. Tally finally allowed herself a slow breath of relief. Watching the scenery pass below, the pleasure of accomplishing a really icy trick washed through her.

Tally's fingers brushed the old metal belly of the helicopter—Zane was only a few meters from her. He had accomplished quite a trick as well. Despite his lesions and his brain damage, he had almost made it to the New Smoke. Whatever Shay thought of Tally now, she couldn't deny that Zane had earned the right to join Special Circumstances.

After all this, Tally wouldn't take no for an answer.

By Tally's internal software, it was an hour later that the first signs of their destination began to appear below.

Although the forest was still dense, a few rectangular fields came into view, the trees chopped down and stacked to make way for some sort of building project. Then more marks of new construction: huge diggers tearing at the earth and magnetic lifters moving hoverstruts into place. Tally frowned. The New Smoke was crazy if they thought they could get away with clear-cutting.

But then more familiar sights began to pass below. The low buildings of a factory belt, then the dense row houses of suburbia. Then a cluster of taller buildings rose up on the horizon, and the air began to fill with hovercars. A ring of soccer fields and dormitories passed below, exactly like Uglyville back in her own city.

Tally shook her head. All this couldn't have been built by Smokies. . . .

Then she remembered Shay's words the night they'd snuck into New Pretty Town to see Zane, about how David and his pals had acquired sneak suits from mysterious allies, and she realized the truth.

The New Smoke wasn't some hidden encampment in the wild, where people crapped into holes and ate dead rabbits, burning trees for fuel. The New Smoke was right here, spread out below her.

An entire city had joined the rebellion.

HARD LANDING

Tally had to get off before the helicopter landed.

She didn't want to be found clinging to the underside when they touched down. Zane would see her, and the rangers would probably know that her cruel beauty marked her as an agent of another city. But as the helicopter settled into a circling approach, headed toward a landing pad, Tally could see nowhere safe to drop.

In her own city, a river wrapped around the island of New Pretty Town. But she saw no convenient bodies of water to jump into, and she was too high to use crash bracelets safely. The sneak suit's armor might protect Tally, but the landing pad was nestled between two large buildings, surrounded by crowded slidewalks full of fragile pedestrians.

As the helicopter made its final approach, she spotted the tall hedges surrounded the landing pad—sturdy enough to dampen the wind from the helicopter's blades. They looked prickly, but a few thorns were nothing the sneak suit's armor couldn't handle.

The helicopter slowed as the pad loomed below, and Tally pulled her hood down to protect her face. As the helicopter banked to bring itself to a halt, she let herself drop, rolling into a ball as she fell, like a littlie jumping into a swimming pool.

Her left shoulder hit the hedge with a sudden *crunch*, branches snapping off against the suit's armor, and she bounced away from the barrier in an explosion of leaves, spinning through the air. She managed to land on her feet, but found herself stumbling across an unsteady surface . . . the quick-moving slidewalk she'd seen on the way down.

Tally waved her arms, almost regaining her balance, but one last step took her onto another slidewalk going the opposite way, which spun her around and dumped her on her back, spread-eagled and staring dumbfoundedly up at the sky.

"*Ouch,*" she murmured. Specials might have unbreakable ceramic bones, but there was still plenty of flesh to be bruised and nerve endings to complain.

Two tall buildings crowded the sky above her. They seemed to be moving gracefully past. . . . She was still being carried along by the slidewalk.

A middle-pretty face came into view, looking down at her with a stern expression. "Young lady! Are you all right?"

"Yeah. Mostly."

"Well, I am aware that standards of conduct have

changed. But you could still be reported to the wardens for a stunt like that!"

"Oh, sorry," Tally said, rising painfully to her feet.

"I suppose that suit was meant to protect you?" the man continued sternly. "But did you ever stop to think of the rest of us!"

Tally rubbed her probably bruise-covered back with one hand, held up the other in defense. For a middle pretty, this guy wasn't very understanding. "I said I was sorry. I had to get off that helicopter."

The man snorted. "Well, if you can't wait to land, next time use a bungee jacket!"

A sudden wave of annoyance came over Tally. This average, aging middle pretty just wouldn't shut up. She decided she was bored with the conversation and pulled off the sneak suit's hood, baring her teeth. "Maybe next time, I'll aim for *you*!"

The man looked straight back into her black and wolfen eyes, her lacework tattoos and razor smile, and only snorted again. "Or maybe you'll break your pretty neck!"

He made a satisfied little noise and stepped onto the faster lane of the slidewalk, which whisked him away without another glance back at Tally.

She blinked. That hadn't been the reaction she'd been expecting. In the windows of the passing building, her warped reflection drifted by. She was still a Special, her face still marked with all the signs of cruel beauty, designed to call up all humanity's ancient fears. But the man had hardly noticed.

Tally shook her head. Maybe in this city Special Circumstances agents didn't keep themselves hidden, and he'd seen cruel pretties before. But what was the point of looking terrifying if everyone had a chance to get used to it?

She played the conversation back in her mind, realizing how close the man's accent was to how she remembered the rangers'—fast, clipped, and precise. This had to be their home city.

But if this whole city really was the New Smoke, where was Shay? Tally boosted her skintenna range, but got no answering ping. Of course, cities were big—she might simply be out of range. Or maybe she had switched off, still sulking over Tally's latest betrayal.

Tally glanced back toward the landing pad. The helicopter's engines were still idling. Perhaps this city *wasn't* the New Smoke, and was only a refueling stop. Stepping over onto the opposite slidewalk, Tally headed back toward the pad.

A couple of new pretties glided by, and Tally noticed that they were wearing costume surge. One had skin much paler than any Pretty Committee would ever allow, with red hair and a smattering of freckles across her face, like one of those littlies who always had to worry about sunburn. The other's skin was so dark it was almost black, and his muscles were way too obvious.

Maybe that explained the middle-pretty man's reaction, or lack of it. There had to be some sort of costume bash happening tonight, one that all the new pretties were surging up for. The costume surgery was more extreme than would ever be allowed back in Tally's city, but at least it meant she wouldn't stick out like a sore thumb while she tried to figure out what was going on.

Of course, the armored black of her sneak suit wasn't exactly fashionable. With a little fiddling, she tuned it to resemble the clothing the two new pretties had been wearing: striped patterns in bold colors, like you'd dress a littlie in back at home. The garish hues made her feel even more conspicuous, but when a few more young pretties glided past—with translucently pale faces, oversize noses, and wildly colored clothes—Tally almost felt as if she was starting to fit in.

The buildings here didn't look too different from those she'd grown up with. The two on either side of the landing pad looked like typical government monoliths. In fact, the closer of the two had stone letters cut into it spelling out TOWN HALL, and most of the slidewalk step-offs were labeled with the names of city agencies. Ahead of Tally were the hovering party towers and sprawling mansions of what had to be New Pretty Town, and she could see ugly-dorms and soccer fields in the distance.

It seemed strange, though, not having a river between New Pretty Town and Uglyville. It would be too easy to sneak across, hardly a challenge at all. How would you keep party-crashers out?

She hadn't seen any wardens so far. Would *anyone* here know what her cruel beauty meant?

A young pretty stepped onto the slidewalk beside her, and Tally decided to see if she could pass for a local.

"Where's the bash tonight?" she asked, trying to imitate the local accent and hoping she didn't sound too random for not knowing.

"The *bash*? You mean a party?"

Tally shrugged. "Yeah, sure."

The young woman laughed. "Take your pick. There's mountains of them."

"Right, mountains. But which one's all the costume surge for?"

"Costume surge?" The woman looked at Tally like she'd said something totally random. "Did you just get off the chopper or something?"

Tally's eyebrows rose. "Um, the helicopter? Yeah, sort of."

"With a face like that?" The woman frowned. Her own skin was dark brown, her fingernails decorated with tiny video screens, each showing a different flickering image.

Tally could only shrug again.

"Oh, I see. Couldn't wait to look like one of us?" She laughed again. "Listen, kid, you should really be hanging out with the other newbies, at least until you know what's going on here." She squinted her eyes, her fingers making an interface gesture. "Diego says they're all up at the Overlook tonight."

"Diego?"

"The city." She laughed again, her fingernails flashing in tandem with the sound. "Wow, kid, you really are just off the chopper."

"Yeah, I guess. Thanks," Tally said, suddenly feeling very average and helpless, not special at all. Trying to navigate this new city, her strength and speed meant nothing, and even her cruel beauty didn't seem to impress anyone. It was like being an ugly again, when things like knowing the best bashes and how to dress had been more important than being superhuman.

"Well, welcome to Diego," the young pretty called, and stepped into a high-speed lane, waving good-bye with the vague embarrassment of ditching a loser at a party.

As she approached the landing pad, Tally kept a wary eye out for the runaway Crims. She stepped off the sidewalk where the hedge showed damage from her collision, and peeked through one of the gaps she'd left behind.

The runaways had unloaded from the helicopter, but they were still getting themselves sorted. Like typical bubbleheads, they were having trouble figuring out which hoverboard was whose. They clustered around the ranger who was trying to organize things, like littlies after ice cream.

Zane was waiting patiently, looking the happiest Tally had seen him since they'd escaped the city. A few of the other Crims crowded around him, slapping him on the back and congratulating one another.

One of the Crims brought Zane his board, and all eight of them set off toward the huge building across from Town Hall.

Tally saw that it was a hospital. That made sense. Anyone from outside would be checked for diseases, and for injuries and food poisoning from the trip. And since this city really was the New Smoke, newcomers would have their bubblehead lesions taken away as well.

Of course, Tally thought. Maddy's pills didn't have to work perfectly anymore. The runaways would all wind up here, where a city hospital staffed with real doctors could take care of their lesions.

She took a step back, breathing out slowly, finally admitting it to herself: The New Smoke was a thousand times larger and more powerful than she and Shay had expected.

The authorities here were taking in other cities' runaways, curing them of bubbleheadness. Now that she thought about it, *none* of the people she'd met so far had the lesions. All of them had expressed their opinions openly, not like bubbleheads at all.

That would explain why this city—"Diego," the woman had called it—had thrown out the Pretty Committee's standards, letting everyone look the way they wanted. They'd even started to build new structures in the surrounding forests, expanding out into the wild.

If that was all true, it was no wonder that Shay was no longer here. She'd probably gone home to report all this to Dr. Cable and Special Circumstances.

But what could they do about it? Cities couldn't tell one another how to run their affairs, after all.

This New Smoke could last forever.

RANDOM TOWN

Tally spent the day walking around the city, marveling at how different it was from her own.

She saw new pretties and uglies hanging out together, friends that the operation hadn't separated. And littlies clinging to their ugly older brothers and sisters instead of being stuck in Crumblyville with their parents. Those small changes were almost as surprising as the wild facial structures, skin textures, and body mods she encountered. *Almost.* It might take a while to get used to coats of downy feathers, pinkie fingers replaced with tiny snakes, skin every shade between deep black and alabaster, and hair that writhed like some sinuous creature under the sea.

Whole cliques wore the same skin color, or shared similar faces, like families used to before the operation. It reminded Tally uncomfortably of how people grouped themselves back in pre-Rusty days, into tribes and clans and so-called races who all looked more or less alike, and made a big point of hating anyone who didn't look like them.

But everyone seemed to be getting along so far—for every clique of people who looked alike, there was another of wild variations.

Diego's middle pretties seemed less crazy about the whole surgery thing. Most of them looked more or less like Tally's parents, and she heard more than a little grumbling about "new standards," how current fads were an eyesore and a disgrace. But they did so in such a forthright way that Tally had no doubt their own lesions were gone.

Disconcertingly, the crumblies seemed to be further into surgery than anyone else. A few wore the wise, calm, trustworthy faces that the Pretty Committee enforced at home, but others looked weirdly young. Half the time Tally wasn't exactly sure what age people were supposed to be, as if the city's surgeons had decided to let all the stages of life blur together.

She even heard a few people who, from the sound of their conversation, were still bubbleheads. For some reason—whether it was a philosophical position or a fashion statement—they had elected to keep the lesions in their brains.

Apparently, you could do just about anything you wanted here. It was like she'd landed in Random Town. Everyone was so different that her own special face practically faded into . . . nothing.

How had this all happened?

It couldn't have been very long ago. The transformations seemed to be still rippling all around her, as if a stone had been hurled into a small pond.

Once she managed to tune her skintenna to the city newsfeeds, Tally found them full of arguments. There were discussions about the wisdom of taking in the runaways, about standards of beauty, and most of all about the new construction at the city's edge—and not everyone bothered with the pleasant, civil debating style of home. Tally had never heard squabbling among adults like this before, not even in private. It was as if a bunch of uglies had taken over the airwaves. Without the lesions making everyone agreeable, society was left roiling in a constant battle of words, images, and ideas.

It was overwhelming, almost like the way the Rusties had lived, debating every issue in public instead of letting the government do its job.

And the changes already in place here in Diego were just a beginning, Tally realized. All around her she felt the city seething, all those unfettered minds bouncing their opinions off each other, like something ready to explode.

That night, she went to the Overlook.

The city interface guided her to the highest point in town, a stretch of parkland atop a chalk-faced cliff that overlooked the city center. The first young pretty she'd met had been right: The park was crowded with runaways, about half uglies and half new pretties. Most wore the faces they'd brought with them, not yet ready to plunge into extremes of cosmetic fashion. Tally could understand why the newbies were hanging out together; after a day on the streets of Diego, the sight of old-fashioned, Pretty Committee–designed faces was a relief.

Tally hoped that Zane would be here. Today had been the longest he'd spent out of her sight since his escape, and she wondered exactly what they'd done to him at the city hospital. Would removing Zane's lesions make him any less shaky? How would he decide to remake himself, here where anyone could look like anything, where the very *possibility* of being average had disappeared?

Maybe they would be able to fix him better than her own city's hospital. With all their practice in crazy surgery, Diego's surgeons might be almost as good as Dr. Cable.

Maybe the next time they kissed, things would be different.

And even if Zane was exactly the same, at least Tally could show him how much *she* had changed. Her journey through the wild and what she'd seen in Diego had already made a difference. Maybe this time she could show him what was really inside her, deeper than any operation could reach.

Tally stalked the darkness outside the hoverglobes' reach, listening to the newcomers. The music wasn't loud—the bash was more about getting to know each other than drinking and dancing—and she heard all kinds of accents, even other languages from the deep south. All the runaways were telling the stories of how they'd gotten here—comic, arduous, or terrifying voyages through the wild to reach pickup spots all over the continent. Some had come by hoverboard, some had walked, and a few even claimed they'd stolen warden hovercars with lifting fans, flying in comfort across the wild.

The party grew as she watched, like Diego itself, more runaways arriving all the time. Soon Tally spotted Peris and a few of the other Crims near the cliff edge. Zane wasn't with them.

She retreated farther into the shadows, eyes searching the crowd, wondering where he was. Maybe she should have stayed close; this city was so strange. Of course, he probably thought she'd lost the helicopter and was still behind in the wild. Was probably relieved to be rid of her. . . .

"Hey, I'm John," came a voice from behind.

Tally spun around, finding herself face-to-face with a standard new pretty. His eyebrows rose at the sight of her cruel beauty and tattoos, but the reaction was slight. He had already gotten used to seeing crazy surge here in Diego.

"Tally," she said.

"That's a funny name."

Tally frowned. She'd thought "John" sounded pretty random, herself, though his accent wasn't too unfamiliar.

"You're a runaway, right?" he asked. "I mean, that's new surge you're trying on?"

"This?" Her fingers brushed her face. Since she'd woken up at Special Circumstances headquarters, the cruel beauty had felt like something that defined her, made her what she was, and this average boy was asking if she was *trying it on*, like some new hairstyle?

But there was no point in giving herself away. "Yeah, I guess. Like it?"

He shrugged. "My friends say it's better to wait until you know the fashions. Don't want to look like a mountainous dork."

Tally let out a slow breath, trying to remain calm. "You think I look like a dork?"

"What do I know? I just got here." He laughed. "I'm not sure what look I'll go for. But probably something less, I don't know, *scary*."

Scary? Tally thought, her anger building. She could show this arrogant little pretty what scary was.

"I wouldn't keep those scars, if I were you," he added. "Kind of grim."

Tally's hands lashed out to grab the boy by his new and

brightly colored jacket. Her fingernails ripped into its fabric as she lifted him from the ground, her razor smile as fierce as she could make it.

"Listen, you bubblehead-until-five-minutes-ago, this is not a *fashion statement*! Those scars are something you'll never even—"

A soft ping sounded in her head.

"Tally-wa," a familiar voice came. "Put that kid down."

She blinked, lowering the pretty to the ground.

Her skintenna had picked up another Cutter.

The boy was giggling. "Hey, neat trick! Didn't see the teeth before."

"Quiet!" Tally loosened her grip from the ruins of his jacket, spinning around to scan the crowd.

"Are you in a clique?" the pretty babbled on. "That guy over there looks just like you!"

She followed his gesture and saw the familiar face coming toward her through the crowd, tattoos spinning with pleasure.

It was Fausto, smiling and special.

REUNION

"Fausto!" she cried, then realized she didn't have to shout. Their skintennas had already connected, creating a network of two.

"So you still remember me?" he joked, his voice whisper-close in her ears.

The intimacy she'd missed for the last weeks—the feeling of being a Cutter, of belonging to something—sent a shiver through her, and Tally ran toward Fausto, forgetting about the pretty who'd insulted her.

She gathered him into a hug. "You're okay!"

"I'm better than okay," he said.

Tally pulled away. She was so overwhelmed, her brain exhausted by everything it had absorbed that day—and now here was Fausto right in front of her, safe and sound.

"What happened to you? How did you escape?"

"That's a long story."

She nodded, then shook her head and said, "I'm so confused, Fausto. This place is all so random. What's going on?"

"Here in Diego?"

"Yeah. It doesn't seem real."

"It's real."

"But how did this all happen? Who *let* it happen?"

He looked out toward the cliff, gazing thoughtfully at the city lights. "As far as I can tell, it's been happening for a long time. This city was never like ours. They didn't have the same barriers between pretties and uglies."

She nodded. "No river."

He laughed. "Maybe that had something to do with it. But they've always had fewer bubbleheads than us."

"Like the rangers I met last year. They didn't have the lesions."

"Even the *teachers* didn't, Tally. Everyone here grew up being taught by non-bubbleheads."

Tally blinked. No wonder the Diego government had been sympathetic to the Smoke. A little colony of free-thinkers wouldn't seem threatening to them at all.

Fausto leaned closer. "And you know what the weird thing is, Tally? They don't have any kind of Special Circumstances here. So when the pills started coming in,

Diego didn't have a way stop them. They couldn't keep control."

"You mean the Smokies *took over*?"

"They didn't exactly take over." Fausto laughed again. "The authorities are still in charge. But the change came a lot faster here than it will at home. It only took a month or so after the first pills came in before most people were waking up, the whole system falling apart. It's *still* falling apart, I guess."

Tally nodded, remembering all the things she'd seen in the last twelve hours. "You got that right. This whole place has gone crazy."

"You'll get used to it." The smile grew on his face.

Tally narrowed her eyes. "And none of this bothers you? Didn't you notice that they're clear-cutting out on the edge of the city?"

"Of course, Tally-wa. They have to expand. The population's going up fast."

The words hit her like a punch in the stomach. "Fausto . . . populations don't go *up*. They can't *do that*."

"It's not like they're breeding, Tally. It's just runaways." He shrugged, like it was no big deal, and Tally felt something start to spin inside her. His cruel beauty, the intimacy of his voice in her ears, even his flash tattoos and razor teeth didn't excuse what Fausto was saying. This was the *wild* he was talking about, being chewed up and spat out to make way for a bunch of greedy pretties.

"What did the Smokies do to you?" she said, her voice suddenly dry.

"Nothing I didn't ask for."

She shook her head furiously, not wanting to believe.

Fausto sighed. "Come with me. I don't want any city

kids to hear us—there are some weird rules here about being special." He placed a hand on Tally's shoulder, guiding her toward the far end of the party. "Remember our big escape last year?"

"Of course I remember. Do I look like a bubblehead?"

"Hardly." He smiled. "Well, something happened after that tracker in Zane's tooth went off, and you insisted on staying behind with him. While we were all running away, us Crims came to an agreement with the Smokies." He paused as they passed a clique of young pretties all comparing their new surge—skin that flashed from paper white to pitch black, following the music's beat.

Letting their skintennas carry the words, Tally hissed, "What do you mean, an agreement?"

"The Smokies knew that Special Circumstances had been recruiting. There were more Specials every day, most of them the same uglies who'd run away to the Old Smoke."

Tally nodded. "You know the rules. Only the tricky ones become special."

"Sure. But the Smokies were just starting to figure that out." They had almost reached the shadows at the other edge of the party, where a stand of trees cast deep shadows. "And Maddy still had Dr. Cable's data, so she thought she could make a cure for being special."

Tally froze in her tracks. "A *what*?"

"A cure, Tally. But they needed someone to test it on. Someone who could give them informed consent. Like you gave consent to be cured, before you let yourself be turned pretty."

She looked into his eyes, trying to peer into their black depths. Something was different in them . . . they were flatter, like champagne with no bubbles.

Just like Zane, Fausto had lost something.

"Fausto," she said softly. "You're not special anymore."

"I gave my consent as we were running away," he said. "We all agreed. If we got caught and turned into Specials, Maddy could try to cure us."

Tally swallowed. So that was why they'd kept Fausto and let Shay escape. Informed consent—Maddy's excuse for playing with people's brains. "You let her experiment on you? Don't you remember what happened to *Zane*?"

"Someone had to, Tally." He held up an injector. "It works, and it's perfectly safe."

Her lips slid back from her teeth, her skin crawling at the thought of nanos eating away at her brain. "Don't touch me, Fausto. I'll hurt you if I have to."

"No, you won't," he said softly, then his hand darted toward her neck.

Tally's fingers shot up, catching the injector a few centimeters from her throat. She twisted hard, trying to make him drop it, and a cracking sound came from his fingers. Then his other hand moved, and she realized it held another injector. Tally dropped to the ground, his swing passing inches from her face.

Fausto kept coming, both hands trying to land a needle in her. She scrambled backward on the grass, barely staying clear. He flailed at her desperately, but she fended him off with a kick to his chest, then another that connected with his chin, sending him stumbling back. He wasn't the same—still faster than a random, maybe, but no longer as fast as Tally. Something ruthless and sure had been sucked out of him.

Time slowed down, until she saw an opening in his predictable attack. She lashed out with a well-aimed kick that knocked one of the injectors from his hands.

By now the sneak suit had detected Tally's rush of adrenalin; its scales rippled across her, hardening to armored mode. She rolled to her feet, throwing herself straight at Fausto. His next swing made contact with her elbow, the suit's armor crushing the injector, and Tally landed a blow on his cheek with an open palm. He stumbled backward, his tattoos spinning wildly.

A flicker of sound from the darkness caught Tally's ear—something headed her way through the air. Her infrared overlay fell into place, senses expanding as she dropped again to the ground. A dozen glowing figures appeared in the trees, half of them in archers' stances.

The flutter of feathers passed overhead—arrows with needle tips glittering—but Tally was already scrambling back toward the mass of the party. She scrambled through the crowd, knocking down runaways around her, creating a barrier of fallen bystanders. Beer spilled across her, and startled cries filled the air over the music.

Tally sprang to her feet and weaved her way deeper into the crowd. There were Smokies in all directions, figures that moved confidently among the baffled runaways, enough to overwhelm her with sheer numbers. Of course, dozens of the Smokies must be here at the Overlook; they had made Diego their home base. All they needed was one hit with an injector, and the chase would be over.

She'd been a fool to let her guard down, to walk around gawking at this city like a tourist. And now she was caught . . . trapped between her enemies and the cliff that gave the Overlook its name.

Tally ran toward the darkness at its edge.

She passed through an open space and more arrows

flew at her, but she ducked and blocked and rolled, all of her senses and reflexes engaged. With every seamless movement Tally became more certain she didn't want to become like Fausto—only half a Special, flat and empty, *cured*.

She was almost there.

"Tally, wait!" Fausto's voice came over the network. He sounded breathless. "You haven't got a bungee jacket!"

She smiled. "Don't need one."

"Tally!"

A last volley of arrows flew, but Tally dropped beneath them, another roll taking her almost to the edge. She leaped up and threw herself between two runaways staring down onto their new home, into the empty air. . . .

"Are you *crazy*?" Fausto shouted.

She fell, staring out at the lights of Diego. The pale cliff-face rushed past, gridded with metal to keep climbers' harnesses aloft. Directly below Tally was the darkness of more parkland, lit only with a few lampposts, probably studded with trees and other things to be impaled on.

Angling her hands in the wind, Tally spun herself around in midair to peer back up at her pursuers, a row of silhouettes arriving one by one on the cliff's edge. None of them had jumped after her—too confident in their ambush to have brought bungee jackets. They'd have hoverboards somewhere close by, of course. But by the time they could get to them, it would be too late.

Tally turned herself around again, facing the ground for the last few seconds of the fall, waiting. . . .

At the last moment she hissed, "Hey, Fausto, how's this for crazy? *Crash bracelets*."

*

It hurt like hell.

Over a city grid, bracelets could stop a fall, but they were designed for tumbles from cruising height, not cliff-jumping. They didn't distribute the force across your entire body like a well-strapped bungee jacket, just grabbed you by both wrists, swinging you in tight circles until your momentum was expended.

Tally had taken some bad spills back in ugly days—shoulder-wrenching, wrist-spraining doozies that made her wish she'd never set foot on a hoverboard, crashes that felt like an unfriendly giant were ripping her arms out of her sockets.

But nothing had ever hurt like this.

The crash bracelets kicked in five meters before she struck the ground. No warning, no smooth buildup from the magnetics. It felt like Tally had tied two cables to her wrists, just long enough to *snap* her to a halt at the last possible moment.

Her wrists and shoulders screamed with pain, the sensation so sudden and extreme that blackness washed over her mind for a moment. But then her special brain chemistry shoved her back to consciousness, forcing Tally to face the clamoring of her injured body.

She was twirling by her wrists, the landscape whirling around and around, her wild momentum sending the whole city spinning. With every rotation her agony grew, until finally Tally slowed to a halt, the force of her fall expended, the bracelets lowering her slowly and painfully to the ground.

Her feet were unsteady underneath her, the grass mockingly soft. A few trees stood close by, and she heard the sounds of a stream. Her arms dropped to her sides, hanging useless and burning with pain.

"Tally?" Fausto's voice came, close in her ears. "Are you okay?"

"What do you think?" she hissed at him, then turned her skintenna off. That's how the Smokies had known where she was, of course. With Fausto on their side, they could have been tracking her since the first moment she'd arrived in town. . . .

Which meant they also would have spotted Shay. Had they gotten her already? Tally hadn't seen her among the pursuers. . . .

She took a few more steps, every movement sending waves of agony through her injured shoulders. Tally wondered if her ceramic bones had been shattered, the monofilament muscles damaged beyond repair.

She gritted her teeth, straining to lift one hand. The simple motion hurt so much that Tally gasped aloud, and when she closed her fingers the grip felt pathetically weak. But at least her body was still responding to her will.

This was no time to congratulate herself for making a fist, though. The Smokies would be here soon, and if any of them had the guts to jump off the cliff on a hoverboard, she didn't have much time.

Tally ran toward the nearby trees, every step sending a jolt of pain through her. In the dark foliage, she set her sneak suit to camouflage mode. Even the rippling of its scales across her wrists and shoulders felt like fire.

The buzz of repair nanos had started up, a tingling all down her arms, but as bad as her injuries were, they would take hours to heal. She reached up, both arms screaming in pain, to pull the sneak-suit hood over her head. She almost blacked out, but again Tally's special brain kept her conscious.

Panting, she stumbled toward a tree whose lowest branches were close to the ground. She jumped up, landing unsteadily on one foot, and leaned against the trunk, gasping for breath. After a long moment she started the arduous process of climbing higher without using her hands, stepping from one branch to the next, grippy-soled shoes scrabbling to stay on.

It was slow and painful going, her teeth gritted and heart racing. But Tally somehow managed to push herself upward slowly. One meter higher, then another . . .

Her eyes caught a flicker of infrared through the leaves, and she froze.

A hoverboard was moving silently past, exactly at her eye level. She could see the glowing rider's head swivel from side to side, listening for any sound among the treetops.

Tally's breath slowed, and she allowed herself a grim smile. The Smokies had expected Fausto, their tamed Special, to bag her for them—they hadn't even bothered with sneak suits. This time around, *she* was the invisible one.

Of course, the fact that the invisible one couldn't lift her arms kind of evened things out.

Finally the pain had been replaced by the buzz of nanos gathering in her shoulders, starting on their repairs and squirting anesthetic around. As long as she didn't move too much, the little machines would keep the agony down to a dull ache.

In the distance, Tally heard other searchers bashing at the leaves, thinking they could flush her out like a flock of birds. But the closest Smokey was hunting quietly, listening and watching. The rider stood in profile, head still moving slowly from side to side, scanning the trees. Its silhouette revealed infrared glasses.

Tally smiled to herself. Night vision wasn't going to work any better than banging at the trees. But then the figure froze, staring right at her. The hoverboard slid to a halt.

Barely moving her head, Tally glanced down at herself. What was showing?

Then she saw it. After all the days she'd lived in the sneak suit, all the thrills and spills she'd put it through . . . finally, that one last leap from the Overlook had done it in.

On her right shoulder, the seam had split. It glowed almost white in infrared, heat from her metabolism gushing out like sunlight.

The figure slid closer through the air, slow and cautious.

"Hey," she called nervously. "I think I've got something here."

"What is it?" came the answer.

Tally recognized the answering voice. *David,* she thought, a little shiver going through her. So close to him, and Tally could hardly make a fist.

The Smokey girl paused, still staring right at Tally. "There's a hot spot in this tree. Baseball-size."

Laughter came from David's way, and someone else shouted, "Probably just a squirrel."

"Way too hot for a squirrel. Unless it's on fire."

Tally waited, squeezing her eyes closed and willing her body to slow down, to stop generating so much energy. But the Smokey girl had got it right: Between the racing engine of her heart and the nanos busily repairing her shoulders, Tally felt like she was on fire.

She tried to move her left hand up to cover the rip, but her muscles would no longer respond. All she could do was stand there and try not to move.

More glowing figures glided her way.

"David!" someone else called from the distance. "They're coming!"

He swore, spinning his hoverboard in midair. "They won't be happy with us. Come on, let's get out of here!"

The girl who'd spotted her let out a frustrated snort, then banked her board and shot away after him. The other Smokies trailed behind the two, flitting through the leafy treetops and into the distance.

Who's coming? Tally wondered. Why had they just left her here? Who were the Smokies afraid of in Diego?

Then the sound of running feet came through the forest, and Tally saw flashes of bright yellow on the ground. She'd seen that exact color in the uniforms of safety workers and wardens earlier today—yellow with bold black stripes, like littlies costumed as bumblebees.

She remembered what Fausto had said, about how the Diego authorities were still in charge, and smiled. They might tolerate the Smokies' presence here, but the wardens probably didn't appreciate kidnapping attempts at parties.

Tally pressed herself harder against the tree trunk, feeling the tear in her sneak suit like a bleeding wound. If they had night vision, they'd spot her just as the Smokies had. Once more, Tally tried to lift her left hand to cover the open seam. . . .

A startling moment of agony sent a wave of dizziness through her, and Tally heard herself utter a racking gasp of pain. She squeezed her eyes shut, trying not to cry out again.

Suddenly, the world was listing to one side. Tally opened her eyes, realizing too late that one foot had slipped from its branch. Instinctively her hands scrambled for a hold, but the attempt only sent fresh agony through her. And then she was tipping over, out of control and crashing through the tree, injuries wailing as she seemed to hit every branch on the way down.

She landed with a grunt, arms and legs splayed like a dummy thrown to the ground.

A circle of yellow-suited wardens quickly formed around her.

"Don't move!" one said gruffly.

Tally looked up and groaned with frustration. The wardens were unarmed, average middle pretties, nervous as a gaggle of cats surrounding a rabid Doberman. Uninjured, she could have laughed in their faces, danced among them, flicking them over like dominoes.

But as things were, the wardens construed her immobility as surrender.

VIOLATIONS OF MORPHOLOGY

She woke up in a padded cell.

The place smelled exactly like the big hospital at home: the chemical tang of disinfectant, the unpleasant scent of too many humans who'd been washed by robots instead of taking showers. And somewhere out of sight, Tally detected bedpans quietly stewing.

But most hospital rooms didn't have padded walls, and they weren't missing a door. Probably that was hidden under the padding somewhere, seamlessly fitted. Soft light in mixed pastel colors, probably meant to be soothing, filtered down from filaments sprinkled across the high ceiling.

Tally sat up and flexed her arms, rubbing her shoulders. The muscles were stiff and achy, but their usual strength had returned. Whatever the wardens had used to knock her out had kept her unconscious for some time. Shay had broken Tally's hand in training once to demonstrate how her self-repair worked, and it had taken hours to feel right again.

Tally kicked the bedcovers off with her feet, then looked down at herself and muttered, "You've got to be kidding."

They'd replaced her sneak suit with a thin, disposable nightgown covered with pink flowers.

Tally got up and tore it off, crumpling the garment into a ball. Dropping it to the floor, she kicked it under the bed. Better to be naked than look ridiculous.

Actually, it felt heavenly to be out of the sneak suit at last. The scales might transport sweat and dead skin cells to its surface, but nothing beat taking a real shower now and then. Tally rubbed at her skin, wondering if she could get one in this place.

"Hello?" she said to the room.

When no answer came, she peered more closely at the wall. The fabric of the padding glittered with a hexagonal pattern of micro-lenses, thousands of tiny cameras woven into it. The doctors could watch anything she did from any angle.

"Come on, guys, I know you can hear me," Tally said aloud, then made a fist and punched the wall as hard as she could.

"Ouch." She swore a few times, waving her hand in the air. The padding had helped a little, but the wall behind it was made of something harder than wood or stone—solid

construction ceramic, probably. Tally wasn't going to break out of here bare-handed.

She returned to the bed and sat down, rubbing her fingers and letting out a sigh.

"Please be careful, young lady," a voice said. "You'll hurt yourself."

Tally glanced at her hand. The knuckles weren't even red. "Just wanted to get your attention."

"Attention? Hmm. Is that what this is all about?"

Tally groaned. If anything was more annoying than being sealed up in a wacko chamber, it was being talked to like a littlie who'd been caught chucking a stink bomb. The voice sounded deep and calming and generic, like some therapy drone. She imagined a committee of doctors behind the wall, typing in answers for the soothing computer voice to speak.

"Actually, this is about my room not having a *door*," she said. "Did I break a law or something?"

"You are being held under controlled observation, as a possible danger to yourself and others."

Tally rolled her eyes. When she got out of here, she was going to be a lot more than a *possible* danger. But she only said, "Who, me?"

"You jumped off the Overlook Cliff with inadequate equipment, for starters."

Tally's mouth dropped open. "You're saying that was *my* fault? I was just talking to an old friend of mine, and suddenly all these random nutcases with bows and arrows started shooting at me. What was I supposed to do? Stand around and get kidnapped?"

The voice paused. "We are reviewing video of the incident. We admit, however, that there are certain immigrant elements here in Diego who can be difficult. We apologize. They've never behaved this badly before. Rest assured that mediation is taking place."

"Mediation? Like, you're *talking* to them about it? Why don't you lock a few of them up, instead of me? After all, *I'm* the victim here."

There was another pause. "That remains to be determined. May I ask your name, city of origin, and exactly how you know this 'old friend' of yours?"

Tally felt the bedcovers between her fingers. Like the wall padding, they were woven through with microsensors, greedy little machines to measure her heart rate, sweat, and galvanic skin response. She took a few slow breaths, getting her anger under control. If she stayed focused, they could polygraph her all day without detecting a flicker of a lie.

"My name's Tally," she said carefully. "I ran away from up north. I heard you guys were *nice* to runaways."

"We welcome immigrants. Under the New System, we allow anyone to apply for Diego citizenship."

"'The New System'? Is that what you call this?" Tally rolled her eyes. "Yeah, well the New System sucks if you lock people up just for running away from psychos. Did I mention the bows and arrows?"

"Rest assured, you are not under observation because of any of your actions, Tally. We're more concerned with certain morphological violations."

Despite her focus, a nervous flicker ran down Tally's spine. "My what?"

"Tally, your body has been constructed around a reinforced ceramic skeleton. Your fingernails and teeth have been weaponized, your muscles and reflex centers significantly augmented."

With a sickening feeling, Tally realized what the wardens had done. Thinking she was seriously hurt, they'd brought her to the hospital for deep scanning, and what the doctors had found had made the authorities very nervous.

"I'm not sure what you're talking about," she said, trying to sound innocent.

"There are also certain structures in your higher cortex, apparently artificial, which seemed designed to change your behavior. Tally, do you ever suffer from sudden flashes of anger or euphoria, countersocial impulses, or feelings of superiority?"

Tally took another deep breath, fighting to remain calm. "What I'm suffering from is being *locked up*," she said in a slow, deliberate voice.

"Why do you have scars on your arms, Tally? Did someone do that to you?"

"What, *these*?" She laughed, running her fingers down the row of cutting scars. "Where I come from, they're just a fashion statement!"

"Tally, you may not be aware of what has been done to your mind. It may seem natural for you to cut yourself."

"But they're just . . ." Tally groaned and shook her head. "After all the crazy surgery I've seen around here, you're worried about a few *scars*?"

"We're only worried about what they indicate regarding your mental balance."

"Don't talk to me about mental balance," Tally growled, deciding to give up on acting calm. "I'm not the one who locks people up!"

"Do you understand the political disputes between your city and ours, Tally?"

"Political disputes?" she asked. "What does that have to do with *me*?"

"Your city has a long history of dangerous surgical practices, Tally. That history, and Diego's policy on runaways, have often been a source of diplomatic conflict. The advent of the New System has only made things worse."

Tally snorted. "So you're locking me up because of where I come from! Have you guys gone totally *Rusty*?"

There was a long pause after that. Tally imagined the doctors arguing over what to type into their voice software. "Why are you torturing me?" she shouted, trying to sound like a harmless, whining pretty. "Let me see your faces!"

She curled up on the bed and made sobbing noises, but readied herself to leap in any direction. These dimwits probably didn't realized that her arms had completely fixed themselves while she was asleep. All she needed was one door open half a centimeter and she would be out of this hospital in a heartbeat, naked or not.

After another moment's silence, the voice returned. "I'm afraid, Tally, that you cannot be allowed to go free. Because of your body modifications, you meet our criteria for a dangerous weapon. And dangerous weapons are illegal in Diego."

Tally stopped her crying act, her jaw dropping open. "You mean, I'm *illegal*?" she cried. "How can a *person* be illegal?"

"You are not accused of any crime, Tally. We believe the authorities of your city are responsible. But before you leave this hospital, your morphological violations must be corrected."

"Forget it! You're not touching me!"

The voice didn't react to her anger, just droned on soothingly. "Tally, your city has often meddled in the affairs of other cities, especially on the issue of runaways. We believe that you were unknowingly altered and sent here to create instability among our immigrant population."

They thought she was a dupe, not even a conscious agent of Special Circumstances. Of course, they had no idea how complicated the truth really was.

"Then let me go home," she said softly, trying to turn her frustration into tears. "I'll leave, I promise. Just let me go." She squeezed her teeth down harder on her lower lip. Her eyes burned, but as always, no tears came.

"We cannot allow you to go free in your current morphological configuration. You're simply too dangerous, Tally."

You have no idea, she thought.

"You're free to leave Diego if you want," the voice continued, "but not until we make some physical adjustments."

"No." A chill washed over her. They couldn't.

"We cannot legally release you without disarming you."

"But you can't operate on me if I don't want you to." She imagined herself weak again, pathetic and puny and *average*. "What about . . . informed consent?"

"If you prefer, we will make no experimental attempts to change your altered brain chemistry. With counseling, you may learn to control your behavior. But your dangerous body modifications will be corrected using proven surgical techniques. Informed consent is not required."

Tally opened her mouth again, but nothing came out. They wanted to make her average again without even fixing her *brain*? What sort of nightmare logic was that?

The four impregnable walls around her seemed suddenly suffocating, their glittering eyes hungry and mocking.

Tally imagined cold metal instruments reaching into her and tearing out everything special from inside.

For those few moments kissing Zane, she'd imagined that she wanted to be normal. But now that someone was threatening to grind her down to averageness, she couldn't stand the thought.

She wanted to be able to look at Zane without disgust, to touch him, kiss him. But not if it meant being changed against her will *again* . . .

"Just let me go," she whispered.

"I'm afraid we can't, Tally. But when we're done, you'll be as beautiful and healthy as everyone else. Think of it, here in Diego you can look any way you want."

"This isn't about how I *look*!" Tally sprang to her feet and ran to the nearest wall. She pulled her fist back and gave it the hardest blow she could. Pain shot through her again.

"Tally, please stop."

"Forget it!" She set her teeth and grimly punched the wall again. If she started hurting herself, someone would *have* to open the door.

And then they'd see how dangerous she really was.

"Tally, please."

Again, she drew back her hand and struck the wall, felt her knuckles threatening to shatter against the iron hardness behind the padding. A gasp of pain slipped through her lips, and spatters of blood marked the padding, but Tally couldn't hold back. They knew how strong she was, and this had to look real.

"You leave us no choice."

Good, she thought. *Just come on in and try to stop me.*

She struck the wall again, another cry escaping . . . more blood.

Then Tally felt something through the pain: a dizziness washing over her.

"No," she said. "Not fair."

From under all the hospital smells of disinfectant and bedpans, so slight that no average human would have detected it, it filtered into her nostrils. Specials were usually immune to knockout gas, but Diego knew her secrets now. They could have designed this just for her. . . .

Tally sank to her knees. She slowed her breathing to a minimum, trying desperately to calm herself, to suck in as little air as possible. They might not have guessed how thoroughly she was designed to deal with every form of attack, how quickly she could metabolize toxins.

Tally leaned against the wall, feeling weaker every second. The padding was suddenly *so* comfortable, as if someone had put pillows everywhere. She managed a few interface gestures with her left hand, setting her software to ping her every ten minutes. Tally had to wake up before they were ready to operate.

She tried to focus, to plan, but the sparkling of the little lenses in the padding was so lovely. Her eyes slid closed. She had to escape, but first Tally needed to sleep.

Sleep wasn't that bad, really, like being a bubblehead again, nothing to worry about, no anger deep inside. . . .

VOICES

It was nice here. Nice and quiet.

For the first time in a long while, Tally felt no fury, no frustration. The tension in her muscles had gone, along with the feeling that she had to *be* somewhere, *do* something, *prove* herself again. Here in this place, she was just Tally, and that simple knowledge flowed across her skin like a pleasant breeze. Her right hand felt particularly nice—all bubbly, as if someone were dribbling warm champagne over it.

She half-opened her eyes. Everything was pleasantly out of focus, not all sharp and edgy like usual. In fact, it was pretty much all clouds around here, white and fluffy. Like a littlie staring up into the sky, Tally could see any shape she wanted. She tried to imagine a dragon, but her brain couldn't make the wings look real . . . and the teeth were sort of complicated.

Besides, dragons were too scary. Tally, or maybe it was someone she knew, had once had a bad experience with one.

It was better to imagine her friends: Shay-la and Zane-la, everyone who loved her. That's all she really wanted, to go and see them once she'd gotten a little more sleep.

She closed her eyes again.

Ping.

There was that sound again. It came back every once in a while, like an old friend checking up on her.

"Hi, ping-la," she said.

The ping never answered. But Tally liked to be polite.

"Did she just say something, Doctor?" someone asked.

"Couldn't have. Not with what we gave her."

"Did you *see* her metabolic chart?" a third voice said. "We're not taking any risks. Check those straps."

Someone grumbled, then started fiddling with Tally's hands and feet one by one, in a circle that started with her bubbly right hand and went clockwise. Tally imagined that she was a clock, lying there and quietly ticking.

"Don't worry, Doctor. She's not going anyplace."

The voice was wrong about that, because a moment later Tally *was* going places, floating along on her back. She couldn't open her eyes, but it felt like being on some kind of hovercarrier. Lights pulsed overhead, bright enough to see even through her eyelids. Her inner ear felt the hovercarrier take a left turn, slow down, then rumble across a bump in the magnetic grid. Then she was accelerating upward, fast enough that her ears popped a little.

"All right," one of the voices said. "Wait here for the prep team. Do *not* leave her alone, and call me if she moves."

"Okay, Doctor. But she's not moving."

Tally smiled. She decided to play a game where she didn't move. Somewhere in the back of her mind was the idea that fooling the voice would be lots of fun.

Ping.

"Hi," she answered, then remembered about not moving.

Tally lay still for a moment, then started to wonder where the pings were coming from. They were starting to get annoying.

She shifted her fingers, until an interface dropped down over the inside of her eyelids. Her internal software wasn't as fuzzy as everything else, and she didn't have to do anything but twitch her fingers to make it work.

Tally saw that the pings were a wake-up reminder. She was supposed to get up and do something.

She let out a slow sigh. Lying here was *so* nice. Besides, she couldn't remember what it was she had pinged herself about. Which made the whole ping pretty pointless. In fact, the whole ping was silly. Tally would have giggled, if giggling weren't so difficult. Suddenly, every ping was silly.

She twitched a finger to switch off the wake-up cycle, so it wouldn't bother her again.

But the question kept bugging Tally: What was she was supposed to *do*? Maybe one of the other Cutters would know. She flicked on her skintenna feed.

"Tally?" a voice asked. "Finally!"

Tally smiled. Shay-la always knew what to do.

"Are you okay?" Shay said. "Where've you *been*!"

Tally tried to answer, but talking was too hard.

"Are you *all right*, Tally?" Shay said after a few moments, sounding worried now.

Tally remembered that Shay had been mad at her, and her smile grew. Shay-la didn't sound mad anymore, just concerned.

Tally tried hard, and managed to drawl, "I'm sleepy."

"Oh, crap."

That was weird, Tally thought. Two voices had said "Oh, crap" at exactly the same time, in exactly the same scared way. One voice was Shay's inside her head, and the other was that *other* voice she kept hearing.

This was getting complicated, like the dragon's teeth she'd tried to imagine.

"Need to wake up," she said.

"Oh, *crap*!" said the other voice.

At the same time, Shay was saying, "Stay where you are, Tally. I think I've got your feed located. You're in the hospital, right?"

"Uh-huh," Tally murmured. She recognized the hospital smell, even though the other voice was making it hard to concentrate. It was shouting stuff in a way that hurt Tally's head. "I think she's waking up! Someone get something to put her back down!" Blah, blah, blah . . .

"We're close by," Shay said. "We figured you were somewhere in there. You're scheduled for despecialization in an hour."

"Oh, right," Tally said, remembering now what she was supposed to do: escape from this place, which was going to be *really* difficult. Much harder than moving her fingertips. "Help, Shay-la."

"Just hang on, Tally, and try to *wake up*! I'm coming for you."

"Yay, Shay-la," Tally whispered.

"But turn off your skintenna, *now*. If they've scanned you, they might be listening in. . . ."

"Okay," Tally said, and as her fingers gestured, the voice in her head went quiet. The other voice was still shouting, still complaining in its worried way. It was starting to give Tally a headache.

"Doctor! She just said something! Even after that last dose! What the hell *is* she?"

"Whatever she is, this should keep her down," someone else said, and sleepiness swept over her again.

So Tally went back to not thinking at all.

LIGHT

Consciousness returned in a burst of light.

Adrenaline shot through Tally, like waking up from a nightmare screaming. The world was suddenly diamond clear, as sharp as the teeth in her mouth, as bright as a spotlight in her eyes.

She sat bolt upright, breathing hard and clenching her fists tight. Shay stood at the end of the hospital bed, fiddling with the straps around her ankles.

"Shay!" she shouted. Tally felt everything so brilliantly she *had* to shout.

"That woke you up, didn't it?"

"Shay!" Her left arm stung; someone had just given her a shot. Energy was boiling through her, all her fury and strength returned. She jerked one foot against an ankle strap, but the metal restraint held.

"Calm down, Tally-wa," Shay said. "I'll get it."

"Calm *down*?" Tally muttered, her eyes scanning the room. The walls were lined with machines, all of them flickering with activity. In the room's center was an operating tank, life-support liquid slowly gurgling into it, a breathing tube hanging loosely, waiting to be put to use. Scalpels and vibrasaws waited on a nearby table.

Lying on the floor were a pair of unconscious men in hospital scrubs—one a middle pretty, the other young enough to sport leopard spots all over his downy fur. At the sight of them, the past twenty-four hours came rushing back to Tally: Random Town, being captured, the threatened operation to make her average again.

She twitched against the ankle restraints, needing to escape this room *now*.

"Almost got it," Shay said soothingly.

Tally's right arm itched, and she found a braid of wires and tubes stuck into it, life support for major surgery. She hissed and ripped them out. Blood spattered across the spotless white floor, but it didn't hurt—the collision between anesthetic and whatever Shay had used to awaken her had filled Tally with a pain-numbing fury.

When Shay finally got the second ankle strap unlocked, Tally leaped up, her fingers curled.

"Um, maybe you better put this on," Shay said, tossing her a sneak suit. Tally looked down at herself. She was wearing another disposable nightgown: pink with blue dinosaurs.

"What *is* it with hospitals?" she shouted, ripping the gown off and sticking one foot into the suit.

"Quiet down already, Tally-wa," Shay hissed. "I've plugged the sensors, but even randoms can hear you shouting like that, you know. And don't turn on your skintenna yet. It'll give us away."

"Sorry, Boss." A sudden wave of dizziness came over Tally; she'd stood up too fast. But she managed to slide her legs into the sneak suit and pull it up around her shoulders. Detecting her wild heart rate, it booted up straight into armored mode, scales rippling, then lying flat and hard.

"No, tune it this way," Shay whispered, one hand on the door. Her own suit was set to a pale blue, the color of hospital scrubs.

As Tally tuned her suit, trying to match the color of Shay's, her head still spun with wild energy. "You came for me," she said, trying to keep her voice low.

"I couldn't let them do this to you."

"But I thought you hated me."

"I hate you *sometimes*, Tally. Like I've never hated anybody else before." Shay snorted. "Maybe that's why I keep coming back for you."

Tally swallowed, looking around once more at the operating tank, the table full of cutting instruments, all the tools that would have turned her average again—*despecialized* her, as Shay had put it. "Thanks, Shay-la."

"No problem. Ready to get out of here?"

"Wait, Boss." Tally swallowed. "I saw Fausto."

"So did I." There was no anger in Shay's voice, simply a statement of fact.

"But he's . . ."

"I know."

"You know . . ." Tally took a step forward, her mind still spinning from waking up, from everything that was happening. "But what are we going to do about him, Shay?"

"We have to *go*, Tally. The rest of the Cutters are waiting for us on the roof. Something big is coming. A lot bigger than the Smokies."

Tally frowned. "But what—?"

The shriek of an alarm split the air.

"They must be getting close!" Shay cried. "We have to *go*!" She grabbed Tally's hand and pulled her through the door.

Tally followed, her mind reeling, her feet still unsteady beneath her. Outside the room, a long, straight hallway stretched in both directions, the alarm echoing down its length. People in hospital scrubs were spilling out of doors on either side, filling the hallway with confused babble.

Shay sprinted away, slipping among the stunned doctors and orderlies like they were statues. She was so light-footed and quick, the milling crowd hardly noticed the matching pale blue streak hurtling through them.

Tally thrust aside her questions and followed, but her just-woken-up dizziness was fading very slowly. She dodged people as best she could, plowing straight through any who got in her way. She caromed off bodies and the walls, but managed to keep moving, letting her wild energy carry her.

"Stop!" a voice shouted. "Both of you!"

In front of Shay, a cluster of wardens stood in their yellow-and-black uniforms, shock-sticks glowing in the soft, pastel light.

Shay didn't hesitate, her suit turning black as she plunged into them, hands and feet flashing. The air filled with the smell of fresh lightning as shock-sticks struck her armored scales, sizzling like mosquitoes frying on a bug light. She spun wildly amid the fracas, sending yellow figures staggering in all directions.

By the time Tally reached the struggle, only two wardens were left standing, backing down the hall and trying to ward off Shay, their shock-sticks flailing through the air. Tally stepped up behind one and grabbed her by the wrist, twisting it with a *snap* and pushing her into the other, sending them both sprawling to the floor.

"No need to *break* them, Tally-wa."

Tally looked down at the woman, who was clutching her wrist, a pained cry spilling from her lips. "Oh, sorry, Boss."

"It's not your fault, Tally. Come on." Shay pushed through the stairwell door and headed upward, taking each flight in two long bounds. Tally trailed behind, her dizziness almost under control, the manic energy from the wake-up shot fading a little as she ran. The stairwell doors closed behind them, dampening the earsplitting shriek of the alarm.

She wondered what had happened to Shay, where she had been all this time. How long had the other Cutters been here in Diego?

But the questions could wait. Tally was simply glad to be free again, fighting alongside Shay and being special. Nothing could stop the two of them together.

A few flights up, the stairs came to an end. They burst through the last door and onto the roof. The night overhead glittered with thousands of stars, beautifully clear.

After the padded cell, it felt glorious to be out under the open sky. Tally tried to suck in a breath of fresh air, but the smell of hospital still poured from the forest of exhaust chimneys around them.

"Good, they're not here yet," Shay said.

"Who isn't?" Tally asked.

Shay led her across the roof, toward the huge, darkened building next to the hospital—Town Hall, Tally remembered. Shay peered over the edge.

People were streaming out of the hospital, staff in pale blue and white, and patients in flimsy gowns—some walking, some being pushed along on hovercarriers. Tally heard the alarm echoing out of the windows below, and realized that the sound had changed to a two-toned evacuation signal.

"What's going on, Shay? They're not evacuating just because of us, are they?"

"No, not us." Shay turned to her, put a hand on her shoulder. "I need you to listen carefully, Tally. This is important."

"I'm *listening*, Shay. Just tell me what's going on!"

"All right. I know all about Fausto—I tracked down his skintenna signal the moment I got here, more than a week ago. He explained everything."

"Then you know . . . he's not special anymore."

Shay paused. "I'm not sure if you're right about that, Tally."

"But he's different, Shay. He's *weak*. I saw it in his . . ."

Tally's voice faded as she peered closer, breath catching in disbelief. In Shay's eyes was a softness that had never been there before. But this was *Shay*, still so fast and deadly—she'd cut through those wardens like a scythe.

"He's not weak," Shay said. "Neither am I."

Tally shook her head, pulled away, and stumbled back. "They got you too."

Shay nodded. "It's okay, Tally-wa. It's not like they turned me into a bubblehead." She took a step forward. "But you have to *listen*."

"Don't come near me!" Tally hissed, her hands curling.

"Wait, Tally, something big is happening."

Tally shook her head. She could hear the weakness in Shay's voice now. If she hadn't been so groggy, she would have seen it from the start. The real Shay wouldn't have been so worried about some random warden's wrist. And the real Shay—*special* Shay—would never have forgiven Tally so easily.

"You want to make me like you! Like Fausto and the Smokies tried to do!"

"No, I don't," Shay said. "I need you the way you—"

Before Shay could utter another word, Tally turned and started running for the opposite edge of the roof as quickly as she could. She had no crash bracelets, no bungee jacket, but she could still climb like a Special. If Shay was as soft as Fausto, she would no longer be as reckless. Tally could just escape this crazy city, and get help from home. . . .

"Stop her!" Shay cried.

Faceless human forms flickered into being among the shapes of exhaust chimneys and antennas. They leaped out of the darkness at Tally, grabbing at her arms and legs.

This was all a trap. "Don't turn on your skintenna,"

Shay had said, so the rest of them could talk to each other silently, plotting against her.

Tally threw a punch, her wounded fist connecting painfully with an armored suit. A faceless Cutter gripped her arm, but Tally turned her suit slippery and pulled away. She let her momentum carry her into a backward roll, springing up from the ground, leaping to the top of a tall exhaust pipe.

She struggled to pull her suit hood down over her face, to turn invisible before they reached her, but a pair of gloved hands grasped Tally's ankles, pulling her feet out from under her. As she fell from the pipe, another figure caught her. Still more hands grabbed her arms, checking her wild flurry of blows, and with a gentle strength dragged her back down to the roof.

Tally struggled, but special or not, there were too many of them.

They pulled off their hoods—Ho, Tachs, all the other Cutters. Shay had gotten every one of them.

They smiled softly at her, an awful, average kindness in their eyes. Tally struggled, waiting for the sting of an injection in her bare neck.

Shay stood before her, shaking her head. "Tally, would you just relax?"

Tally spat at her, "You said you were *saving* me."

"I *am*. If you'd settle down and listen." Shay let out an exasperated sigh. "After Fausto gave me the cure, I called the Cutters. I told them to meet me halfway here. On our way back to Diego, I cured them one by one."

Tally looked around at their faces—a few of them grinning at her as if she were some littlie who wasn't in on a joke—and saw no doubts, no hint of rebellion against

Shay's words. They were sheep now, no better than bubble-heads.

Her anger faded into despair. All of their brains had been infected with nanos, made weak and pitiful. Tally was completely alone.

Shay spread her hands. "Listen, we just got back here today. I'm sorry that the Smokies tried to jump you; I wouldn't have let them. This cure isn't what you need, Tally."

"Then let me *go*!" Tally growled.

Shay paused for a moment, then nodded. "Okay. Let her go."

"But Boss," Tachs said. "They're through the defenses already. We've got less than a minute."

"I know. But Tally's going to help us. I know she will."

One by one, the others cautiously released their grip. Tally found herself free, still glaring at Shay, unsure what to do next. She was still surrounded and outnumbered.

"There's no point running, Tally. Dr. Cable's on her way here."

Tally raised an eyebrow. "To Diego? To get you all back?"

"No." Shay's voice broke, almost like some littlie about to cry. "It's all our fault, Tally. Yours and mine."

"*What* is?"

"After what we did to the Armory, no one believed it was Crims or Smokies. We were too icy, too special. We terrified the whole city."

"Since that night," Tachs said, "everyone in town goes by to see the smoking crater you two left. They bring classes of littlies out to gawk at it."

"And Cable's coming here?" Tally frowned. "Wait, you mean, they figured out it was *us*?"

"No, they have another theory." Shay pointed at the horizon. "Look."

Tally turned her head. In the distance beyond Town Hall, a mass of bright lights had filled the sky. As she watched, they grew closer and brighter, shimmering like stars on a hot night.

Just like when Tally and Shay had been chased from the Armory.

"Hovercraft," Tally said.

Tachs nodded. "They've given Dr. Cable control of the city military. Everything that's left, anyway."

"Get your boards," Shay said. The others scattered in all directions across the roof.

Shay pushed a pair of crash bracelets into Tally's hands. "You have to stop trying to run away, and face what we started."

Tally didn't flinch at Shay's touch, suddenly too confused to worry about being cured. She could hear the approaching craft now, a swarm of lifting fans humming like some vast engine warming up. "I still don't get it."

Shay adjusted her own bracelets, and a pair of hoverboards rose up from the darkness. "Our city has always hated Diego. Special Circumstances knew about them helping the runaways, about the helicopters carrying people to the Old Smoke. So after the Armory was destroyed, Dr. Cable decided it must have been a military attack. She blamed Diego."

"So those hovercraft . . . they're coming to attack this *city*?" Tally murmured. The lights grew larger and larger until they swirled overhead, dozens of hovercraft, a great vortex of them surrounding Town Hall. "Even Dr. Cable wouldn't do that."

"I'm afraid she would. And the other cities will just sit back and watch, for now. The New System has them all totally scared." Shay pulled her sneak-suit hood down over her head. "Tonight we have to help them here, Tally, we have to do whatever we can. And tomorrow, you and I need to go home and stop this war we started."

"*War?* But cities don't . . ." Tally's voice faded. The roof under her feet had begun to rumble, and under the drone of a hundred lifting fans she heard a small, thin sound from the streets below.

People were screaming.

A few seconds later, the armada overhead opened fire, filling the sky with light.

Part III

UNMAKING WAR

One faces the future with one's past.
—Pearl S. Buck

PAYBACK

Streams of cannon fire ripped through the air, their traces burning across Tally's vision. Explosions battered her ears, and shock waves thudded against her chest, like something trying to tear her open.

The hovercraft armada rained its fire down onto Town Hall, cascades of projectiles flaring so brightly that for a moment the building disappeared. But Tally could still hear the sound of shattering glass and the shriek of tearing metal through the blinding display.

After a few seconds, the furious onslaught paused, and Tally glimpsed Town Hall through the smoke. Huge holes had appeared—the fires burning inside the building made it look like some insane jack-o'-lantern carved with dozens of glowing eyes.

From below, the cries rose up again, full of terror now. For a dizzying moment she remembered what Shay had said: *"It's all our fault, Tally. Yours and mine."*

She shook her head slowly. What she was seeing couldn't be true.

Wars didn't happen anymore.

"Come *on*!" Shay cried, leaping onto her board and rising into the air. "Town Hall's empty at night, but we have to get everyone out of the hospital. . . ."

Tally broke from her paralysis, jumping onto her hoverboard as the bombardment began once more. Shay hurtled over the edge of the roof, silhouetted for a moment against the firestorm before dropping out of sight. Tally followed, vaulting the guardrail to hover a few seconds, peering down at the chaos below.

The hospital hadn't been hit, not yet anyway, but crowds of terrified people were still spilling from its doors. The armada didn't have to shoot anyone for people to wind up dead tonight—panic and chaos would do the killing. The other cities would see only a proportionate response to the attack on the Armory: one mostly empty building for another.

Tally cut her lifting fans and dropped, kneeling to hold her board tight. The pounding concussions from the attack had turned the air into something palpable and shuddering, like a choppy sea.

The other Cutters were already below, their sneak suits set to the yellow and black of Diego's warden uniforms. Tachs and Ho were herding the crowd around to the other side of the hospital, away from the debris spilling from Town Hall. The others were rescuing the pedestrians who had fallen between the two buildings; all the slidewalks had jammed, throwing their late-night passengers to the ground.

Tally spun for a moment in the air, overwhelmed and wondering what to do. Then she spotted a stream of littlies pouring from the hospital. They were lining up along the hedgerow barrier around the helicopter landing pad, their minders stopping to count them all before moving on to safety.

She angled her board toward the landing pad and

dropped as fast as gravity would take her. Those helicopters had carried runaways from other cities to the Old Smoke and now here to the New System—Tally somehow doubted Dr. Cable's attack was going to leave them untouched.

She brought her descent to a halt just over the littlies' heads, lifting fans screaming, terrified faces staring up open-mouthed.

"Get out of here!" she yelled down at the minders, two middle pretties with classic faces: calm and wise.

They looked up at her in disbelief, then Tally remembered to switch her sneak suit to a rough approximation of warden yellow. "The helicopters could be a target!" she cried.

The minders' dumbfounded expressions didn't change, and Tally swore. They hadn't realized yet what this war was about—runaways and the New System and the Old Smoke—all they knew was that the sky had exploded overhead and they had to account for all of their charges before moving on.

She looked up and spotted a glittering hovercraft breaking from the armada. It swept through a wide, leisurely turn, descending toward the landing pad like a lazy bird of prey.

"Get them to the other side of the hospital, *now*!" she yelled, then reversed course, climbing toward the approaching hovercraft, wondering exactly what she could do against it. This time she had no grenades, no hungry nano-goo. She was alone and bare-handed against a military machine.

But if this war really was her fault, she had to try.

Tally pulled her hood down over her face and switched the suit to infrared camouflage, then shot toward Town Hall. Hopefully, the hovercraft wouldn't see her coming against the background heat of cannon fire and explosions.

As she grew nearer to the disintegrating building, the air shuddered around her, explosive concussions beating against her body. She could feel the searing heat of the fires now, and heard the thunderous sound of floors collapsing one upon another as Town Hall's hoverstruts began to fail. The armada was destroying the entire building, razing it to the ground, just as she and Shay had done to the Armory.

With the inferno at her back, Tally pulled level with the hovercraft and followed its descent, looking for some weakness. It was like the first one she'd seen rising up from the Armory: four lifting fans carrying a bulbous body bristling with weaponry, wings, and claws, its dull black armor reflecting nothing of the firestorm behind her.

It showed scars from recent damage, and Tally realized that Diego must have thrown up some resistance against the armada—a fight that hadn't lasted very long.

Though all the cities had given up war, maybe some had given it up more than others.

Tally glanced down. The landing pad wasn't far below, the line of littlies inching away from it with maddening slowness. She swore and shot toward the hovercraft, hoping to distract it.

The machine detected her approach at the last moment, insectlike metal claws reaching out toward the white-hot board. Tally tipped back into a steep climb, but she'd changed course too late. The hovercraft's claws jammed into her forward lifting fan, which ground to a noisy halt, and she was thrown from the riding surface. Other claws grasped blindly in the air, but Tally in her sneak suit soared over them.

She landed on the machine's back, and it tipped wildly, her weight and the force of the hoverboard's impact almost rolling the craft over backward. Tally waved her arms as she skidded across the armor, her sneak suit's grippy soles barely keeping her from falling. She bent her knees and grabbed the first handhold she could find, a thin piece of metal sticking up from the hovercraft's body.

Her ruined board sailed past—one lifting fan working, the other destroyed, making it spin through the air like a throwing knife.

As the hovercraft tried to steady itself, the object that had saved Tally suddenly swiveled in her hand, and she jerked away. A little lens glittered at its tip, like an eye-stalk on a crab. She scooted to the center of the machine's back, hoping it hadn't seen her.

Three other camera-stalks pivoted madly around Tally, looking in all directions, searching the sky for more threats. But none of them turned toward her—they were all pointed outward, not back at the hovercraft itself.

Tally realized that she was sitting in the machine's blind spot. Its eye-stalks couldn't turn to see her, and its armored skin had no nerves to sense her feet. Apparently the hovercraft's designers had never imagined an adversary *standing right on top of it.*

But the machine knew something was wrong—it was too heavy. The four lifting fans tilted wildly as Tally shifted from side to side, scrambling to stay on. The metal claws that hadn't been mangled by her hoverboard swung randomly in the air, searching like a blind insect's for an opponent.

Under her extra weight, the hovercraft began to descend. Tally leaned hard toward Town Hall, and the machine began to drift in that direction as it dropped. It was like riding the world's wobbliest, most uncooperative hoverboard, but gradually she guided it away from the landing pad and the slow-moving line of littlies.

As Town Hall grew nearer, shock waves from the attack rumbled through the machine. Heat from the burning building began to penetrate her sneak suit, and she felt a film of sweat spring up all over her body. Behind her the littlies seemed to have finally moved clear of the landing pad. All she had to do now was get off the hovercraft without it spotting her and opening fire.

When the ground was only ten meters below, Tally jumped from the machine's back, grabbing one of the damaged claws as she sailed past, yanking that side of the machine downward with the force of her fall. The hovercraft spun in midair over her head, lifting fans screeching in an attempt to keep it upright. But it had already tipped too far over; after a brief struggle, her weight on the lifeless claw flipped the machine over and upside down.

She dropped the short distance, and her crash bracelets stopped her fall, depositing her gently on the ground.

Above, the hovercraft spun sideways toward Town Hall, still careening out of control, claws flailing mindlessly. It crashed into the building's lowest floor, disappearing into a gout of flame that swept across Tally, her sneak suit reporting malfunctions all across its skin. The scales that had absorbed the explosion rippled to a halt, and Tally smelled her own hair singeing inside the hood.

As she ran back toward the hospital, fierce concussions shook the earth, knocking Tally's feet out from under her. Looking back, she saw that Town Hall was finally crumbling. After the long minutes of bombardment, even its alloy skeleton was melting, bowing under the weight of the burning building.

And it was practically on top of her.

She rose to her feet again, turning her skintenna on, her head filling with the Cutters' chatter as they organized the hospital evacuees.

"Town Hall's collapsing!" she said, running. "I need help!"

"What are you doing way over *there*, Tally-wa?" Shay's voice answered. "Roasting marshmallows?"

"Tell you later!"

"We're on our way."

The rumbling grew, the heat behind her redoubling as tons of burning building collapsed in upon itself. A chunk of fiery debris flew past, setting fire to the motionless slidewalks' grippy surface as it bounced to a halt. The light behind her brightened, Tally's flickering shadow stretching out like a giant's in front of her.

From the direction of the hospital, a pair of shapes shot into view. Tally waved her arms. "Over here!"

They swept around her and circled back, the collapsing building silhouetting their black forms.

"Hands up, Tally-wa," Shay said.

Tally jumped into the air, both hands reaching. The two Cutters grabbed her wrists, pulling her away from Town Hall and toward safety.

"You okay?" Tachs's voice cried.

"Yeah, but it's . . ." Tally's voice faded. Carried backward, she found herself watching the building's final collapse in awestruck silence. It seemed to fold into itself, like a balloon deflating, then a vast billowing cloud of smoke and debris gushed outward, like a dark tidal wave swallowing the fiery remains.

The wave raced toward them, closer and closer. . . .

"Uh, guys?" Tally said. "Can you go any—?"

The shock wave broke over the Cutters, full of swirling debris and furious winds, knocking Shay and Tachs from their boards and hurling all three of them to the ground. As she rolled, the burn-damaged scales of Tally's sneak suit jabbed into her like sharp elbows, until she finally tumbled to a halt.

She lay on the ground, her breath knocked out of her. Darkness had swallowed them.

"You guys okay?" Shay asked.

"Yeah, icy," said Tachs.

Tally tried to speak, but wound up coughing; her sneak-suit mask had stopping filtering the air. She pulled it off, the smoke stinging her eyes, and spat out the taste of burnt plastic. "No board, and my suit's ruined," she managed. "But I'm okay."

"You're welcome," Shay said.

"Oh, yeah. Thanks, guys."

"Hang on," Tachs said. "You hear that?"

Tally's ears were still ringing, but a moment later she realized that the barrage of cannon fire had ceased. The quiet was almost eerie. She flicked down an infrared overlay and looked up. A glowing vortex of hovercraft was forming above, like a galaxy gathering itself into a spiral.

"What are they going to do now?" Tally asked. "Destroy something else?"

"No," Shay said softly. "Not yet."

"Before we came here, we Cutters were in on Dr. Cable's plans," Tachs said. "She doesn't want to demolish Diego. She wants to remake it. Turn it into another city just like ours: strict and controlled, *everyone* a bubblehead."

"When things start to fall apart," Shay said, "she'll be here to take over."

"But cities don't take each other over!" Tally said.

"Not normally, Tally, but don't you see?" Shay turned toward the still-burning wreck of Town Hall. "Runaways running free, the New System out of control, and now the city government in ruins . . . *this* is a Special Circumstance."

BLAME

The hospital was full of broken glass.

All the windows on the Town Hall side had been blown inward by the building's final collapse. Their shattered remains crunched underfoot as Tally and the other Cutters checked each room for anyone left behind.

"Got a crumbly up here," Ho said from two floors above.

"Does he need a doctor?" Shay's voice asked.

"Just a few cuts. Medspray should do it."

"Let a doctor take a look, Ho."

Tally tuned out the skintenna chatter and peered into the next abandoned hospital room, staring once more through the empty window frames at the glowing wreckage. Two helicopters hovered overhead, spraying foam down onto the fire.

She could escape now, simply turn off her skintenna and disappear into the chaos. The Cutters were too busy to chase her, and the rest of the city was hardly functioning at all. She knew where the Cutters' hoverboards waited, and the crash bracelets Shay had given her were keyed to unlock them.

But after what had happened here tonight, there was nowhere left to go. If Special Circumstances was really behind this attack, running back to Dr. Cable was out of the question.

Tally would almost have understood if the armada had gone after the new developments, teaching Diego a lesson about expanding into the wild. Whatever else was happening in Random Town, that had to be stopped. Cities couldn't just start grabbing land whenever they wanted.

But cities couldn't just attack each other like this either, blowing up buildings in the middle of town. That was how the insane, doomed Rusties had solved their disputes. Tally wondered how her own city had forgotten the lessons of history so easily.

On the other hand, she couldn't bring herself to doubt what Tachs had said, that Dr. Cable's purpose in destroying Town Hall was to bring the New System to its knees. Of all the cities, only Tally's had bothered to hunt down the Old Smoke. Only Tally's would think that a few runaways were worth obsessing over.

She was beginning to wonder if all cities had Special Circumstances, or whether most were like Diego, willing to let people come and go. Maybe the special operation—the one that had made Tally the way she was—was something Dr. Cable had invented herself. Which would mean that Tally really was an aberration, a dangerous weapon, someone who needed to be cured.

She and Shay had started this bogus war, after all. Normal, healthy people wouldn't do something like that, would they?

The next room was also empty, strewn with the remains of a late meal interrupted by the evacuation. The windows were decorated with curtains stirring in the wind from the distant helicopter. They had been shredded by flying glass, and now they were like tattered white flags waving in surrender. A pile of life-support equipment sat in the corner, still thrumming but disconnected. Tally hoped that whoever was supposed to be attached to all those tubes and wires was still okay.

It was strange, worrying about some nameless, fading crumbly. But the aftermath of the attack had been head-spinning: People didn't look like crumblies or randoms anymore. For the first time since Tally had become a Cutter, being *average* didn't seem pathetic to her. Seeing what her own city had done had somehow made her feel less special, at least for now.

She remembered back in ugly days, how living in the Smoke for a few weeks had transformed the way she saw the world. Perhaps coming to Diego, with all its messy discords and differences (and its absence of bubbleheads), had already started to make her a different person. If Zane was right, she was rewiring herself once again.

Maybe the next time she saw him, things would be different.

Tally flicked her skintenna to a private channel. "Shay-la? I need to ask you a question."

"Sure, Tally."

"How is it different? Being cured."

Shay paused, and through the skintenna Tally heard her slow breathing and the crunch of glass underfoot. "Well, when Fausto first stuck me, I didn't even notice. It took a couple of days to realize what was happening, that I was starting to see things differently. The funny thing was, when he explained what he'd done to me, it was mostly a *relief*. Everything's less intense now, less extreme. I don't have to cut myself just to make sense of it all; none of us do. But even though things aren't as icy, at least I don't get furious over nothing anymore."

Tally nodded. "When they had me in my padded cell, that's how they described it: anger and euphoria. But right now, I just feel numb."

"Me too, Tally-wa."

"And there was one other thing the doctors said," Tally added. "Something about 'feelings of superiority.'"

"Yeah, that's the whole point of Special Circumstances, Tally-wa. It's like they always taught us in school, how in Rusty days some people were 'rich'? They got all the best stuff, lived longer, and didn't have to follow the usual rules—and everyone thought that was perfectly okay, even if these people hadn't done anything to deserve it except have the right crumblies. Thinking like a Special is partly just human nature. It doesn't take much convincing to make someone believe they're better than everyone else."

Tally started to agree, then remembered what Shay had yelled at her when they'd split up back on the river. "But you said I was already that way, didn't you? Even back in ugly days."

Shay laughed. "No, Tally-wa. You don't think you're *better* than everyone else, just that you're the center of the universe. It's totally different."

Tally forced a laugh. "So why didn't you cure me? You had the chance, when I was out cold."

There was another pause, the faraway whirr of the helicopter filtering through Shay's skintenna link. "Because I'm sorry about what I did."

"When?"

"Making you special." Shay's voice was shaking. "It's all my fault what you are, and I didn't want to force you to change again. I think you can cure yourself this time."

"Oh." Tally swallowed. "Thanks, Shay."

"And there's one other thing: It'll help if you're still a Special when we go back home to stop this war."

Tally frowned. Shay hadn't explained that plan in detail yet. "How exactly will me being a psycho help?"

"Dr. Cable will scan us, to see if we're telling the truth," Shay said. "It would be better if one of us was still a real Special."

Tally came to a halt at the next doorway. "Telling the truth? I didn't know we were going to *talk* about this with her. I was imagining something involving hungry nanos. Or grenades, at least."

Shay sighed. "You're being a Special-head, Tally-wa. Violence isn't going to help. If we attack, they'll just think it's Diego fighting back, and this war will only get worse. We have to confess."

"Confess?" Tally found herself facing another empty room, lit only by the flickering fires of Town Hall. Flowers were everywhere, their vases shattered on the floor, colorful shards and dead flowers mixing with the broken window-glass.

"That's right, Tally-wa. We have to tell everyone that it was you and me who attacked the Armory," Shay said. "That Diego didn't have anything to do with it."

"Oh. Great." Tally stared out the window.

The fires inside Town Hall still glowed, no matter how much foam the helicopters sprayed. Shay had said the wreckage would burn for days, the pressure of the collapsed building creating its own heat, as if the attack had given birth to a tiny sun.

The awful sight was *their* fault—the realization kept hitting Tally, as if she would never get used to it. She and Shay had made this happen, and only they could undo it.

But at the thought of confessing to Dr. Cable, Tally had to fight the urge to flee, to run toward the open windows and jump, letting her crash bracelets catch her. She could disappear into the wild and never be caught. Not by Shay. Not by Dr. Cable. Invisible again.

But that would mean leaving Zane behind in this battered, threatened city.

"And if they're going to believe you," Shay continued, "it can't look like anyone's been messing with your brain. We need to keep you special."

Suddenly, Tally needed fresh air. But as she walked toward the window, the sweet scent of dead and dying flowers assaulted her nose like a crumbly's perfume. Her eyes watered, and Tally closed them, crossing the room using the echoes of her own footsteps.

"But what will they *do* to us, Shay-la?" she asked softly.

"I don't know, Tally. No one's ever admitted starting a bogus war before, not as far as I know. But what else can we do?"

Tally opened her eyes and leaned out the blown-out window. She sucked up fresh air, though it was tainted with the smell of burning. "It's not like we *meant* for it to go that far," she whispered.

"I know, Tally-wa. And it was all my idea, my fault that you were special in the first place. If I could go alone, I would. But they won't believe me. Once they scan my brain, they'll see I'm different, cured. Dr. Cable would probably rather think Diego messed with my head than admit she started a war over nothing."

Tally couldn't argue with that; she could hardly believe herself that their little break-in had caused all this destruction. Dr. Cable wouldn't take anyone's say-so without a full brain-scan.

She looked out at the burning Town Hall again, and sighed. It was too late to run, too late for anything but the truth.

"Okay, Shay, I'll go with you. But not until I find Zane. I need to explain something to him."

And maybe try again, she thought. *I'm different already.* Tally stared out the frame of shattered glass, imagining Zane's face.

"After all, what's the worst they can do, Shay-la? Make us both bubbleheads again?" she said. "Maybe that wasn't so bad. . . ."

There was still no response, but Tally heard a small, insistent beeping from Shay's end of the skintenna link.

"Shay? What's that sound?"

The answer came in a tense voice. "Tally, you better come down here. Room 340."

Tally turned away from the window, stepping quickly across the broken vases and dead flowers, heading for the door. The beeping sound grew louder as Shay moved closer to something, and a sense of dread began to fill Tally. "What's going on, Shay?"

Shay popped the channel open to the other Cutters, panic in her voice. "Someone get a doctor up here." She repeated the room number.

"What *is* it, Shay?" Tally cried.

"Tally, I'm so sorry . . ."

"What?"

"It's Zane."

PATIENT

Tally ran, heart racing in her chest, the beeping sound filling her head.

She jumped the handrail of the fire stairs, descending in a controlled fall down the center of the stairwell. When she burst out into the third-floor hallway, she saw Shay and Tachs and Ho outside a room marked RECOVERY, staring through the door like a crowd gawking at an accident.

Tally pushed between them, skidding to a halt on shards of shattered window glass.

Zane lay in a hospital bed, his face pale, his arms and head hooked up to a collection of machines. Each was making its own beeping noise, bright red lights keeping time with the sounds. A middle pretty in white doctor's scrubs stood over Zane, pulling back his lids to peer into his eyes.

"What happened?" she cried. The doctor didn't look up.

Shay stepped up behind her, taking her shoulders in a firm grip. "Stay icy, Tally."

"Icy?" Tally pulled herself from Shay's grasp. Adrenaline and anger surged through her blood, chasing away the numbness that had come over her after the attack. "What's *wrong* with him? What's he doing in here?"

"Could you bubbleheads be *quiet*?" the doctor snapped.

Tally spun back to face him, teeth bared. *"Bubbleheads?"*

Shay wrapped her arms around Tally and pulled her off

her feet. In one swift movement, she carried her backward out of the room, set her down, and shoved her hard away from the door.

Tally regained her footing, crouching low with fingers curled. The Cutters stared her down, while Tachs gently closed the door.

"I thought you were rewiring yourself, Tally," Shay said in a hard, even voice.

"I'll rewire *you*, Shay!" Tally said. "What's going on?"

"We don't know, Tally. The doctor just got here." Shay placed her palms together. "Control yourself."

Tally's mind spun, seeing only angles of attack, strategies for fighting her way through the three of them and back into the recovery room. But she was outnumbered, and as the standoff continued, her flash of anger was transforming into panic.

"They operated on him," she whispered, her breath quickening. The hall began to spin as she remembered the Crims all headed into the hospital, straight from the helicopter.

"That's what it looks like, Tally," Shay said, her voice even.

"But he arrived in Diego *two days* ago," Tally said. "The other Crims were at a party the night they got here—I saw them."

"The other Crims didn't have brain damage, Tally. Just the bubblehead lesions. You know Zane was different."

"But this is a city hospital. What could go *wrong*?"

"Shhh, Tally-wa." Shay took a step forward and put her hand gingerly on Tally's shoulder. "Be patient, and they'll tell us."

In a flash of anger, Tally's focus narrowed to the door of the recovery room. Shay was close enough to punch in the face; Ho and Tachs were momentarily distracted by the arrival of a second doctor—Tally could get past them all if she struck now. . . .

But anger and panic seemed to cancel each other out, paralyzing her muscles and twisting her stomach into a knot of despair.

"This is because of the attack, isn't it?" Tally said. "That's why it's going wrong."

"We don't know that."

"It's *our* fault."

Shay shook her head, her voice soothing, as if Tally were some littlie who'd woken from a nightmare. "We don't know what's happening, Tally-wa."

"But you found him in there all alone? Why didn't they evacuate him?"

"Maybe he couldn't be moved. Maybe he was safer here, hooked up to those machines."

Tally's hands tightened into fists. Since becoming special, she'd never felt so helpless and average, so powerless. Everything was suddenly going *random*. "But . . ."

"Shush, Tally-wa," Shay said in her maddeningly calm voice. "We just have to wait. That's all we can do for now."

An hour later, the door opened.

There were five doctors now, leftover from a steady stream of hospital staff that had moved in and out of Zane's room. A few had given Tally nervous looks, realizing who she was: the dangerous weapon who had escaped earlier that night.

Tally had passed the time fretfully, half-expecting someone to jump her, put her to sleep, and schedule her for despecialization again. But Shay and Tachs had stayed close by, staring down the wardens who'd arrived to keep an eye on them. One thing about Maddy's cure, it had made the other Cutters a lot better at waiting than Tally. They remained eerily calm, but she hadn't been able to stop moving for the whole hour, and half-moons of blood covered her palms where fingernails had driven into flesh.

The doctor cleared his throat. "I'm afraid I have bad news."

Tally's mind didn't process the words at first, but she felt Shay's grip upon her arm, iron hard, as if she thought Tally was about to leap at the man and tear him apart.

"At some point during the evacuation, Zane's body rejected his new brain tissue. His life support tried to alert the staff, but of course there was no one nearby. It tried to ping us, but the city interface was too overloaded by the evacuation to get a message through."

"Overloaded?" Tachs said. "You mean the hospital doesn't have its own network?"

"There is an emergency channel," the doctor said. He looked in the direction of Town Hall, shaking his head like he still didn't believe it was gone. "But it goes through the city interface. Of which nothing remains. Diego's never had a disaster like this before."

It was the attack . . . the war, Tally thought. *It* is *my fault.*

"His immune system thought the new brain tissue was an infection, and responded accordingly. We did all we could, but by the time you found him, the damage had already been done."

"How much . . . damage?" Tally said. Shay's hands squeezed tighter.

The doctor looked at the wardens, and in Tally's peripheral vision, she saw them readying nervously for a fight. They were all terrified of her.

He cleared his throat. "You realize that he arrived here with brain damage, don't you?"

"We know," Shay said, her voice still soothing.

"Zane said he wanted to be fixed: no more shakes or lapses in cognition. And he requested a physical control upgrade—as far as we could push it. It was risky, but he gave informed consent."

Tally's gaze fell to the floor. Zane had wanted his old reflexes back, and better, so that she wouldn't see him as weak and average.

"That's where the rejection hit him hardest," the doctor continued. "The functions we were trying to repair. They're all gone now."

"Gone?" Tally's mind reeled. "His motor skills?"

"And higher functions, more importantly: speech and cognition." The doctor's wariness faded, his expression now set to classic middle-pretty concern, calm, and understanding. "He can't even breathe on his own. We don't think he'll regain consciousness. Not ever."

The wardens had glowing shock-sticks in their hands now. Tally could breathe in the electricity.

The doctor took a slow breath. "And the thing is . . . we need the bed."

Tally sagged toward the floor, but Shay's grip didn't let her fall.

"We have dozens of casualties," the doctor continued. "A few night workers who escaped Town Hall have terrible burns. We need those machines, the sooner the better."

"What about Zane?" Shay said.

The doctor shook his head. "He'll stop breathing once we take him off. Normally, we wouldn't move this quickly, but tonight . . ."

"Is a special circumstance," Tally said softly.

Shay pulled her close, whispered in her ear. "Tally, we have to go now. We have to leave this place. You're too dangerous."

"I want to see him."

"Tally-wa, it's not a good idea. What if you lose it? You could kill someone."

"Shay-la," Tally hissed. "Let me see him."

"No."

"Let me see him or I'll kill them all. You won't be able to stop me."

Shay's arms were wrapped around her now, but Tally knew she could break the grip. Enough of her sneak suit still worked that she could turn it slippery, slide out, and start swinging, go straight for their throats. . . .

Shay's grip shifted, and something pressed lightly against Tally's neck. "Tally, I can inject you with the cure right now."

"No, you can't. We have a war to stop. You need my brain the messed-up way it is."

"But *they* need those machines. All you're doing is—"

"Let me be the center of the universe for *five more minutes*, Shay. Then I'll go away and let him die. I promise."

Shay let out a long sigh between her teeth. "Everyone, get out of our way."

His head and arms were still connected, the wild chorus of beeping replaced by a steady beat.

But Tally could see that he was dead.

She'd seen a dead body once before. When Special Circumstances had come to destroy the Old Smoke, the ancient keeper of the rebels' library had been killed trying to escape. (That death had been her fault too, Tally remembered now; how had *that* little fact slipped her mind?) The old man's body had looked misshapen in death, so twisted that the entire world had distorted around it. Even the sunlight had looked wrong that day.

But this time, staring at Zane, everything was much worse—her eyes were special now. Every detail was a hundred times clearer: the wrong color of his face, the too-steady pulse in his throat, the way his fingernails were slowly fading from pink to white.

"Tally. . ." Tachs's voice choked off.

"I'm so sorry," Shay said.

Tally glanced back at her fellow Cutters, and realized that they couldn't understand. They might still be strong and fast, but Maddy's cure had made their minds average again. They couldn't see how maddening death really was, how colossally *pointless* in every way.

The fires still burned outside, mockingly beautiful against the dark and perfect sky. That was what no one else could see, that the world was too bubbly and gorgeous for Zane to be missing from it.

Tally reached out and touched his hand. Her exquisitely sensitive fingertips told her that his flesh was cooler than it should be.

This was all her fault. She'd coaxed him here to become what *she* wanted; she had wandered around the city instead of watching over him; she had started the war that had torn him apart.

This was the final price of her massive ego.

"I'm sorry, Zane." Tally turned away. Five minutes was suddenly too long to stand here, eyes burning, unable to cry.

"Okay, let's go," she whispered.

"Tally, are you sure? It's only been—"

"Let's *go*! On our boards. This war has to stop."

Shay put a hand on her shoulder. "Okay. First light. We can fly without stopping—no bubbleheads to slow us down, no Smokey position-finder taking us on the scenic route. We'll be home in three days."

Tally opened her mouth, about to demand that they head for home right now, but the exhaustion on Shay's face silenced her. Tally had been unconscious most of the last twenty-four hours, but Shay had traveled to meet the Cutters and cure them, had rescued Tally from being despecialized, had led them through this long and terrible night. Her eyes were barely open.

Besides, this wasn't Shay's battle anymore. She hadn't paid the price that Tally had.

"You're right," Tally said, realizing what she had to do. "Go get some sleep."

"What about you? Are you okay?"

"No, Shay-la. I'm not okay."

"Sorry, I mean . . . are you going to hurt anyone?"

Tally shook her head and held out her hand, which didn't tremble at all. "See? I'm under control, maybe for the first time since I became a Special. But I can't sleep. I'll wait for you."

Shay paused, unsure, perhaps sensing what Tally had in mind. But then fatigue fell across her worried expression, and she hugged Tally one more time. "I only need a couple of hours. I'm still special enough."

"Of course." Tally smiled. "First light."

She walked with the other Cutters out of the room, past the doctors and nervous wardens, away from Zane forever, from all their imagined futures. And with every step, Tally knew she had to leave not just Zane, but everyone, behind.

Shay would only slow her down.

GOING HOME

Tally left the moment Shay was asleep.

It was pointless, both of them giving themselves up. Shay had to stay here in Diego; at this point the Cutters were the closest thing this city had to a military. Dr. Cable wouldn't believe Shay, anyway. Her brain would show the marks of Maddy's cure—she was no longer special.

But Tally was. She ducked and weaved among branches in the forest, knees bent and arms stretched out like wings, flying faster than she ever had before. Everything was icy clear: the warm wind across her bare face, the shifting gravities of flight beneath her feet. She'd taken two boards, riding one while the other followed, jumping back and forth every ten minutes. With her weight shared between them, top speed wouldn't burn out the lifting fans for days.

She reached the edge of Diego long before the sun began to rise, when the orange sky was just becoming radiant overhead, like an immense vessel emptying its light down upon the wild. The world's beauty hurt like razors, and Tally knew she'd never have to cut herself again.

She carried a knife inside herself now, one that was always cutting her. She could feel it every time she swallowed, every time her thoughts strayed from the splendor of the wild.

The forest thinned as Tally reached the great deserts left

by the white weed. As the wind against her face became rough with airborne sand, she angled toward the sea, where her magnetics could grip the railroad line, lending her more speed.

She only had seven days to end this war.

According to Tachs, Special Circumstances planned to wait a week for the situation in Diego to grow worse. The destruction of Town Hall would impair the city's workings for months, and Dr. Cable seemed to think that non-bubbleheads would rise up against any government if their needs weren't met.

And if the rebellion didn't happen on schedule, Special Circumstances could simply attack again, destroying more of the city to make conditions still worse.

Tally's software pinged—another ten minutes gone by. She called the empty board closer and leaped across the void, for a moment nothing but sand and scrub below, then landing in a perfect riding stance.

She found herself smiling grimly. If she fell, there was no grid below to catch her, only hardpacked sand racing by at a hundred kilometers per hour. But the doubts and uncertainties she had always suffered, the ones Shay had complained about even after Tally had become a Cutter, had finally been burned away.

Danger didn't matter anymore. Nothing did.

She was truly special now.

As dusk began to fall, Tally reached the coastal railroad line.

Clouds had glowered at her from the sea all afternoon, and as the sun went down, a black veil rolled in, covering the stars and moon. An hour after nightfall, the day's heat stored in the railroad tracks began to fade, leaving the path invisible even in infrared. Tally navigated by ear, using only the roar of the surf to stay on course. Here over the metal rails, her bracelets would save her if she fell.

Just as dawn broke, she shot over a camp full of sleepy-looking runaways. She heard shouting in her wake, and glanced back to see that the wind of her passage had scattered embers from their campfire across the dry grass. The runaways were scampering around trying to keep the fire from spreading, beating the flames with their sleeping bags and jackets, screeching like a bunch of bubbleheads.

Tally kept flying. She didn't have time to turn back and help.

She wondered what would become of all the runaways still making their way across the wild. Could Diego still spare its meager fleet of helicopters to bring them in? How many more citizens could the New System handle, now that it was fighting for its own existence?

Of course, Andrew Simpson Smith wouldn't realize there was a war on. He would still hand out his position-finders, guides to nowhere. The runaways would reach their collection points, but no rides would come. They would slowly lose faith, until they ran out of food and patience, then head back home.

Some might make it, but they were all city kids, clueless about the dangers out here. Without a New Smoke to welcome them, most would be consumed by the wild.

On her second night of flying without rest, Tally fell.

She had just noticed that one board was acting up, some microscopic flaw in its forward lifting fan causing it to run hot. She'd been watching it carefully for the last few minutes, a detailed infrared overlay blotting her normal vision, and she never even noticed the tree.

It was a lone pine, its upper leaves sheered by salt spray like a bad haircut. The board she was riding struck a branch dead center, snapping it clean, sending Tally flying head over heels.

Her crash bracelets found the metal in the rail line just in time. They didn't snap her up short, like they would have in a straight-down fall, but bounced her along the tracks at speed. For a few wild moments, Tally felt like she'd been strapped to the front of some ancient train, the world rushing by on either side, the dark rails stretching before her into blackness, cross-ties a blur beneath her feet.

She wondered what would happen if the railroad line curved suddenly, whether the bracelets would carry her through a turn, or dump her unceremoniously on the ground. Or off the cliff . . .

The track ran doggedly straight, though, and after a hundred meters her momentum petered out. The bracelets set Tally down; her heart was pounding, but she was unhurt. Both boards found her signal a minute later, nosing out of the darkness like sheepish friends who'd run off without telling her.

Tally realized that she should probably get some sleep. When her next lapse of concentration came, she might not be so lucky. But the sun would be rising soon, and the city was less than a day's travel away. She stepped onto the overheated board and rode it hard, keeping herself alert by listening carefully to every shift in the sound of the damaged fan.

Just after dawn, a high-pitched squeal erupted, and Tally leaped from the stricken hoverboard as it disintegrated into a white-hot mass of shrieking metal. She landed on the other board, turning to watch the screaming remains of the first spin out sideways and fall into the sea, where its impact threw up a geyser of spray and steam.

Tally faced home again, never even slowing.

When the Rusty Ruins came into sight, she headed inland.

The ancient ghost city was full of metal, so for the first time since leaving Diego, Tally let herself slow down, resting the lifting fans of her remaining board. She moved in silence through the empty streets, staring down at the burnt-out cars that marked the Rusties' last day. Crumbling buildings rose up around her, all the familiar spots where she had hidden back in her Smokey days. Tally wondered if tricky uglies still snuck out here at night. Maybe the ruins didn't seem so exciting anymore, now that there was a real-live city to run away to.

They still felt creepy, though, as if the vast emptiness was full of ghosts. The gaping windows seemed to stare at Tally, taking her back to that first night Shay had brought her here, back when they were both uglies. Shay had learned the secret route from Zane, of course—he was the ultimate reason that Tally Youngblood wasn't just another bubblehead, happy and clueless among the spires of New Pretty Town.

Maybe after she confessed to Dr. Cable, Tally would wind up there again, all these unhappy-making memories erased at last. . . .

Ping.

Tally slowed to a halt, not quite believing what she'd heard. The ping was on the Cutters' frequency, but none of them could have made it here before her. The ID was blank, as if the ping had come from no one. It had to be some abandoned beacon left behind on a training mission, nothing but a random signal in the ruins.

"Hello?" she whispered.

Ping . . . ping . . . ping.

Tally raised her eyebrows. That hadn't been random; it had sounded like an answer. "Can you hear me?"

Ping.

"But you can't say anything?" Tally frowned.

Ping.

Tally sighed, realizing what was going on. "Fine. Nice trick, ugly. But I've got more important things to do." She started up her lifting fans again, angling toward town.

Ping . . . ping.

Tally slid to a halt, unsure about ignoring this. Any bunch of uglies smart enough to trick the Cutters' frequency might have useful information. It wouldn't hurt to find out how things were going in the city before confronting Dr. Cable.

She checked the signal strength. It was strong and clear. Whoever had rigged it up wasn't far away.

Tally drifted down the empty street, watching the signal carefully. It grew slightly stronger on the left. She turned in that direction and glided a block farther.

"Okay, kid. One means yes, and two means no. Got that?"

Ping.

"Do I know you?"

Ping.

"Hmm." Tally kept going until the signal weakened, then turned around and made her way slowly back. "Are you a Crim?"

Ping . . . ping.

The signal's strength peaked, and Tally looked up.

Towering above her was the tallest building left standing in the ruins, an old Smokey hangout and the logical place to set up a broadcasting station.

"Are you an ugly?"

There was a long pause. Then a single ping.

Tally began her silent ascent, the hoverboard's magnetics taking hold of the tower's ancient metal skeleton. Her senses expanded, listening for every sound.

The wind shifted, and she smelled something familiar, her stomach clenching.

"SpagBol?" She shook her head. "So you come from this city?"

Ping . . . ping.

Then she heard a sound, movement in the rubble of some ruined floor above. Tally stepped from her board through an empty window frame, setting her damaged sneak suit to a rough approximation of broken stone. She took both sides of the frame and leaned in, peering upward.

There he was above, looking down at her. "Tally?" he called.

She blinked. It was David.

DAVID

"What are you *doing* here?" she called.

"Waiting for you. I knew you'd come this way . . . through the ruins one more time."

Tally climbed toward him, swinging from one iron beam to the next, covering the distance in a few seconds. He was huddled in the corner of a floor that hadn't completely collapsed, barely enough room for the sleeping bag splayed out beside him. His sneak suit was set to match the shadows inside the ruin.

A self-heating meal in his hand chimed that it was ready, and the revolting smell of SpagBol hit Tally again.

She shook her head. "But how did you . . . ?"

David held up a crude device in one hand, a directional antenna in the other. "After we cured him, Fausto helped us rig this up. Every time you guys got close, we detected your skintennas. We could even listen in."

Tally squatted on a rusty iron beam, her head suddenly spinning from three days of constant travel. "I wasn't asking how you pinged me. How did you get here so quickly?"

"Oh, that was easy. When you left without her, Shay realized that you were right: Diego needs her more than you do. But they don't need me." He cleared his throat. "So I took the next helicopter to a pickup spot about halfway here."

Tally sighed, closing her eyes. "*Special-head*," Shay had called her. She could have gotten a ride most of the way. That was one problem with dramatic exits: Sometimes they wound up making you look like a bubblehead. But she was relieved to hear that her fears about the runaways had been unfounded. Diego hadn't abandoned them yet.

"So *why* exactly did you come?"

David wore a determined look. "I'm here to help you, Tally."

"Listen, David, just because we're *sort of* on the same side now doesn't mean I want you around. Shouldn't you be back in Diego? There's a war on, you know."

He shrugged. "I don't like cities much, and I don't know anything about wars."

"Well, I don't either, but I'm doing what I can." She signaled for her board, which still hovered below. "And if Special Circumstances catches me with a Smokey, it's not going to make it any easier convincing them I'm telling the truth."

"But Tally, are you okay?"

"That's the second time someone's asked me that stupid question," she said softly. "No, I'm not okay."

"Yeah, I guess it was stupid. But we're worried about you."

"We who? You and Shay?"

He shook his head. "No, my mother and me."

Tally let out a short, sharp laugh. "Since when was Maddy worried about me?"

"She's been thinking about you a lot lately," he said, setting his untouched SpagBol on the floor. "She had to study the special operation to cure it. She knows quite a bit about what it's like, being what you are."

Tally leaped up, hands curling, and jumped across the void between them in a single bound, sending a shower of rust down into the chasm of the building's core. Her teeth bared, she said straight to his face, "*No one* knows what it's like to be me right now, David. I promise you: no one."

He held her gaze without flinching, but Tally could *smell* his fear, all the weakness leaking out of him.

"I'm sorry," he said evenly. "I didn't mean it that way. . . . This isn't about Zane."

At the sound of his name, something fractured inside Tally, and her fury faded. She sank onto her haunches, breathing raggedly. For a moment, it felt as though the burst of rage had shifted something heavy and leaden inside her. It was the first time since Zane's death that anything, even anger, had broken through her despair.

But the feeling had lasted only a few seconds, then the

fatigue from her uninterrupted days of travel came tumbling down.

She lowered her head into her hands. "Whatever."

"I brought you something. You might need it."

Tally looked up. In David's hand was an injector.

She shook her head tiredly. "You don't want to cure me, David. Special Circumstances won't listen to me unless I'm one of them."

"I know, Tally. Fausto explained your plan to us." He placed a cap over the needle, snapping it down. "But keep this. Maybe after you tell them what happened, you'll want to change yourself."

Tally frowned. "There doesn't seem like much point thinking about what happens *after* I confess, David. The city might be a little upset with me, so I might not have much say in the matter."

"I doubt it, Tally. That's what's so amazing about you. No matter what your city does to you, you always seem to have a choice."

"Always?" She snorted. "I didn't *seem* to have a choice when Zane died."

"No . . ." David shook his head. "I'm sorry, again. I keep saying stupid things. But remember when you were a pretty? You changed yourself, and *you* led the Crims out of the city."

"Zane led us."

"He'd taken a pill. You hadn't."

She groaned. "Don't *remind* me. That's how he wound up in that hospital!"

"Wait, wait." David put up his hands. "I'm trying to say something. *You* were the one who thought your way out of being pretty."

"Yeah, I know, I know. A lot of good that did me. Or Zane."

"Actually, it did more than a lot of good, Tally. After seeing what you'd done, my mother realized something important about how the operation could be reversed. About the bubblehead cure."

Tally looked up, remembering Zane's theories back in pretty days. "You mean about making yourself bubbly?"

"Exactly. My mother realized that we didn't have to get rid of the lesions, all we had to do was stimulate the brain to work around them. That's why the new cure is much safer, and why it works so fast." He was talking quickly, his eyes bright in the shadows. "That's how we got Diego to change in only two months. Because of *what you showed us*."

"So I'm to blame for those people turning their little fingers into snakes? Great."

"You're to blame for the freedom they've found, Tally. For the end of the operation."

She laughed bitterly. "The end of Diego, you mean. Once Cable gets her hands on them, they'll wish they'd never seen your mother's little pills."

"Listen, Tally. Dr. Cable is weaker than you think." He leaned closer. "This is what I came to tell you: After the New System came into being, some of Diego's industrial managers helped us out. Mass production. We've smuggled two hundred thousand pills into your city over the last month. If you can knock Special Circumstances off-balance, even for a few days, your city will start to change. Fear is the only thing keeping a New System from happening here, too."

"Fear of whoever attacked the Armory, you mean." She sighed. "So it's all my fault again."

"Maybe. But if you can dispel that fear here, every city in the world will start paying attention." He took her hand.

"You aren't just stopping the war, Tally. You're about to fix *everything*."

"Or screw everything up. Has anyone thought what'll happen to the wild if everyone becomes cured all at once?" She shook her head. "All I know is I have to stop this war."

He smiled. "The world is changing, Tally. You made it happen."

She pulled away, staying silent for a while. Anything she said might set off another speech about how wonderful she was. She didn't feel wonderful, just exhausted. David seemed content to sit there, probably thinking that his words were sinking in, but Tally's silence meant nothing except that she was too tired to speak.

For Tally Youngblood, the war had already come and gone, leaving a smoking ruin in its wake. She couldn't fix everything, for the simple reason that the only person she cared about was past fixing.

Maddy could cure every bubblehead in the world, and Zane would still be dead.

But one question was niggling at her. "So, are you saying your mother actually *likes* me now?"

David smiled. "She finally realizes how important you are. To the future. And to me."

Tally shook her head. "Don't say things like that. About you and me."

"I'm sorry, Tally. But it's true."

"Your father *died* because of me, David. Because I betrayed the Smoke."

He shook his head slowly. "You didn't betray us—you were manipulated by Special Circumstances, like a lot of other people were. And it was Dr. Cable's experiments that killed my father, not you."

Tally sighed. She was too exhausted to argue. "Well, I'm glad Maddy doesn't hate me anymore. And speaking of Dr. Cable, I need to go see her and stop this war. Are we done here?"

"Yes." He picked up his meal and chopsticks, dropping his eyes to the food, his voice soft. "That's everything I wanted to say. Except . . ."

She groaned.

"Listen, Tally, you're not the only person who ever lost someone." His eyes narrowed. "After my father died, I wanted to disappear too."

"I'm not disappearing, David, I'm not running away. I'm doing what I have to, all right?"

"Tally, I'm just saying: I'll be here when you're done."

"You?" She shook her head.

"You're not alone, Tally. Don't pretend you are."

Tally tried to stand up, to get away from this nonsense, but suddenly the ruined tower seemed to sway around her. She sank back to her haunches.

Another lame dramatic exit.

"Okay, David, turns out I'm not going anywhere until I get some sleep. Guess I should have taken that helicopter."

"Use my sleeping bag." He scooted aside and held up the antenna. "I'll wake you up if anyone comes sniffing around. You're safe here."

"Safe." Tally squeezed past David, for a moment feeling the heat of his body and faintly remembering his smell from when they'd been together, what seemed like years ago.

It was strange. His ugly face had revolted her the last time she'd seen it, but after seeing so many insane surgeries in Diego, his scarred eyebrow and crooked smile just seemed like one more fashion statement. And not an awful one at that.

But he wasn't Zane.

Tally crawled into the sleeping bag, then peered down through the rotted floors of the building to the rubble-filled foundation a hundred meters below.

"Um, just don't let me roll over in my sleep, okay?"

He smiled. "All right."

"And give me that." She took the injector from his hand, zipping it into a pouch of her sneak suit. "I might need it one day."

"Maybe you won't, Tally."

"Don't confuse me," she murmured.

Tally laid down her head, and slept.

EMERGENCY MEETING

She took the river home.

Crashing through white water, the familiar skyline of New Pretty Town before her, Tally wondered if this would be the last time she'd ever see her home from the outside. How long did they lock you up for attacking your own city, accidentally destroying its armed forces, and getting it into a bogus war?

The moment she reached the city's repeater network, the newsfeeds rolled over Tally's skintenna like a tidal wave. More than fifty channels were covering the war, describing breathlessly how the hovercraft armada had broken through Diego's defenses and sent its Town Hall tumbling to the ground. Everyone was so *happy* about it, as if the bombardment of a helpless foe had been fireworks at the end of some long-awaited celebration.

It was weird hearing Special Circumstances mentioned

every five seconds—how they'd stepped in after the Armory had been destroyed, how they would keep everyone safe. Until a week ago, most people hadn't even *believed* in Specials, and suddenly they were the saviors of the city.

The new wartime regulations actually had their own channel, a cheerless scrolling list of rules to be memorized. Curfew restrictions on uglies were stricter than ever, and for the first time in Tally's memory, new pretties had limits on where they could go and what they could do. Ballooning was completely forbidden, hoverboards restricted to parks and sports fields. And ever since the disintegrating Armory had lit the sky, New Pretty Town's nightly fireworks displays had been canceled.

No one seemed to be complaining, though, not even cliques like the Hot-airs, who practically lived in their balloons during the summer. Of course, even if two hundred thousand people had been cured, that still left about a million bubbleheads. Maybe those who wanted to protest were still too outnumbered to make themselves heard.

Or perhaps they were too afraid of Special Circumstances to raise their voices at all.

As she passed through the outer ring of Crumblyville, Tally's skintenna connected with a drone patrolling the city limits. The machine gave her a quick electronic frisk before realizing that she was an agent of Special Circumstances.

She wondered if anyone had figured out how to get past the new patrols yet, or whether all the tricky uglies were gone by now, either run away to Diego or drafted into Special Circumstances. Everything had changed so much in the few weeks she'd been gone. The closer she got to the city, the less it felt like she was home at all, especially now that Zane would never see this skyline again. . . .

Tally took a deep breath. Time to get this over with. "Message to Dr. Cable."

The ping bounced back to announce that the city interface had put her in a holding queue. Apparently, the head of Special Circumstances was busy these days.

But a moment later, another voice answered, "Agent Youngblood?"

Tally frowned. It was Maxamilla Feaster, one of Cable's subcommanders. The Cutters had always reported directly to Dr. Cable.

"Let me talk to the doctor," Tally said.

"She's not available, Youngblood. She's meeting with the City Council."

"She's downtown?"

"No. At headquarters."

Tally slowed her board to a halt. "Special Circumstances headquarters? Since when does the City Council meet out there?"

"Since we went to war, Youngblood. A lot's happened while you and your miscreants have been wandering around in the wild. Where on earth have you Cutters been?"

"That's a long story, one I have to tell the doctor face-to-face. Tell her I'm coming, and that what I have to say is extremely important."

There was a brief pause, then the woman's voice came back, annoyed. "Listen, Youngblood. We are at war, and Dr. Cable is currently acting chair of the Council. She's got a whole city to run, and doesn't have time to give you Cutters your usual special treatment. So tell me what this is all about, or you won't be seeing 'the doctor' anytime soon. Understand?"

Tally swallowed. Dr. Cable was running the whole city?

Maybe confessing to her wasn't going to be enough. What if she was enjoying being in charge too much to believe the truth?

"Okay, Feaster. Just tell her that the Cutters have been in Diego the last week—fighting the war, okay?—and that I have some very important intelligence for the Council. It concerns the safety of the city. Is that good enough for you?"

"You've been in Diego? How did you—" the sub-commander started, but Tally gestured to cut the feed. She'd said enough to get the woman's attention.

She leaned forward and engaged the board's lifting fans, heading for the factory belt at top speed, hoping to get there before the City Council meeting had ended.

They were the perfect audience for her confession.

Special Circumstances headquarters stretched across the plain of the factory belt, low and flat and unimpressive. But it was bigger than it looked, descending twelve stories down into the earth. If the City Council was afraid of another attack, it was the logical place to hide. Tally was certain that Dr. Cable had welcomed the Council with open arms, happy to have the city government cowering in her basement.

Tally stared down from the summit of the long, tilted hill that overlooked the headquarters. Back in ugly days, she and David had jumped on hoverboards from here down to the roof. Since then, motion sensors had been installed to keep another break-in like theirs from happening again. But no fortress was designed to keep one of its own out, especially when she had important news to deliver.

Tally opened her skintenna feed again. "Message to Dr. Cable."

This time, Subcommander Feaster's response was instantaneous. "Quit playing around, Youngblood."

"Let me talk to Cable."

"She's still with the Council. You have to speak with *me* first."

"I don't have time to explain everything twice, Maxamilla. My report concerns the entire Council." She paused to take a long, slow breath. "There's another attack coming."

"Another *what*?"

"An attack, and *very* soon. Tell the doctor I'll be there in two minutes. I'll come straight to the Council meeting."

Tally cut her skintenna feed again, choking off more sputtering replies. She spun her hoverboard around and shot down the long, sloping side of the hill, then turned to face the summit once more, flexing her fingers.

The trick was to make her entrance as dramatic as possible, blustering past everyone and straight into the City Council meeting. Dr. Cable would probably enjoy one of her pet Cutters dashing in to deliver vital intelligence, proof that Special Circumstances was on the job.

Of course, the announcement wasn't going to be what Dr. Cable expected.

Tally urged her hoverboard forward, fans and magnetics fully engaged. She climbed the hill, building speed all the way.

At the top, the horizon suddenly slipped away, the ground disappearing beneath her, and Tally soared into the sky.

She cut the fans and bent her knees, grasping the board with her fingers.

The silence stretched out, the roof of the headquarters

growing as Tally fell. She felt a grin spreading on her face. This might be the last time she would do something this icy, with all her special senses sucking up the world; she might as well enjoy it.

A hundred meters from impact, her lifting fans spun to life. They pressed the board up against her, struggling to bring Tally to a halt. Her crash bracelets pushed against her wrists, straining against the force of the fall.

The hoverboard smacked hard and flat against the roof, and Tally rolled from its riding surface and straight into a run. Alarms were sounding all around her, but with a single gesture, her skintenna placated the security system. She shouted for emergency access through the hovercar doors ahead.

There was a short pause, then Feaster's anxious voice replied, "Youngblood?"

"I need in, double-quick!"

"I told Dr. Cable what you said. She wants you to head straight for the Council meeting. They're in the Level J operating theater."

Tally let herself smile. Her plan was working. "Got you. Open this door up."

"Right." With a lurching metal scrape, the landing pad beneath Tally began to part, as if the roof were splitting in two. She dropped through the widening seam, falling from bright sunlight into semidarkness and landing on top of a Special Circumstances hovercar. Ignoring the startled hangar workers around her, Tally rolled to the floor and kept running.

The voice popped into her ear again. "I've got an elevator waiting. Right in front of you."

"Too slow," Tally panted, coming to a halt before the elevator bank. "Just open an empty shaft."

"Are you kidding, Youngblood?"

"No! Seconds count here. Do it!"

A moment later, another door slid open, revealing darkness.

Tally stepped into the shaft.

Her grippy-soled shoes shrieked as she bounced from one side of the shaft to the other, her fall barely controlled, descending ten times faster than any elevator. On the headquarters' skintenna channel, she heard Feaster's voice warning everyone out of her way. Light spilled up into the shaft—the door to Sublevel J already open for her.

Tally caught the ledge of the floor above and swung herself through the opening, landing at a dead run. She dashed down the hallway at top speed, Specials pressing themselves against the wall to make way for her, as if Tally were some pre-Rusty messenger bringing news to the king.

At the entrance to the floor's main operating theater, Maxamilla Feaster waited with two Specials in full battle gear. "This had better be important, Youngblood."

"Believe me, it is."

Feaster nodded, and the door slid open. Tally ran through.

She skidded to a halt. The theater was silent, a great ring of empty seats staring down at her from all directions—no Dr. Cable, no City Council.

No one but Tally Youngblood, winded and alone.

She spun around. "Feaster? What is this—?"

The door slid closed, trapping her in the room.

Through her skintenna, she could hear the amusement in Feaster's voice. "Just wait in there, Youngblood. Dr. Cable will be with you once she's done with the Council."

Tally shook her head. Her confession would be useless

if Cable didn't want to believe it. She needed witnesses. "But this is happening *now*! Why do you think I ran all this way?"

"Why? Perhaps to tell the Council that Diego had nothing to do with the Armory attack? That it was really you?"

Tally's mouth dropped open, her next plea silenced on her lips. She replayed Feaster's words in her mind slowly, unable to believe she'd really heard them.

How could they have known?

"What are you talking about?" she finally managed.

The cruel sound of delight grew in Maxamilla Feaster's voice. "Be patient, Tally. Dr. Cable will explain."

Then the lights flicked off, leaving her in total darkness. Tally started to speak again, then realized that her skintenna had gone dead.

CONFESSION

The absolute darkness lasted what seemed like hours. A white-hot rage built inside Tally, a forest fire gaining strength with every passing second. She fought an urge to run blindly through the blackness, destroying everything she could lay her hands on, tearing her way through the ceiling and then the next floor, upward until she reached the open sky.

But Tally forced herself to sit down on the floor, breathing deep and trying to stay calm. The thought kept spinning in her mind that she was going to *lose* to Dr. Cable once again. Just like she had lost when the Smoke had been invaded, when she had given herself up to be made pretty, and when she and Zane had escaped together, only to be recaptured.

Again and again, Tally pushed the rage down, clenching her fists so hard it felt like her fingers would break. She felt powerless, just like when Zane had lain before her, dying. . . .

But she couldn't afford to lose again. Not this time, when the future was at stake.

So she waited in the darkness, struggling.

Finally, the door opened, framing Dr. Cable's familiar silhouette. From the ceiling, four spotlights popped on, shining directly into Tally's eyes. Blinded for a moment, she heard more Specials slip through before the door slid closed behind them.

Tally jumped to her feet. "Where's the City Council? It's urgent that I speak to them."

"I'm afraid that what you have to say might upset them, and we can't have that. Very jumpy these days, the Council." A chuckle came from Dr. Cable's silhouette. "They're up on Level H, still droning to each other."

Two floors above . . . She'd gotten so close, only to fail again.

"Welcome home, Tally," Dr. Cable said softly.

Tally looked around the empty auditorium. "Thanks for the surprise party."

"You were the one planning to surprise us, I believe."

"What, by telling the truth?"

"The truth? From you?" Dr. Cable laughed. "What could be more surprising?"

A flash of anger went through Tally, but she took a long, slow breath. "How did you know?"

Dr. Cable stepped into the light, drawing a small knife from her pocket. "I believe this is yours." She threw the knife into the air. It spun, glittering in the spotlights, and sunk deep into the floor between Tally's feet. "The skin cells we found on it certainly were."

Tally stared down at the knife.

It was the one Shay had thrown to set off the Armory's alarm, the same one Tally had used to cut herself that night. Tally opened her clenched fist and stared at her palm; the flash tattoos still spun in their halting rhythm, broken by the scar. She had seen Shay wipe it for fingerprints, but some tiny trace of her flesh must have lingered. . . .

They must have found it and run her DNA soon after the attack, and known all along that Tally Youngblood had been there at the Armory.

"I knew that nasty habit would eventually get you Cutters into trouble," Dr. Cable murmured. "Does it really feel so wonderful, cutting yourself? I must look into that, next time I make Specials so young."

Tally knelt and pulled the knife out of the floor, weighing it in her hand, wondering if a well-aimed throw could find its way into Dr. Cable's throat. But the woman was just as fast as Tally, just as special.

She couldn't afford to be a Special-head any longer. Tally had to *think* her way out of this.

She threw the knife aside.

"Just answer me one question," Dr. Cable said. "Why did you do it?"

Tally shook her head. Telling the whole truth would mean bringing Zane into it, which would only make it harder to keep control.

"It was an accident."

"An accident?" Dr. Cable laughed. "That's quite some accident, destroying half the city's military."

"We weren't planning to let loose those nanos."

"We? The Cutters?"

Tally shook her head—no point in mentioning Shay either. "One thing just sort of led to another. . . ."

"Indeed. That's how it always works with you, isn't it, Tally?"

"But why did you lie to everyone?"

Dr. Cable sighed. "That should be obvious, Tally. I couldn't very well tell them that *you* had almost dismantled the city's defenses. The Cutters were my pride and joy, my *special* Specials." Her razor smile spread across her face. "Besides, you'd given me a splendid opportunity to get rid of an old opponent."

"What did Diego ever do to you?"

"They supported the Old Smoke. They've taken in our runaways for years. Then Shay reported that someone was supplying the Smokies with sneak suits and huge quantities of those appalling pills. Who else could it have been?" Her voice grew stronger. "The other cities were just waiting for someone to take Diego down, with their New System and their flouting of morphological standards. You simply provided me with the ammunition. You've always been so *useful*, Tally."

Tally squeezed her eyes shut, willing Dr. Cable's words to somehow be heard up in the Council meeting. If only they knew how they'd been lied to. . . .

But this whole city was too scared to think clearly, too thrilled by their own counterattack, too ready to accept the rule of this twisted woman.

Tally shook her head. She'd spent the last few days focused on rewiring herself, but she needed to rewire *everyone*.

Or maybe just the right someone . . .

"When does it all end?" she asked quietly. "How long does this war go on?"

"It never ends, Tally. I'm getting too much done that I could never do before, and believe me, the bubbleheads are having such fun watching it on the newsfeeds. And all it took was a *war*, Tally. I should have thought of this years ago!" The woman stepped closer, her cruelly beautiful face aglow at the edge of the spotlights. "Don't you see, we've entered a new era. From now on, *every day* is a Special Circumstance!"

Tally nodded slowly, then let a smile creep onto her face. "Nice of you to explain that to me. And to everyone else."

Dr. Cable raised an eyebrow. "Pardon me?"

"Cable, I didn't come here to tell the City Council what happened. They're a bunch of wimps, if they put you in charge. I came to make sure that *everyone* knows about your lies."

The woman let out a low, rumbling laugh. "Don't tell me you made some sort of video of yourself, Tally, explaining that *you* started the war? Who'll believe it? You may have been famous once among the bubbleheads and uglies, but no one over the age of twenty even knows you exist."

"No, but they know you, now that you've put yourself in charge." Tally reached into her sneak suit's carrying pouch and pulled out the injector. "And now that they've watched you explain that this entire war was bogus, they'll remember you *forever*."

Dr. Cable frowned. "What is that thing?"

"A satellite transmitter, one that can't be jammed." Tally pulled the cap from the injector's top, exposing the needle. "See that little antenna? Amazing, isn't it?"

"You couldn't . . . not from down here." Dr. Cable's eyes closed, her lids fluttering as she checked the feeds.

Tally kept talking, her own bare-toothed smile growing. "They do the craziest surgery in Diego. They replaced my eyes with stereo cameras, and my fingernails with microphones. The whole city has been watching you explain what you've done."

Cable's eyes opened. She snorted. "There's nothing on the feeds, Tally. Your little toy doesn't work."

Tally raised her eyebrows, glancing at the bottom of the injector in puzzlement. "Oops. Forgot to press send." She shifted her fingers. . . .

Dr. Cable leaped forward, one hand darting for the injector, and in the same split second Tally turned the needle to exactly the right angle. . . .

The blow smacked the injector from her hand, and Tally heard it clatter in the corner, broken into pieces.

"Really, Tally," Dr. Cable said, smiling. "For someone so clever, you're such a little fool sometimes."

Tally lowered her head and closed her eyes. But she was breathing in slowly through her nose, searching the air. . . .

Then she smelled it—the barest scent of blood.

She opened her eyes, and saw Dr. Cable glance down at her hand, mildly annoyed by the needle's prick. Shay had said she'd hardly noticed the cure at first, that it took days to manifest.

In the meantime, Tally didn't want Cable wondering how she'd stabbed herself on the "antenna," or taking a closer look at the shattered injector. Perhaps a distraction was in order.

Tally set a look of rage on her face. "You're calling me a *fool*?"

She lashed out a foot, catching Dr. Cable in the stomach and knocking the breath from her.

The other Specials reacted instantly, but Tally was

already in motion, darting toward where she'd heard the injector fall. She landed one foot squarely on its remains, smashing it as hard as she could, then turned the motion into a roundhouse kick that landed on the jaw of the closest pursuer. She leaped up to the first row of seats, running along their backs without touching the floor.

"Agent Youngblood," another guard called. "We don't want to hurt you!"

"I'm afraid you'll have to!" She doubled back toward where the first guard lay. The door to the operating theater exploded open then, a swarm of gray silk uniforms storming into the room.

Tally jumped down near the fallen guard, landing once more on the shards of the injector. The other guard in battle gear landed a punch on her shoulder, rolling her back into the first row of seats. She leaped up and threw herself at him, ignoring the mass of Specials descending on her.

A few seconds later, Tally found herself thrown facedown on the floor, her arms pinned under her. She squirmed, crushing the last pieces of the injector beneath her into powder. Then someone kicked her in the ribs, driving her breath out in a grunt.

More of them piled on, like an elephant sitting on her back. The room grew dim; Tally felt herself being squashed against the edge of consciousness.

"It's okay, Doctor," one of the Specials said. "We have her under control."

Cable didn't respond. Tally craned her neck to see. The doctor was doubled over, still gasping for breath.

"Doctor?" the Special asked. "Are you all right?"

Just give her time, Tally thought. *And she'll be much, much better. . . .*

CRUMBLING

Tally watched it all happen from her cell.

The changes came slowly at first. For a few days, Dr. Cable seemed her usual psychotic self when she visited, arrogantly demanding information about what was happening in Diego. Tally was happy to oblige, spinning tales about how the New System was crumbling, while watching for any sign of the cure.

But decades of vanity and cruelty faded slowly, and time itself seemed to come to a halt inside the four walls of Tally's cell. Cutters weren't designed to live indoors, especially not in tiny spaces, and Tally had to focus most of her strength on not going crazy. She stared at the cell door, filled with despair, fighting the rage that came in waves inside her, always resisting the urge to cut herself with her own fingernails and teeth.

That was how she'd managed to rewire herself for Zane—not cutting anymore—and she couldn't give in to weakness now.

Hardest was when Tally thought about how far below the earth she was, twelve stories down, as though the cell were a coffin buried deep in the ground. As if she had died, but some evil machinery of Dr. Cable's was keeping her conscious even in the grave.

The cell reminded her of the way the Rusties had lived—the rooms in the lifeless ruins small and cramped, their overcrowded cities like prisons reaching toward the sky. Every time the door opened, Tally expected to be put under the knife, to wake up as a bubblehead or as some still more psychotic form of a Special. She was almost glad when it was Dr. Cable ready to interrogate her again—anything was better than being alone in this empty cell.

And finally she began to see that the cure was working . . . slowly. Gradually Dr. Cable seemed to become less sure of herself, less able to make decisions.

"They're telling *everyone* my secrets!" she started mumbling one day, running her fingers through her hair.

"Who is?"

"Diego." Dr. Cable spat the word. "Last night they put Shay and Tachs on the world feeds. Showing their cutting scars and calling me a monster."

"How bogus of them," Tally said.

Dr. Cable glared at her. "And they're broadcasting detailed scans of your body, calling you a 'morphological violation'!"

"You mean I'm famous again?"

Cable nodded. "You're infamous, Tally. Everyone's terrified of you. The New System may have made the other cities nervous, but they seem to think my little gang of psychotic sixteen-year-olds is worse."

Tally smiled. "We were pretty icy."

"Then how did you let Diego capture you!"

"Yeah, that sucked." Tally shrugged. "And it was just a bunch of wardens, too. They had these stupid uniforms that looked like bumblebees."

Dr. Cable stared at her, beginning to shiver like poor Zane had. "But you were so strong, Tally. So fast!"

Tally shrugged again. "Still am."

Dr. Cable shook her head. "For now, Tally. For now."

After two weeks of solitary silence, someone took unexpected mercy on Tally's boredom and the wallscreen in her cell booted up. She was amazed to see how quickly Dr. Cable's grip on the city had slipped. The newsfeeds had stopped rerunning the military's triumphant battle—

bubblehead dramas and soccer games filled the wallscreen instead of military exploits. One by one, the City Council was letting the new regulations lapse.

Apparently, Maddy's cure had taken hold of Cable's mind just in time: The second attack on Diego had never materialized.

Of course, the other cities may have had something to do with that. They'd never liked the New System, but were even less thrilled about the outbreak of an actual shooting war. People had died, after all.

As Dr. Cable's surgical experiments became infamous, Diego's repeated denials that it had attacked the Armory slowly gained credence. The feeds began to question what had really happened that night, especially after a crumbly museum curator who'd witnessed the attack went public with his story. He claimed that some sort of Rusty nano had been released, not by an invading army, but by two faceless attackers who'd seemed more young and harebrained than deadly serious.

Then stories sympathetic to Diego began to appear on the local feeds, including interviews with wounded survivors of the Town Hall strike. Tally always hurried to flick past those segments, which usually ended by listing the seventeen people who'd died in the attack—especially the one victim who was, ironically, a runaway from this very city.

They always showed his picture, too.

Arguments about the war—and about everything else—began to erupt. The disagreements grew more intense as Tally watched, less polite and measured every day, until the whole debate about the city's future became downright ugly. There was talk of new morphological standards, of letting uglies and pretties mix, even of expansion into the wild.

The cure was taking hold here, just as it had in Diego, and Tally wondered exactly what sort of future she had helped let loose. Were the city pretties going to start acting like Rusties now? Spreading across the wild, overpopulating the earth, leveling everything in their path? Who was left to stop them?

Dr. Cable herself seemed to fade from the newsfeeds, her influence waning, her personality shrinking before Tally's eyes. She stopped coming to the cell, and not long after that, the City Council finally removed her from power, saying that the crisis and her tenure as acting chair were over.

Then the talk of despecialization started.

Specials were dangerous, they were potentially psychotic, and the whole idea of a special operation was unfair. Most cities had never created any such creatures, except for a few reflex-boosted firefighters and rangers. Perhaps in the wake of this ill-considered war, it was time to get rid of them all.

After a long debate, Tally's own city began the process—a gesture of peace to the rest of the world. One by one, the agents of Special Circumstances were remade into normal, healthy citizens, and Dr. Cable never even raised her voice in protest.

Tally felt the walls of her cell pressing closer every day, as if the thought of being changed once more was crushing her. She looked at herself in the wallscreen, imagining her wolfen eyes made watery, her features ground down to averageness. Even the cutting scars on her arm would disappear, and Tally realized she didn't want to lose them. They were a reminder of everything she'd been through, of what she'd managed to overcome.

Shay and the others were still in Diego, still free, and maybe they could slip away before this happened to them. They could live anywhere: Cutters had been designed for the wild, after all.

But Tally had nowhere to run, no way to save herself. Finally one night, the doctors came for her.

OPERATION

She heard them outside, two nervous voices. Tally slipped from her bed and went to the door, placing her palm against the Special-proof ceramic wall. The chips in her hands turned the murmurs into words. . . .

"You sure this will work on her?"

"It's worked so far."

"But isn't she, you know, some kind of superfreak?"

Tally swallowed. Of course she was. Tally Youngblood was the most famous psychotic sixteen-year-old in the world; her body's lethal details had been broadcast far and wide.

"Relax, they whipped up this batch special, just for her."

Batch of what? she wondered.

Then she heard the hissing sound . . . gas leaking into the cell.

Tally jumped back from the door, sucking in a few quick gulps of air before the gas spread throughout the cell. She turned frantically in place, glaring at the four crushingly familiar walls, trying for the millionth time to find some weakness. Searching again for some way to escape . . .

Panic rose in Tally. They couldn't *do* this to her, not again. It wasn't her fault how dangerous she was. *They* had made her this way!

But there was no way out.

As she held her breath, the adrenaline pumping

through her, Tally's vision began to swarm with red dots. She hadn't breathed in almost a minute now, and the iciness of her panic was fading. But she couldn't give up.

If only she could think straight. . . .

She looked down at her arm, at the row of scars. It had been more than a month since her last cut, and it felt as though all the heartbreaks since were ready to burst from her veins. Maybe if she cut herself one more time, she could think of a way out of here.

At least her last moments as a Special would be icy. . . .

She put her fingernails against the flesh, gritted her razor teeth. "I'm sorry, Zane," she whispered.

"Tally!" came a hissing voice in her head.

She blinked. For the first time since they'd thrown her in the cell, her skintenna wasn't jammed.

"Don't just stand there, you little moron! Act like you're passing out!"

Tally's aching lungs sucked in a breath. The smell of the gas filled her head. She sat down on the floor, red spots swarming across her eyes.

"Yes, much better. Keep pretending."

Tally breathed deeply—she could hardly stop herself anymore. But something strange was happening: The dark clouds were fading from her vision, the much-needed oxygen making her more alert.

The gas was doing nothing.

She leaned back against the wall, eyes closed, heart still pounding hard. What was going on here? Who was in her head? Shay and the other Cutters? Or was it . . .

She remembered David's words: *"You're not alone."*

Tally closed her eyes and slumped to one side, letting her head crack against the floor. She waited there, unmoving.

A long moment later, the door slid open.

"That took long enough." The voice was nervous, lingering hesitantly in the hallway.

A few footsteps. "Well, like you said, she's some kind of superfreak. But she's headed for normalville now."

"And you're *sure* she's not going to wake up?"

A foot prodded her in the side. "See? Out cold."

The kick sent a flash of rage through Tally, but in her month of solitude she'd learned to control herself. When the foot nudged at her again, Tally allowed herself to be rolled over onto her back.

"Don't move, Tally. Don't do anything. Wait for me. . . ."

Tally wanted to whisper, *Who are you?* but she didn't dare. The two who'd gassed her were kneeling over her now, shifting her weight onto a hovercarrier.

She let them take her away.

Tally listened to the echoes carefully.

The halls of Special Circumstances were much emptier now; most of the cruel pretties had already been changed. She caught a few words of passing conversations, but none carried the razor sharpness of a Special's voice.

She wondered if they had saved her for the very last.

The elevator trip was short, probably only one floor up, where the main operating rooms were. She heard a double door slide open, and felt her body turning at a sharp angle. The carrier glided into a smaller room filled with metal surfaces and antiseptic smells.

Tally's entire being ached to leap from the hovercarrier, to fight her way to the surface. She'd escaped from this very building as an ugly. If the other Specials really were all gone, no one could stop her now. . . .

But she kept control, waiting for the voice to tell her what to do.

Repeating to herself: *I'm not alone.*

They stripped her clothes off and lifted her into an operating tank, the room's sounds muted by its plastic walls. She felt the cold smoothness of the table against her back, the metal claw of a servo-arm poking into her shoulder. She imagined it sprouting a scalpel, cutting the Cutter one last time, tearing her specialness out of her.

A dermal braid was pressed against her arm, its needles spraying a flash of local painkiller before sliding into her veins. She wondered when they'd start pumping serious anesthetic into her, and if her metabolism could keep her awake.

As the tank was sealed, Tally's breathing grew panicked. She hoped the two orderlies didn't notice the flash tattoos spinning all over her face.

They sounded very busy, though. Machines were booting up all around the room, beeping and humming, servo-arms stirring around her, their little saws buzzing through test patterns.

Two hands reached in and shoved a breathing tube into her mouth. The plastic tasted like disinfectant, and the air that flowed from it was sterile and unnatural. As the tube booted up, reaching tendrils around her nose and head, it almost made her gag.

She wanted to rip the thing out and *fight*.

But the voice had told her to wait. Whoever had made her knockout gas harmless must have a plan. She had to remain calm.

Then the tank began to fill.

Liquid poured in from all sides, pooling around her

naked body, thick and viscous, full of nutrients and nanos to keep her tissues alive while the surgeons were shredding her to pieces. Its temperature matched her body's, but when the solution ran into her ears, a shiver traveled through Tally. The sounds of the room were muffled almost into silence.

The fluid rose above her eyes, over the tip of her nose, covering her completely. . . .

She sucked the recycled air from the tube, fighting to keep her eyes closed. Now that she was practically deaf, keeping herself blind was torture.

"On my way, Tally," the voice in her head hissed.

Or had she just imagined it?

She was trapped now, immobilized, and the city could take its final revenge on her: grinding down her bones to reduce her to average pretty height; cutting the harsh angles from her cheeks; stripping out the beautiful muscles and bones, the chips in her jaw and hands, her lethal fingernails; replacing her black and perfect eyes. Making her a bubblehead again.

Only this time she was awake, and would feel it all . . .

Then Tally heard a sound, something smacking hard against the plastic side of the tank—she opened her eyes.

The operating solution made everything blurry, but through the transparent tank walls she saw furious movement, heard another muffled crash. One of the blinking machines toppled over.

Her rescuer was here.

Tally leaped into motion, tearing the dermal braid from her arm, then reaching up to yank the breathing tube out of her mouth. The device squirmed, its tendrils tightening across the back of her head, trying to stay on. She bit down on it, her ceramic teeth rending the plastic, and it died in her hand, spitting out a final spray of air bubbles into Tally's face.

She scrambled for a grip on the tank's edges, trying to pull herself up and out. But a transparent barrier barred her way.

Crap! she thought, fingers scrabbling for any gap in the plastic walls. She'd never seen an operating tank in use; when they were empty, the top was always *open*! Tally scratched the sides with her nails, scoring them as her panic built.

But the walls didn't break. . . .

Her shoulder brushed against a servo-arm's scalpel, already deployed, and a pink cloud of blood blossomed across her vision. The nanos in the operating fluid took only seconds to staunch the bleeding.

Well, that's convenient, she thought. *Of course, breathing would be nice too!*

She peered out through the blurry solution. The fight was still going on, one figure against many. *Hurry up!* she thought, scrambling to find the breathing tube again. She shoved it into her mouth, but it was dead, clogged by the operating fluid.

At the top of the tank was a bare centimeter of airspace, and Tally pushed herself up to suck in the tiny bit of oxygen. But it wouldn't last long. She had to get *out* of this thing!

She tried to pound her way through the tank wall, but the solution was too thick and viscous. Tally's fist moved in slow motion, like punching through molasses.

Red dots sparkled at the edge of her vision . . . her lungs were empty.

Then she saw a blurry figure stumbling straight toward

her, thrown back from the fight. It crashed against the side of the tank, making the whole thing wobble unsteadily on its stand.

Maybe that was the way.

Tally began to rock herself from side to side, setting the solution sloshing around her, the tank swaying a little farther each time. Scalpels tore at her shoulders as she threw herself one way and then the next, the buzz of repair nanos matching the swarming dots before her eyes, a pink tinge of blood filling the liquid.

But finally the tank was tipping over.

The world seemed to tilt around her, liquids swirling as she tumbled, the whole tank turning as it fell. Tally heard the muffled smack of plastic as she hit the floor, saw the tank's walls webbing with cracks. Solution drained from around her, sound rushing back into her ears as she drew her first breath of air.

She dug her fingernails into the fractured plastic and tore, pulling her way free from the operating tank.

Bleeding and naked, Tally stumbled forward, gasping for more air, the solution clinging to her as if she'd stepped from a bathtub full of honey. Unconscious doctors and orderlies lay in a pile, the solution rolling across them.

Her rescuer stood before her.

"Shay?" Tally wiped the liquid from her eyes. "David?"

"Didn't I tell you to lie still? Or must you always destroy *everything*?"

Tally blinked, unable to believe her eyes.

It was Dr. Cable.

TEARS

She looked a thousand years old. Her eyes had lost the blackness in their depths, their evil sparkle. Like Fausto, she had become champagne without bubbles. Cured at last.

But she still managed to sneer.

Gasping for air, Tally said, "What are you . . . ?"

"Rescuing you," Dr. Cable said.

Tally looked at the door, listening for alarms, for footsteps.

The old woman shook her head. "I built this place, Tally. I know its tricks. No one's coming. Let me rest a moment." She sat heavily on the soaking floor. "I'm too old for this."

Tally stared down at her old enemy, hands still curled into deadly claws. But Dr. Cable was panting, a cut on her lip beginning to bleed. She looked like a very old crumbly, one whose life extension treatments were running out.

Except for the three unconscious doctors who lay at her feet.

"You still have special reflexes?"

"I'm not special at all, Tally. I'm pathetic." The old woman shrugged. "But I'm still *dangerous*."

"Oh." Tally wiped more operating solution from her eyes. "Took you long enough, though."

"Yes, that was clever Tally, taking out your breathing tube *first*."

"Sure, great plan, leaving me in there until they almost . . ." Tally blinked. "Um, *why* are you doing this again?"

Dr. Cable smiled. "I'll tell you, Tally, if you answer me a

question first." Her eyes grew sharp for a moment. "What did you do to me?"

It was Tally's turn to smile. "I cured you."

"I know that, you little fool. But *how*?"

"Remember when you snatched my transmitter? It wasn't a transmitter at all—it was an injector. Maddy's made a cure for Specials."

"That miserable woman again." Dr. Cable's gaze sank back to the soaking floor. "The Council's reopened the city's borders. Her pills are everywhere."

Tally nodded. "I can tell."

"Everything's going to pieces," Dr. Cable hissed, glaring up at Tally. "It won't be long before they start chewing up the wild, you know."

"Yeah, I know. Just like in Diego." Tally sighed, remembering Andrew Simpson Smith's forest fire. "Freedom has a way of destroying things, I guess."

"And you call this a *cure*, Tally? It's letting loose a cancer on the world."

Tally shook her head slowly. "So that's why you're here, Dr. Cable? To blame me for everything?"

"No. I'm here to let you go."

Tally looked up—this had to be a trick, some way for Dr. Cable to get her final revenge. But the thought of being out under the open sky again sent a painful ping of hope through her.

She swallowed. "But didn't I, you know, destroy your world?"

Dr. Cable stared at her for a long time with her unfocused, watery eyes. "Yes. But you're the last one, Tally. I've watched Shay and the others on the Diego propaganda feeds—they aren't right anymore. Maddy's cure, I suppose."

She sighed slowly. "They're no more right than I am. The Council has despecialized almost all of us."

Tally nodded. "But why me?"

"You're the only real Cutter left," Dr. Cable said. "The last of my Specials designed to live in the wild, to exist outside the cities. You can escape this, can disappear forever. I don't want my work to become extinct, Tally. Please . . ."

Tally blinked. She'd never thought of herself as some sort of endangered animal. But she wasn't about to argue. The thought of freedom made her head spin.

"Just get out, Tally. Take any elevator to the roof. The building's almost empty, and I've shut down most of the cameras. And frankly, no one can stop you. Leave, and for my sake, *keep yourself special*. The world may need you, one day."

Tally swallowed. Just walking out seemed too simple. "What about a hoverboard?"

"It's waiting for you on the roof, of course." Dr. Cable snorted. "What is it about you miscreants and those things?"

Tally looked down at the three unconscious forms on the floor.

"They'll be fine," Cable snorted. "I am a doctor, you know."

"Sure you are," Tally muttered, kneeling to gently peel the scrubs from one of the orderlies. When she pulled them on, the operating solution soaked through in dark blotches, but at least she wasn't naked anymore.

She took a step toward the door, but turned back to face Dr. Cable.

"Aren't you worried I'll get myself cured? Then there won't be any of us left."

The woman looked up, and her defeated expression

changed, a glint of the old evil returning to her eyes. "My faith in you has always been rewarded, Tally Youngblood. Why should I start worrying now?"

When she reached the open air, Tally stood for a long minute looking up at the darkened sky. She didn't worry about pursuers. Cable had been right: Who was left to stop her?

The stars and the crescent moon glowed softly, the wind carrying scents from the wild. After a month of recycled air, the cool summer breeze tasted alive on her tongue. Tally breathed in the icy world.

She was finally free of her cell, of the operating tank, of Dr. Cable. No one would change her against her will, not ever again. There would be no more Special Circumstances.

But even as relief spread through her, Tally felt herself bleeding inside. Freedom was cutting her.

Zane was still dead, after all.

The taste of salt found its way to Tally's lips, a reminder of that last bitter kiss by the sea. The scene that she'd reimagined every hour in her underground cell: the last time she'd spoken to him, the test she'd failed, pushing him away. But somehow the memory played differently this time, long and slow and sweet in her mind—as if she hadn't felt Zane trembling, as if she'd let that kiss go on and on. . . .

She tasted salt again, and finally felt the heat streaming down her cheeks. Tally reached her hands up, not quite believing until she saw her own fingertips glistening in the starlight.

Specials didn't cry, but her tears had finally come.

RUINS

Before she left the city Tally booted her skintenna, and found three messages waiting for her.

The first was from Shay. It told her that the Cutters were staying in Diego. After their help in the Town Hall attack, they had become the city's defense force, not to mention its firefighters, rescue workers, and heroes of last resort. The City Council had even changed the laws to let them keep their morphological violations, for the moment, anyway.

Except the fingernails and teeth. Those had to go.

With Town Hall still a pile of rubble, Diego needed all the help it could get. Though the cure was already invading other cities, slowly changing the entire continent, new runaways still arrived in Diego every day, ready to embrace the New System.

The old static bubblehead culture had been replaced by a world where change was paramount. So one day some other city would catch up—from now on fashions were guaranteed to shift—but for the moment, Diego was still the place that changed faster than everywhere else. It was the place to be, and it grew larger every day.

Shay's original message had been appended hourly, a diary of the challenges the Cutters faced as they helped to rebuild a city even as it transformed before their eyes. It seemed that Shay wanted Tally to know everything, so that she could jump right in and help when she was freed at last.

Shay was sorry about one thing, though. They'd all heard about the despecializations. They were public knowledge, a gesture of peace. The Cutters desperately wanted to come and rescue Tally, but they couldn't just rush in and attack the city now that they had become Diego's official defense force. They couldn't reignite this war when it was so close to fizzling out. Tally could see that, right?

But Tally Youngblood would always be a Cutter, whether she was special or not. . . .

The second message was from David's mother.

She said that David had left Diego, had struck out into the wild. The Smokies were spreading across the continent, still working to smuggle the cure into those cities that clung to the bubblehead operation. In not too long, they would be sending an expedition into the deep south, and another across the seas to the eastern continents. Everywhere, it seemed, runaways were already streaming from their cities, setting up their own New Smokes, inspired by ugly rumors from afar.

There was an entire world waiting to be liberated, if Tally wanted to lend a hand.

Maddy ended with the words, "Join us. And if you see my son, tell him I love him."

The third message was from Peris.

He and the other Crims had left Diego. They were working on a special project for the city government, but they didn't much like staying in town. It was really bogus, it turned out, living in a place where *everyone* was Crim.

So they traveled across the wild, gathering up the villagers that the Smokies had released. They were teaching them about technology, about how the world outside their reservations worked, and about how *not* to start forest fires. Eventually, the villagers they worked with would go back to their own people and help bring them out into the world.

In return, the Crims were learning everything about the wild, how to hunt and fish and live off the land, gathering the knowledge of the pre-Rusties before it was lost again.

Tally smiled as she read the last lines:

> This one guy, Andrew Something, says he knows you? How did that happen? He says to tell you, "Keep challenging the gods." Whatever.
>
> Anyway, see you soon, Tally-wa. Best friends forever, finally!
>
> —Peris

Tally didn't answer any of them, not yet. She hoverboarded up the river, taking one last ride through the rapids that she would never see again.

Moonlight illuminated the white water, each burst of spray glittering around her like an explosion of diamonds. The icicles had all melted in the warm air of early summer, releasing the pine smell of the forest to coat her tongue like syrup. Tally didn't gesture for infrared vision, letting her other senses probe the darkness unassisted.

Amid all this beauty, Tally knew exactly what she had to do.

Her lifting fans sprang to life as she took the old familiar path, down the trail that led to the natural vein of iron discovered by some tricky ugly generations ago. She skimmed across it on magnetics, down into the dark bowl of the Rusty Ruins.

The dead buildings rose up around her, towering monuments to the people who had once let themselves grow too greedy and too many, hungry billions of them spreading across the globe.

Tally stared long and hard as she passed the burnt-out cars and gaping windows, her special eyes returning the blank gaze of a crumbling skull. She never wanted to forget this place.

Not with all these changes coming . . .

Her hoverboard climbed the iron frame of the tallest building, the place Shay had brought her that first night she'd been Outside, almost exactly a year ago. On silent magnetics, Tally drifted up through its empty shell, the silent city sprawling around her through the empty window frames.

But when she reached the top, David was gone.

His sleeping bag and other equipment had all disappeared, only empty self-heating meals remained scattered around the half-crumbled section of floor. There were a lot of them—he'd waited for her a long time.

He'd also taken the crude antenna he'd pinged her with.

Tally flicked on her skintenna and felt it reach out across the dead and empty city, waiting with her eyes closed for some kind of reply.

But no ping came. A kilometer was nothing in the wild.

She went higher, up to the summit of the tower, slipping through one of the gaping holes in the roof up into the rushing wind. Her board kept climbing until its magnetics lost their grip on the skyscraper's iron frame. Then her lifting fans spun to life, turning red-hot as they strained to push her higher.

"David?" she said softly.

Still no answer.

Then she remembered Shay's old trick, back in ugly days.

Tally knelt on the wavering, windblown board and reached a hand into its storage compartment. Dr. Cable had loaded it with medspray, smart plastic, firestarters, and even a single meal of SpagBol, just for old times' sake.

Then Tally's fingers closed around a safety flare.

She lit it, raising it in one hand, the fierce wind scattering a stream of sparks behind her as long as a kite string. "I'm not alone," she said.

She held it there until the hoverboard grew white-hot beneath her feet, the flare finally sputtering out to a single glowing ember.

Then Tally dropped back into the Rusty skyscraper and curled up on the high section of broken floor, suddenly overwhelmed by her escape, almost too exhausted to care if anyone had seen her signal.

David came at dawn.

THE PLAN

"Where were you?" she said sleepily.

He stepped from his board, exhausted and unshaven. But David's eyes were wide. "I've been trying to get into the city. Trying to find you."

Tally frowned. "The borders are open again, aren't they?"

"Maybe if you know how cities work . . ."

She laughed. David had spent all of his eighteen years out in the wild. He didn't know how to deal with simple things like security drones.

"I made it in finally," he continued. "But then I had some trouble finding Special Circumstances headquarters." He sat down wearily.

"But you saw my flare."

"Yeah, I did." He smiled, but he was watching her closely. "The reason I was trying to . . ." He swallowed. "I can pick up the city feeds on my antenna. It said they were going to change you all. Turn you into something less dangerous. Are you still . . . ?"

She gazed at him. "What do you think, David?"

He peered into her eyes for a long moment, then sighed and shook his head. "You just look like Tally to me."

She looked down, her vision blurring.

"What's the matter?"

"Nothing, David." She shook her head. "You just took on five million years of evolution again."

"I *what*? Did I say something wrong?"

"No." She smiled. "You said something right."

They ate a meal of city food, Tally swapping the SpagBol in her storage compartment for a can of David's PadThai.

She told him how she'd used his injector to change Dr. Cable, and about her month of captivity, and how she'd finally escaped. She explained that the debates David had heard on the newsfeeds meant that the cure was taking hold, the city transforming at last.

The Smokies had won, even here.

"So you're still special?" he finally asked.

"My body is. But the rest of me, I think that's all . . ." She had to swallow before using Zane's word. "Rewired."

David smiled. "I knew you'd manage."

"That's why you waited here, isn't it?"

"Of course. Someone had to." He cleared his throat. "My mom thinks I'm busy seeing the world, spreading the revolution."

Tally looked out at the ruined city. "The revolution's going pretty well on its own, David. It's unstoppable now."

"Yeah." Then he sighed. "But it's not like I did a very good job of saving you."

"I'm not the one who needs saving, David," Tally said. "Not anymore. Oh, *right*! I forgot to mention, Maddy sent me a message for you."

His eyebrows went up. "She sent *you* a message for me?"

"Yeah. 'I love you . . .'" Tally swallowed again. "She said to say that. So maybe she knows where you are, after all."

"Maybe so."

"You randoms *can* be awfully predictable," Tally said, smiling. She'd been watching him closely, her eyes cataloging all his imperfections, the asymmetry of his features, the pores of his skin, his too-big nose. His scar.

He wasn't an ugly anymore; to her he was just David. And maybe he had been right. Maybe she didn't have to do this alone.

David hated cities, after all. He didn't know how to use an interface or call a hovercar, and his handmade clothes would always look pretty bogus at a bash. And he certainly wasn't cut out to live in a place where people had snakes for pinkies.

Most important, Tally knew that no matter how her plan turned out, whatever awful things the world forced her to do, David would remember who she really was.

"I have this idea," she said.

"About where you're going next?"

"Yeah." Tally nodded. "It's kind of this plan . . . to save the world."

David paused, chopsticks halfway to his mouth, the SpagBol slithering off them and back into the container. His face shifted through emotions, as easy to read as any ugly's: confusion, curiosity, then a hint of understanding. "Can I help?" he asked simply.

She nodded. "Please. You're the right man for the job."

And then she explained everything.

That night, she and David hoverboarded to the very edge of the city, slowing to a halt when the repeater network picked up her skintenna. The three messages from Shay, Peris, and Maddy were still there, waiting for her. Tally flexed her fingers nervously.

"Look at that!" David said, pointing.

The skyline of New Pretty Town was aglow, rockets shooting high and bursting into vast, sparkling flowers of red and purple. The fireworks were back.

Maybe they were celebrating the end of Dr. Cable's rule, or the new transformations sweeping through the city, or the end of the war. Or perhaps this display marked the final days of Special Circumstances, now that the last Special had run off into the wild.

Or maybe they were just acting like bubbleheads again.

She laughed. "You've seen fireworks before, haven't you?"

He shook his head. "Not very many. They're *amazing*."

"Yeah. Cities aren't so bad, David." Tally smiled, hoping that the nightly fireworks displays had returned now that the war was ending. With all the convulsions about to unsettle her city, maybe that one tradition should never change. The world needed more fireworks—especially now that there was going to be a shortage of beautiful, useless things.

As she prepared herself to speak, a shiver of nerves played through Tally. Whether she was a Special-head or not, this message needed to come out icy and convincing. The world depended on it.

Then suddenly, she was ready.

As they stood there watching New Pretty Town glow, their eyes tracking the slow ascent of the rockets and their sudden blossoming, Tally spoke clearly over the water's roar, letting the chip in her jaw catch her words.

She sent them all—Shay, Maddy, and Peris—the same reply. . . .

MANIFESTO

I don't need to be cured. Just like I don't need to cut myself to feel, or think. From now on, no one rewires my mind but me.

Back in Diego, the doctors said that I could learn to control my behavior, and I have. You all helped, in one way or another.

But you know what? It's not my behavior I'm worried about anymore. It's yours.

That's why you won't be seeing me for a while, maybe a long time. David and I are staying out here in the wild.

You all say you need us. Well, maybe you do, but not to help you. You have enough help, with the millions of bubbly new minds about to be unleashed, with all the cities coming awake at last. Together, you're more than enough to change the world without us.

So from now on, David and I are here to stand in your way.

You see, freedom has a way of destroying things.

You have your New Smokes, your new ideas, whole new cities and New Systems. Well . . . we're the new Special Circumstances.

Whenever you push too far into the wild, we'll be here waiting, ready to push back. Remember us every time you decide to dig a new foundation, dam a river, or cut down a tree. Worry about us. However hungry the human race becomes now that the pretties are waking up, the wild still has teeth. Special teeth, ugly teeth. Us.

We'll be out here somewhere—watching. Ready to remind you of the price the Rusties paid for going too far.

I love you all. But it's time to say good-bye, for now.

Be careful with the world, or the next time we meet, it might get ugly.

—Tally Youngblood

Scott Westerfeld is the acclaimed author of numerous best-selling novels for teens, including the UGLIES sequence; *Uglies*, *Pretties*, *Specials* and *Extras* published by Simon and Schuster. His other teen novels include *The Midnighters Trilogy*, *Parasite Positive*, *Last Days* and *So Yesterday* which was named an ALA Best Book for Young Adults.

Scott was born in Texas and now he and his wife, Justine, alternate summers between Sydney, Australia and New York City. Visit Scott's website at www.scottwesterfeld.com.

EXTRAS

Also by Scott Westerfeld:

UGLIES
PRETTIES
SPECIALS

LEVIATHAN
BEHEMOTH
GOLIATH